Scarlet is dedicated to the ones who've passed on
but have never been forgotten.

To Quincy and Olinda—Grandpa and Grandma.

I miss you.

Scarlet

Jordan Summers

TOR®

paranormal romance

A TOM DOHERTY ASSOCIATES BOOK
NEW YORK

This is a work of fiction. All of the characters, organizations, and events portrayed in this novel are either products of the author's imagination or are used fictitiously.

SCARLET

Copyright © 2008 by Toni Allardice

All rights reserved.

A Tor Book
Published by Tom Doherty Associates, LLC
175 Fifth Avenue
New York, NY 10010

www.tor-forge.com

Tor® is a registered trademark of Tom Doherty Associates, LLC.

ISBN: 978-0-7653-5915-5

First Edition: June 2009

Printed in the United States of America

0 9 8 7 6 5 4 3 2 1

Praise for *Red*

"Dark and dangerous and shivering with possibility, *Red*'s a temptation worth indulging."
——Melissa Marr, *New York Times* bestselling author

"Clever and gripping, *Red* kept me guessing at every step. Jordan Summers spins a dangerously exciting tale with a mind-bending twist."
——Cheyenne McCray, *USA Today* bestselling author

"Dark, action-filled, and hot! This heroine is a wolf dressed in Little Red Riding Hood's clothing."
——Jeaniene Frost, *New York Times* bestselling author

"Get in, sit down, shut up, and hold on."
——Lynn Viehl, *New York Times* bestselling author

"Red Santiago is a heroine with fire befitting her name. The murderer she must find makes her question her very sanity and takes the reader along for the ride. Summers has a winner with this one!"
——Cathy Clamp, *USA Today* bestselling author

Books by Jordan Summers

Red
Scarlet
Crimson*

*Forthcoming

ACKNOWLEDGMENTS

As always I have many people to acknowledge for this book. Anna Genoese for believing I had more than one book in me. Heather Osborn and Melissa Frain for working so hard on edits, covers, and copy. Thank you, ladies. You're the reason this book is possible. Chris McGrath for the amazing artwork on both *Red* and *Scarlet*. I am in awe of your talent. The entire Tor art department for branding my covers so well. All the wonderful authors who stepped forward to give me a quote. Thank you for your time. Given your deadlines, I know you didn't have it to spare. To my agent, Ginger Clark, thanks for working so tirelessly. Your faith means more than you'll ever know.

I'd also like to thank my folks and in-laws. I am very lucky and fortunate to have two terrific sets of parents. To my husband, who is my rock, my reason, and my inspiration. Your love amazes me.

And finally, I'd like to thank Julia Templeton and Terri Hendrix. You are two of the best friends a girl could have. This world is a better place because you're in it.

Scarlet

chapter one

Red stood naked in the barren valley. The cool desert air brushed her skin, leaving gooseflesh in its wake. She shivered and took a deep breath, closing her eyes to picture the wolf in her mind.

Eyes the color of autumn stared back at her from a shaggy elongated face. Not quite animal and definitely not human. White teeth glowed against its black pelt. Deadly claws curled into minidaggers, rearing to score the earth. Whether on two legs or on four, the beast looked impressive. And dangerous.

She felt its hunger. Its need for survival. The desire to escape. The urge to run blindly into the darkness rode her hard. She longed to feel the dirt and compacted sand beneath rough pads. Red reached out, drawing the vision nearer, beckoning it to come. She embraced that which she feared.

Close. Closer. Almost there.

Pain seared her flesh, causing her back to contort. Her head jerked to the night sky, her mouth open in a silent scream. Yanked by the fire coursing through her veins, she could no longer control her movements. Her muscles bunched under her skin. Bones in her hand snapped as the beast fought its way out. Red shrieked and threw open her eyes. Tonight was the night. She could feel it. The change had to work.

Her body continued to coil and bulge, twisting into unnatural shapes until Red thought she'd go mad. Her vision dimmed and fear engulfed her. The pain suddenly stopped.

Red looked down at her gnarled, broken hand, expecting to see a smattering of fur—or at least a misshapen paw where her fingers should be. One claw protruded through the top of her fingernail and blood dripped fat drops onto the thirsty desert floor—a glistening scarlet reminder that she'd failed once more.

"Damn it!" she shouted. It had been weeks since she'd moved to Nuria in the Republic of Arizona. Weeks since she'd first attempted the change. And she still couldn't control the wolf inside her.

Red stared at her hand, watching the bones pop back into place. Her body had already started to repair the damage. More excruciating pain followed. It was the same every night. She would've thought that she'd be used to it by now. But she wasn't. Red glanced over at Morgan, who'd been waiting quietly in the distance, just in time to see the disappointment on his face.

Disapproval she could deal with, but disappointment . . .

She'd spent her whole life trying not to disappoint anyone. She had succeeded with her parents and her grandfather. At least Red thought she had. But now, thinking about it, how could she be sure? Maybe they'd lied. Maybe like Morgan, they'd hid their disappointment and she'd been too young to realize it. She debated whether to try one more time. She glanced at the night sky. It was getting late.

They'd been out here for two hours already while she attempted to make the change. Two wasted hours with only a claw to show for it. Red picked up a rock and threw it at a tank, half buried under the desert. It was a rotting reminder of the last world war, which brought about the dissolution of countries and fostered the development of self-governing republics. Those republics now took up 70 percent of the landmass in the world. The other 30 percent fell into no-man's-land, a place of utter lawlessness. The rock pinged off the rusting metal, then dropped with a thud to the ground.

Red picked up another rock and sent it hurling through the air out of sight. She had no doubt that the town would know about her failure by morning. Morgan wouldn't lie, if someone asked. She didn't expect him to, but sometimes she wished he would. How much longer could she go before the townsfolk decided to run her out of Nuria?

She sighed. Werewolves who couldn't control their change were as dangerous to the town as a loaded laser rifle in the hands of a criminal. Then there was the damage they could do to themselves. Since they'd been created by the old order to fight as super soldiers in the last war, adult-size wolves could take several laser pistol blasts before they even realized they'd been hit. It would take a couple of more after that to finish the job. It was easy to injure your body without knowing it when in wolf form. Not that she'd know first-hand, since she'd spent the majority of her time without fur.

Morgan's influence as sheriff would only protect Red for so long. Soon that would end, then it would be open season on her. The pressure from that invisible clock only made things worse. Morgan hid his worry well, but Red could still sense it. Hard to keep things like that from someone you're sleeping with. He hadn't come right out and said anything. Morgan never would. It wasn't his way. There'd be enough people in town to do it for him.

Red glanced over at Morgan's shirtless form. Scars etched his chest and abdomen, carving out a tragic story. He hadn't had those scars when she'd first met him. His cousin Kane had put them there, thanks to her. In his madness, he'd almost killed Morgan.

She couldn't believe how close she'd come to losing him. What would she have done then? Gone back to the International Police Tactical Team? Doubtful. Found a new job?

Who would hire her? She was only qualified to do one job and that was hunt *unknowns*. Maybe she'd have retired. And do what? Live on dirt, since she didn't have enough credits to support herself. And Red absolutely refused to ask her grandfather for help.

The wind picked up. Morgan had his dark head thrown back, letting the desert breeze caress his skin. Wildness surrounded him, oozing out of his pores like the sweet musk that covered his body. The man was magnificent in his rugged beauty. His wolf brushed his flesh in a primitive caress. Despite his civilized reserve, it always lurked just beneath the surface, a barely leashed sexual being that was impossible to ignore. Even now he drew her to him without trying, the aura of dominant power second nature.

Red's body tightened in anticipation.

She wanted to change just to be near him. The sensual creature inside of her itched to embrace this newfound ability, even though she'd never had a sexual nature before coming to Nuria. Everything involving the wolf was happening too fast. What if she couldn't control it? What if she released the beast inside her and it killed someone? Did she want the death of a Nurian citizen on her conscience? What if she killed Morgan? Could she take that chance? Red shuddered at the thought.

There was no way she could live with herself if she killed an innocent. Morgan would be forced to put her down—no matter his feelings for her and their burgeoning relationship. Nuria had survived this long by following a few simple rules: 1. Never tell an outsider that you're an Other. 2. Do not hunt humans. 3. Shape-shifters must be able to control their changes.

Violation of rule number two garnered an automatic death sentence. Breaking rule number three came with two forms of punishment: banishment or death.

Neither was appealing, but Red could live with those

rules. At least she hoped she could. When she'd agreed to the terms, she had thought learning to shift wouldn't take her long. She'd always been a fast learner, even as a child. Her parents had praised her academic and athletic prowess until the day they were killed. Her abilities hadn't changed as far as she could tell. If anything, they'd gotten better. So why was she having problems, when she'd already shifted in her sleep on several occasions? How hard could it be to do it consciously?

Apparently, very hard.

Her finger burned as the claw finished receding into her hand. In two weeks, she'd never so much as gotten a single whisker, much less a pelt of fur. She had to be doing something wrong, but Red didn't know what that might be. She'd followed Morgan's instructions to the letter. She was good at following instructions, when they suited her. Morgan had told her to hold the image in her mind, bring it toward her, then let her body do the rest.

Watching him shift in seconds, seeing all the muscles in his body spring to life, made it seem so easy. His enthusiasm was palpable and addictive enough to fuel her in the beginning. He'd continued their nightly ritual until he realized his presence was more of a hindrance than a help. Maggie Sheppard, his assistant at the sheriff's station, had taken over her lessons. But after a frustrating week of false starts, she'd given up and suggested Red do the same. So Morgan came back, and he'd been with her ever since. Her gaze strayed in his direction.

Morgan stayed in the woods, silently moving along the edge. He'd watched night after night, partly to bear witness and partly to make sure she didn't do anything she shouldn't while in her other form. So far, there wasn't a chance of that happening, since Red had yet to shift.

Red could feel the tension rolling off him in waves. He wanted her to succeed. His support was palpable. He pushed her hard because he knew she could take it. And she loved him for it, even though the pressure had started to get to her.

She stared at him, mesmerized. The wind shifted. Morgan inhaled and his amber eyes flew open, pinning her in place.

"Gina, you're not concentrating," Morgan said, a feral grin on his face. That look alone made her heart skip a beat. He stalked toward her, grace and stealth giving a fluidness to his movements.

Red watched him approach, anticipation coursing through her veins. It was still taking awhile to get used to Morgan using her given name. Everyone at her old job on the International Police Tactical Team had called her Red, a name that had started out as an insult due to her uncanny ability to cause excessive amounts of bloodshed on the job. It wasn't her fault that *unknowns* refused to surrender. She did her best to bring them back alive, but rarely succeeded. She'd embraced the negative nickname, wearing it proudly, and wasn't quite ready to give it up just yet.

"I was concentrating," she said. "Just not on the change." She bent to gather her clothes.

Morgan was behind her before she could straighten. His strong hands gripped her hips, his blunt nails digging into her skin. He leaned forward until his chest scraped her back. "Do you know what you just offered by bending over naked in front of an alpha wolf?"

Gooseflesh rose on her skin and her nipples marbled into two painful peaks. "Maybe." She laughed. The truth was she'd been too distracted by her failure to pay attention. She'd only meant to gather her clothes to cover her embarrassment over another wasted evening.

"You won't be needing your clothes for a while," he rasped in her ear, then nipped her tender lobe.

Red groaned, dropping her clothes onto the ground, her failure temporarily forgotten. She heard a button pop behind her and the slow, teasing purr of a zipper being lowered. His musky scent surrounded her, drowning her senses. The material from his pants brushed the back of her thighs and she bit her lip. It was always like this between them, so heated and urgent. Like they'd never get enough of each other.

"Do you have any idea how hard it is for me to wait in the woods, while you're standing naked forty feet away?" Morgan asked. He trailed kisses along her spine while his callused hands kneaded the round globes of her bottom.

"No," she gasped. "Tell me." She rocked back into his grip, loving the feel of his hands on her.

Morgan's voice strangled in his chest. "Your delicious scent calls to me," he said, inhaling loudly, before catching the tender flesh of her neck in a love bite. Her knees shook. With a flick of his tongue, he released her, only to have his stubbled jaw abrade her shoulder as he nuzzled her skin.

Red practically howled under the onslaught.

"You watch me, when you think that I'm not looking. But my wolf is always aware of your presence. It's so attuned to your body that I know the second you become wet." To prove his point, Morgan ran his finger along the seam of her bottom until he reached her moist center.

Red shimmied, trying to get closer.

"Do you want to know how I know?" he asked.

"Yes," she bit out, as he slipped two thick fingers inside of her, stretching her. He slowly curled them to stroke the hidden nerves that would send her over the edge.

"Because," he gasped, his hot breath bathing her ear. "I get hard the moment your body sends out that signal." He rocked his hips to show her just how hard he was.

"Morgan, please," Red begged, nearly mindless with passion. After failing to shift, she needed this connection.

His hot, throbbing length scalded her as he slid the head of his cock to her entrance. He slowly pushed inside, swirling the tip in her juices. "Please what?"

Red tried to deepen their connection. Morgan growled, his hands tightening on her hips to hold her in place and prevent her from impaling herself. "I want you," she said. Red reached around and brushed his testicles.

The slight caress sent the air rushing out of Morgan's lungs. His entire body clenched. "Stop!"

She stroked him again. This time giving his balls a gentle squeeze.

"Not fair," he said, shuddering.

"That makes us even," Red said. If he didn't move soon, she'd die from the exquisite torture.

"You're mine. Don't ever forget that," he said, then thrust forward, burying himself to the hilt.

Red's knees nearly gave out as Morgan took her roughly from behind. His hands seemed to be everywhere at once, teasing her nipples, stroking her clit, caressing her skin, all while supporting her. His feral grunts only served to ratchet up her need. Moans filled the air as flesh slapped flesh.

Morgan ground his hips into her bottom, lifting her onto her toes. "I love you so much." The words came out as both a curse and a confession. He latched onto the piece of skin where her shoulder met her neck. "Please don't ever leave me again," he murmured almost too low for her to hear, then bit down.

The sensation of him drawing on her flesh and drinking her blood sent Red spinning out of control. She screamed and her body convulsed beneath him. They collapsed onto the ground, Morgan still hard inside of her. His rough tongue lapped the spot he'd bitten as he waited for the flutters of her orgasm to fade. His taste for blood had grown since the vampire Raphael Vega had saved his life after Kane's vicious attack. He hadn't taken on any other vampiric *quirks* that Red could see, but it had only been a couple of months.

"That was incredible," she whispered as she tried to catch

her breath. Morgan pulled her close and rolled them onto their sides.

"I'm just getting started," he said, rocking his hips for emphasis.

They made love for the next two hours, sometimes slow and easy, others fast and heated. The wolf was nothing if not insatiable. Red lost track of her orgasms by the time Morgan was spent. They lay on the desert floor, gasping like a couple of naughty teenagers who'd just discovered sex.

It was like this between them every time. Red had thought the intensity would fade or at least cool, but as she lay there listening to her heart pound in her ears, she realized if anything, the feelings were stronger. Was that her wolf responding?

Eventually her strength returned and she stood, helping Morgan to his feet. They gathered their clothes and began to dress. The air had cooled. Red hadn't noticed while Morgan had been wrapped around her. The breeze chilled her flesh and cleared her love-fogged mind.

"You know I haven't managed to do anything in weeks but produce a claw. I know you're trying to help me, but I've heard the talk that's going around town."

His expression soured. "You can't listen to gossip," Morgan admonished as he yanked on his pants.

"Be that as it may, I know most teenagers can slip easily in and out of form. If the rumors are true, it's never taken anyone this long to learn. What if I can't do it? What if I'm some kind of *freak*?" Red croaked on the last word.

She'd never fit in on the tactical team, even though her grandfather was the commander of IPTT headquarters. When her *gift* was revealed, she'd finally understood why. She thought that she'd found her place among the Others of Nuria, but now she wasn't so sure. What if she couldn't fit in here either?

Not being able to shift made her different. Made her stand

out. Acceptance here was an illusion Red had created in her mind and religiously cultivated because of Morgan's love, and because she'd wanted so badly to belong. Maybe she didn't belong anywhere, and never would.

"Failure isn't an option," Morgan said matter-of-factly. "You keep forgetting you've already done it several times. Now you just have to learn to do it when you're awake. Take learning how to talk for example; it takes some people longer than others. Does it mean the late bloomers' language skills pale in comparison to the early adopters'? Absolutely not. It just took them longer. So don't be too hard on yourself. It'll happen. I have faith in you." He smiled encouragingly.

He might have faith in her, but did she? Red swallowed the lump that had suddenly formed in her throat and finished dressing. She laced up her black combat boots, then turned to Morgan. "All done," she said.

They strolled back to the hydrogen car and drove slowly back to town.

chapter two

Nuria sat nestled on the desert floor of a wide valley just north of where the old city of Phoenix, Arizona, used to stand. The majestic mountains that once dotted the area were reduced to rubble, forming monstrous boulders that were larger than most homes. A boundary fence that separated the Republic of Arizona from no-man's-land could be seen on the horizon. The green glow from its electromagnetic defenses crackled in the darkness like heat lightning before a storm. A constant reminder that danger was only a few miles away.

Largely unscathed by the last world war in 2010, Nuria's buildings stood as a tribute to 21st-century small-town architectural design. Unfortunately, its economy hadn't fared as well. There were only a few businesses remaining in town; the sheriff's station, an emergency care center that treated people in the surrounding republics, too, an outfitter shop, a few share spaces, a food dispensing station, a hydrogen refill, and a water trader. Everyone else in Nuria existed by farming animals, since food was scarce on the dead world.

Lights were blazing in the sheriff's station when they arrived. Maggie had probably left them on because she knew Morgan had planned to work late.

"You going to come in?" he asked. Red stared at the small

concrete structure with its brick facade and hand-painted sheriff's station sign. The solar panels on the roof reflected the stars, giving the place a magical quality. Inside the door, the magic ended. The place went from sparkling to practical. She pictured Morgan sitting behind his utilitarian desk with his dark hair disheveled from their lovemaking and a shadow of beard growth on his jaw.

As much as she longed to stay with him, she knew it was best that she go. He wouldn't get any work done with her looking over his shoulder. "I think I'm going to call it a night," she said.

"Sure?"

Red nodded. "I'm tired and have those interviews to prepare for tomorrow."

"Okay." Morgan leaned down to kiss her, his firm lips lingering long enough to ignite the embers smoldering inside of her. "I'll be over as soon as I can," he said, then reluctantly released her and strolled inside.

Red watched him go, her heart thumping out a quick staccato from the kiss, then headed over to the water trader.

She'd kept the room she had rented from her friend, the late Jesse Lindley, when she first hit Nuria, even though Morgan had offered to let her live with him. She'd been sorely tempted, but thought it best to take things slow given all they'd been through. Someday in the very near future, when she ran out of credits, Red would have to decide on a more permanent living situation. But until that happened, she'd continue with the present arrangement.

That was if the Nurians didn't run her out of town first.

Red opened the door and stepped into the empty bar area. Metal stools bellied up to the counter, waiting for tomorrow's patrons to arrive and place their water orders. There were stairs on the right, leading to the share space. Until last month, Jesse Lindley had run the water trader depot for more than forty years.

She'd died trying to protect Red and the people of Nuria

from Roark Montgomery and Morgan's cousin, Kane Hunter. The place seemed obscenely quiet without her burly presence to fill it. Red climbed the stairs and walked down the yellow hall that led to her room. Normally she stopped to look at the pale red roses that had been stenciled along the way, but not tonight.

The animal furs under her feet silenced her footsteps. As she moved closer, she caught sight of the scanner that glowed next to her door. Red placed her hand against the flat panel and waited while it analyzed her palm. The machine hummed as it processed her identity with the Republic of Arizona's registrar system.

Every legal citizen was scanned and chipped at birth so all the republics could identify them. If you had no scan or identifier chip, you were considered an *unknown*—an outlaw. It had been part of Red's previous job to arrest or eliminate all unknowns. But that seemed like a lifetime ago. The scanner beeped and the door opened.

Red entered the large square room with cheery yellow walls and dropped onto the rest pad. Her muscles ached and no matter how hard she tried, she couldn't form a single coherent thought. She ran her hand over her face and came away with a layer of grit. Red forced herself off the pad. She undressed, then stepped into the chemical shower.

Having a private cleansing unit was still a luxury that took some getting used to. She'd shared for as long as she could remember. Modesty went out in the twenty-first century, when water rationing arrived. It was normal for groups of people to bathe in communal cleansing units. Nudity was regarded as commonplace.

Sex, on the other hand, was still as complicated as ever, Red thought as she rinsed the cleanser out of her hair. At least they didn't have to deal with unwanted pregnancies or sexually transmitted diseases, since births without medical intervention were almost nonexistent and all STDs had been cured.

She finished washing up, then grabbed an e-book reader that contained the files of the applicants she'd be interviewing tomorrow. With any luck, they'd find several promising candidates for the new Nurian Tactical Team. Even if she didn't manage to find anyone, reading the files would at least keep her awake until Morgan arrived.

Red fell asleep the moment her head hit the rest pad.

Suddenly, she was frolicking in a valley with Morgan. Under his loving guidance, she'd shifted into a magnificent black wolflike creature. They chased each other for what seemed like hours, playfully nipping at the other's haunches. The day was sunny and warm. Like most days, there were few clouds in the sky.

Her tongue lolled out of her mouth as she watched Morgan crest a rise and then disappear. Thinking it was part of their precoital game, Red followed, sprinting up the hill. But when she reached the top, he was gone. Charred earth and sand lay below her in an endless sea of nothingness.

She looked around frantically and tried to call out his name, but words evaded her. Instead, the sound erupted in loud, guttural barks. Red coughed and tried again to no avail. What if she never found him? What if she was stuck in her wolf form forever?

Her heart began to pound as panic set in. She didn't like being here alone. Her tail tucked between her legs and she started to whimper. Morgan had to be here somewhere. She lowered her muzzle to the ground and sniffed.

The scent of sweat and fear reached her nostrils, making her dizzy. Was Morgan in trouble? She took off at a run, loping down the hill with ease. Her new form landed quietly as she pursued her quarry's trail. Only after she'd been running for a while did Red realize that the sun had set. Night was upon the desert, embracing the quiet.

Red sniffed the air once more and heard a small cry coming from her right. She scanned the sand dunes, but didn't immediately spot him. With excited yips, she followed his aroma and found him hiding behind the rubble of an old tank.

I've got you now, Red thought as she leapt behind the tank, claws extended. Something was wrong. She sensed his fear of her. She tried to pull back, but it was too late. She was out of control. Her sharp claws hit his neck, slashing the tender flesh easily. Red heard a hiss, then his dark head fell back, dipping into the shadows, exposing the bloody smile that cut across his throat.

Revulsion battled with hunger as the coppery scent of blood filled her nostrils, tempting her feral senses. Red wanted to stop, but she couldn't. Her body's demands were too strong. She leaned closer, until her lips met his warm flesh. Her tongue darted out. One taste and she was mindlessly lost.

Hot, sweet liquid rushed into her mouth, nearly choking her in her fervor to devour. It tasted so salty good she had to force herself to slow down for fear she'd get sick. She savored the next few bites, her hunger far from abated.

Red licked her muzzle and looked at what she'd been feeding upon. Morgan's lifeless face stared up at her, his eyes wide with shock.

No. She shook her head, her mind refusing to believe what she was seeing. *It can't be.* She couldn't have. Yet there was no mistaking the identity of the man lying under her with his throat savagely slit.

Morgan was dead.

Gina woke up screaming, her body tensed in terror. Morgan grabbed her. She flailed until his low, soothing voice finally registered on her sleep-muddled mind.

The sun peeked through the curtains. "Shh, I've got you. It's okay. I've got you," Morgan said, rocking her gently in his arms. This wasn't the first time she'd had nightmares, but they never got any easier for him. He'd been sound asleep beside her, resting peacefully when she'd screamed. For a second, fear had engulfed him, then he'd remembered where they were. He'd scented the surroundings and known they were safe.

"You were dead," she sputtered, as tears streamed from her hazel eyes.

Morgan kissed her forehead. Her skin was hot and soft beneath his lips. "It was only a dream." He brushed the hair away from her face.

She shook her head.

"Look at me."

She pressed her face into his chest and sniffled. Morgan's heart clenched and he pulled her closer. He'd hoped by now her nightmares would've stopped, but if anything, they seemed to be getting worse. He fisted the sheets in helpless frustration. "Gina, look at me."

She scrubbed at her face with the palms of her hands to hide the tears, then met his gaze.

"See? I'm fine," Morgan said.

Without a word, she reached down and grasped his cock.

"What are you doing?" Morgan gasped as her warm fingers stroked his length. He couldn't think when she touched him. Couldn't reason. Could only feel. It was like that every time. He'd never admit it, but the feelings she evoked scared the hell out of him. It had been so long since he'd allowed a woman to get close. Sure, he'd had sex. Plenty of it. But this was different. She was different. Gina had swept past his defenses, laying him bare. He couldn't go back to his old existence, even if he wanted.

"I want to see for myself." She pushed him onto his back.

There was no way he'd stop her, even if he could. "But I'm supposed to be helping you," he said on a gasp as she gently squeezed. The last of his blood left his brain and headed south.

"You already have," she said. "Now stop fighting me."

Resistance was the last thing on Morgan's mind. He stared at the small, pert breasts peeking through her long, black hair. Her nipples grew hard in response. Morgan hadn't intended to seduce her or be seduced by her. He'd only wanted to comfort her after her nightmare. He continued to stare until his mouth started to water. He forced his gaze away from her chest and focused on her face.

From the smile playing on her full lips, Morgan realized that Gina had other plans, and they didn't include comforting. At least the sadness was gone from her eyes. He couldn't handle seeing her like that. It made him want to go into her dreams and kill something, or beat the crap out of the first person who made her frown.

Gina caressed him, drawing his attention to more immediate needs. Morgan licked his lips. "What do you plan to do with that now that you have its full attention?"

She shrugged. "I'll think of something."

Gina straddled his waist, locking her knees tight, then slowly lowered herself onto his bulging erection. She was wet, so wet. God help him, he couldn't resist her. She was temptation incarnate. Maybe if he were a stronger man, he'd be able to push her away. Make her go somewhere safe, somewhere far from him and the Others. But he couldn't. He'd fought for her. Marked her as his own. It had nearly cost him his life, but he'd won. He wasn't about to give her up. Not now. Not ever.

Morgan gritted his teeth as hot, moist woman surrounded him. His heart accelerated as he forced himself to remain still. This one was for Gina.

Once she'd seated herself, she stopped.

The muscles in Morgan's abdomen bunched and his thighs began to twitch. He tightened his hold on the sheets. They ripped as his claws extended.

Gina looked over her shoulder, then arched a questioning brow at him.

"I'm trying, darlin', but I don't know how much longer I can keep the beast inside." Morgan gave her a strained smile.

She rose to her knees until only the tip of him remained inside of her. The sound of shredding reached Morgan's ears as he buried his hands in the rest pad. She stayed there, balanced on his hard cock until he groaned in defeat. The second he did, Gina grinned and plopped down, her bottom slapping his legs.

Morgan's breath whooshed out of his lungs and sweat began to trickle along his hairline. She repeated the movement until he was panting and shallow growls were emanating from his throat. He released the covers, tossing away the shredded material, but still kept his hands to himself.

Gina met his gaze. "I couldn't live with myself if anything happened to you," she said, gyrating her hips.

His heart swelled at her words, snapping his self-control. Morgan grabbed the back of her neck and pulled her mouth down to his in a punishing kiss that left them both reeling. He thrust his tongue inside, tasting her femininity, her warmth, her courage—her love. He pillaged, savagely taking what she would give him and more. He couldn't get enough of her, returning again and again to dip in the warmth of her well. Morgan knew he was being greedy, but he didn't care. He needed Gina and she didn't disappoint. She matched him step for step, returning his passion tenfold.

Reluctantly, he released her, their lips parting in a loud smack. "I love you. And now that I've found you, I'm not going anywhere," he said. "Do you hear me? I'll always be here for you."

Gina grinned and proceeded to ride him into oblivion.

chapter three

Red and Morgan entered the sheriff's station an hour later. They'd showered and changed into fresh clothes in preparation for the long day ahead. Red had interviews to conduct, even though technically she didn't work for the Nuria sheriff's department yet, since her transfer orders hadn't arrived. Her tenuous position made it awkward with the other deputies.

Good thing she was used to awkward.

She looked at the empty desk outside of Morgan's office. Maggie wasn't in yet. She must have had a busy night with Jim Thornton, the director of the dissecting lab, since she normally beat everyone into the office. They'd been carrying on for more than a year and no one had known until last month, when a disheveled Maggie had been spotted coming out of Jim's lab.

Red grabbed a spare metal desk in the back of the room. She'd just opened her notes for the first interview, when Maggie rushed into the room, tossing her oversized purse onto the desk. She was a soft-spoken woman of moderate age, who'd lived and worked in Nuria her whole life. The last twenty years had been spent at the sheriff's station, keeping everything and everyone in tiptop shape. She took her management job seriously. Red thought sometimes too seriously.

"Sorry I'm late," she said, fiddling with her brown curls, which lay in disarray around her head. Half her shirt hung loose, while the other half had been haphazardly tucked in.

"Rough morning?" Red asked.

Maggie blushed and then gave her a once-over. "You're one to talk."

"Touché," she said. Despite the fact Maggie had given up on Red ever controlling her change, they were still comfortable enough with each other to tease on occasion. She hoped that eventually they'd become friends just as she and Jesse had. Red hid her smile behind the compunit on her desk and went back to work. If the applications she'd read through were any indication of the quality of the recruits, it was going to be a long day. . . .

"So why do you want to join the team?" she asked.

"You have pretty eyes, has anyone ever told you that?" the redheaded applicant named Hank asked. He sat across from her with his elbows resting casually on her desk.

Red stared at him until he sat up straight. Why had she volunteered for this job, when she could be cleaning her guns instead? "Yes. Now answer the question," she said.

Undeterred he kept up his onslaught. "Would you like to go to lunch sometime?"

She blinked at his audacity. "You do realize you're at a job interview, right? I mean I know it's confusing given the men running around with badges and laser pistols, but try to stay focused."

"I *am* focused." He gave her what Red was sure was supposed to be an engaging smile, but it came off more like a leer, since his eyes roved over her chest at the same time. "It doesn't have to be *all* business. Does it?"

Red shook her head and typed in the word "reject" by his name. "Next."

That was the fourth applicant who'd tried to ask her out. Normally that wouldn't bother her, but it had never happened before her wolf raised its furry head. She'd been around plenty of male recruits in her last job. Thousands to be exact, and only two had ever asked her to . . . well, it hadn't been to dinner. One she'd accepted. The other she'd told to go to hell. Bannon Richards hadn't liked her since.

But that didn't explain the sudden interest from the recruits. It could be because they thought it would help their chances, but Red didn't think so. There was something in their eyes. In the way they looked at her. It was predatory and she didn't like it one bit. It raised her hackles, made her want to lash out. And for someone not in control of her wolf, that could be a very dangerous prospect.

The morning crawled bloodied and beaten into the afternoon. Red's voice had grown hoarse from shouting "next" so many times. Every applicant she'd interviewed had given her good cause to dismiss them. The faces of the rejected blurred before her tired eyes. Red didn't know how much longer she could keep this up.

Someone cleared their throat. Red glanced up and realized she'd forgotten all about the potential recruit she'd been about to interview. With sandy blond hair and freckles dotting his cheeks, the man across from her didn't look old enough to shave, much less serve on the new tactical team. Maybe she was just jaded. After all, she'd started at about his age.

She looked down at the list of innocuous questions on her compunit, then back at the new recruit. "So why do you want to join the Nurian Tactical Team?" She paused as it dawned on her that she couldn't remember his name. She flicked her gaze at the screen once more. "Anthony."

"I was told you'd give me a laser pistol," he said, grinning like the answer should please her.

Red heard snickers from the people around her, but chose

to ignore them. Someone had to do this, and since Morgan was busy making sure Nuria ran smoothly, that left her. *"And?"* she coaxed, waiting for Anthony to continue. Surely, joining a tactical team meant more to him than carrying a weapon. If not, then this would be a very short interview.

The man fidgeted and looked flustered. "And I thought going on patrol outside of Nuria would be cool." A hopeful expression lit his face.

Red stared at him until he shrank a little under her gaze. "Those aren't exactly the reasons we were looking for. This is a serious job. One where lives are on the line. If you think this is a joke, then you're wasting my time and yours."

"I don't think it's a joke." He sat forward with newfound determination. "I can't spend my life raising hogs like my folks. Just tell me what you want to hear."

"I shouldn't have to," she snapped. "But here's a hint. We want to hear that you want to join so you can look out for your people. That you want to join because you think justice should be for everyone, not just purebloods. That you understand in this line of work death is always just around the corner."

Anthony perked up. "Yeah, that, too."

Red's eyes narrowed. "Next." She typed in the standard rejection by his name.

"Bitch," Anthony spat.

A growl rumbled out of Red's chest before she could stop it. She wasn't sure who was more surprised, her or Anthony. His blue eyes widened with fear and his head lowered. The room grew deathly quiet.

Red straightened her shoulders. She could feel everyone's eyes on her, waiting to see if she'd snap and shift. She pushed the wolf back into the darkness of her mind, then glared at Anthony. "I said next. I suggest you leave while you still can," she said with more force than she'd intended.

Anthony left quickly out the front door, glancing back every now and then to make sure she wasn't following. The urge to give chase caused her to twitch, but she kept the impulse in check.

A shadow passed over her, blocking out the overhead light. Red looked up and up until she met a pair of piercing amber eyes. She cleared her throat.

"Are you here to be interviewed for the team?"

He nodded.

"Then please take a seat."

He draped himself over the chair, flipping his long black hair gracefully away from his face. Red couldn't tell how long it was, but it fell well past his broad shoulders.

"Name?" she asked, trying not to react to his unflinching regard. This was the type of man the new team needed—strong, forceful, self-assured, and dominant. He hadn't even opened his mouth yet and he'd shown more presence and intelligence than all the other applicants combined.

"Takeo Alan Yakamura." He threw open the coat he wore and dust floated through the air.

"Long trip?" she asked.

"Very," he said without expanding his answer.

Red watched the material settle around him, mesmerized by his movements. "Current occupation?" She placed her fingers on the keys, prepared to type.

"Botanist."

Her head jerked up and she stared at him. "Did you say botanist?"

His lips twitched and something in his eyes glittered. "Not what you expected?"

"Uh, actually no," she said. "May I ask why you're interested in joining the NTT?"

"Do I not look capable?" He stood and did a slow turn so Red could get a good look at him.

She swallowed hard as her eyes took in his lean muscular form. He looked more than capable. She inhaled, whether from habit or curiosity she didn't know. His scent was a mix of musk and a spicy floral aroma. Yet in no way could it be described as feminine. Definitely different from the other applicants. Different from anyone she'd ever encountered. The wolf inside her perked with interest and Red quickly leashed it.

"What are you, Mr. Yakamura?" Red sat back and crossed her arms over her chest. "I don't sense wolf in you." She still hadn't perfected detecting the Other in individuals. Some people projected their power, while others kept it hidden.

"No, you wouldn't, but I can sense it in you. Rich, lush, and dare I say, inviting." A smile split his sensual lips, causing his eyes to slant even further. Red's breath caught in her throat. She prayed he hadn't noticed her reaction, but from the subtle change in his expression, she bet he had.

She cleared her throat. "We weren't discussing me. We were talking about you, and you still haven't answered my question."

"I am something very rare." He leaned over the desk until only inches separated them. "Do you really want to know?"

His sweet breath fanned over her face, the heat of it doing strange things to her insides, while at the same time, making her light-headed. Something wasn't right. Red's hand instinctively moved to her pistol. She drew the weapon and brought it up under his chin so fast he didn't have time to move, much less think.

"Yes," she said. "I really want to know."

His golden eyes narrowed dangerously and his pupils went from a circle to a slit. "You shouldn't have done that. It feels threatened."

"That's funny, so do I." Before Red could ask what he was talking about, a snake with diamond patterns on its head and back sprang out from under his coat and came straight for her face, fangs extended and hissing.

"What the hell!" Red shouted as her left hand caught it

around the neck midstrike. It was warm and slick to the touch, utterly foreign. She held on tight, making sure her laser pistol didn't budge an inch.

"I warned you," he said.

The snake twisted and coiled in an attempt to break free. Red refused to release the scaly creature as it continued to hiss and snap. Takeo, she noted, hadn't moved. Smart man. "I'm going to ask you one more time," she said in an overly calm voice. "What are you?"

A look of admiration crossed his features before he carefully schooled his expression. "I'm a chimera. If you let me go," he glanced at the hand holding the snake, "I'll put away my toys."

"One wrong move and I'll blow its head off, then yours." Red released the snake and watched it recede back under the coat. It was already morphing, the color fading from its diamond-patterned skin. By the time it disappeared beneath the fabric, it was flesh colored. "Neat trick," she said, holstering her weapon and sitting once more. "I don't want to know what I was just holding."

His lips quirked. "You're fast," he said. "Faster than I expected. I'd heard rumors, but they were hard to believe."

"You sound surprised, which makes you dumb. Dumber than I expected."

He grinned. "More like pleasantly pleased."

Red stared at him, but didn't respond. What could she say? She'd always had fast reflexes, but they'd never been that fast before. It was the wolf again, exerting its presence in her waking state. Why now? Why not when she was trying to change? She looked at Takeo.

"Why do you want to be part of the NTT?" she asked, as if they'd never had their little altercation.

Takeo smiled. "I wasn't sure I did until now."

"Well you certainly seem capable of defending yourself," she said, nodding at his coat.

"As do you," he added, sizing her up. There was something different in his gaze this time, respect.

"Report here at dawn tomorrow morning," she said. "And keep the snake under wraps."

He nodded. "Is there anyplace in town worth staying?"

"The water trader still has plenty of rooms. They're clean, spacious, and come with private cleansing units."

"Thanks, Commander."

Red's eyes widened. "I'm not your commander."

He shrugged. "Sure act like one to me," Takeo said, then strode out of the office.

After the chimera left, she found two more promising recruits. Randall Jones and Keith Olson would make a nice addition to the team. Red was about to take a break when a flash of color caught her eye. She watched as a man came forward covered from head to toe in white protective clothing. At least she thought it was a man, given the size. She couldn't see his eyes yet, but her body tensed as he neared. One more attack and she was done for the day.

He stepped forward and pressed a button on the side of his mask. The plate cleared enough for her to see his face. Dreadlocks fell in long snaking spirals near his jaw. He smiled, causing his velvety black skin to dimple, and she caught a glimpse of fangs. That explained the protective gear.

Most vampires couldn't handle the sun's rays. It hardened their skin, causing them to expand until they exploded into a thousand tiny pieces of shrapnel. You could kill them, but they'd kill you back. A few, like Raphael Vega and Mike Travers, had developed immunity over the years or maybe they'd always been able to tolerate sunlight. This man was obviously not one of the fortunate souls.

"Hi," he said, grinning from ear to ear, his brown eyes sparkling like onyx.

Red tried to remain stern, but found herself smiling back at him. "Please take a seat."

He sat down, his movements graceful despite the suit. The smile hadn't left his face.

"Name?" she asked.

"Demery Wilson." A lilt flavored his smoky voice.

"Origin?"

"Caribbean, mon. In the Republic of Floridian Islands."

Red looked at him. "You're a long way from home."

"My home is wherever I lay my head," he said cheerfully. "I am a traveler of the world."

"Any family?" she asked, straying from her list of questions. She was genuinely curious what had brought the vamp here.

His expression clouded, dimming his chocolate-colored eyes. It could've been a trick of the light, but Red didn't think so.

Demery shifted in his seat and his smile dropped a fraction. "I had—have a sister, but I haven't seen her in a while."

Red moved on quickly. She should've known better than to ask such a personal question. "Current occupation?"

"Bounty hunter." Demery perked up.

"Really?" Red laughed, not expecting that answer. He seemed too jovial to be a bounty hunter. The ones she'd run across on the job had been stoic and antisocial. "Any good?"

"I've been told I'm the best." He winked at her.

"Are we still discussing bounty hunting?" she asked, her eyes narrowing.

He chuckled. "But of course, mon." The sparkle in his gaze told her that he wasn't about to admit otherwise. "No one can hide from me for long. I'm the best when it comes to remote viewing."

Remote viewing was a talent they could definitely use on the team. Developed back in the twentieth century for military use, remote viewing allowed a person to *mentally* find things. The person doing the viewing could be looking for weapons, secret military locations, or missing individuals.

Practically anything. The program had been dropped publicly, but experiments and training continued to take place behind the scenes and through private organizations. "If you have such a lucrative talent, then why do you want to join the NTT? There are other positions out there that would pay far more than we can offer."

"Just want to do my part for the cause, mon. And who knows, the team may end up helping me in the long run." The cadence in his accent made his words sound almost melodic. Red found herself tapping her toes to the rhythm.

"Aren't you worried you'll be at a disadvantage?" She nodded to his protective suit. It was a valid question. A member that could be easily dispersed wasn't going to be of help to the rest of the team.

"No, mon. I've had it modified. I can see as well during the day through the mask as I can at night and the material allows me to move quickly. I'm lethal in and out of the suit."

Red eyed him and his smile seemed to widen, if that was even possible. "We'll see," she said. "Be here tomorrow at dawn."

She climbed out from behind her desk, rubbing her back. Red hadn't expected the day to be such a waste. At least she'd found a few good candidates. There would be more interviews tomorrow. *Oh goody.* She strode across the station to Morgan's office and knocked.

"Come in."

The door slid open and Red stepped inside and closed it behind her. Morgan sat at his desk, his hair poking out at all angles like he'd been running his fingers through it.

"That good a day, huh?" she asked.

He looked up at her. "You don't look like you fared any better," he said, beckoning her closer.

Red walked over and sat on the corner of his desk. Morgan reached up and pulled her onto his lap. She wrapped her arms around his neck and he kissed her tenderly.

"It's better now," he said, nuzzling her neck. "I've missed you."

"I've missed you, too. I can't wait until we can get out of here."

Morgan grinned and waggled his eyebrows. "Me either."

The viewer in his office glowed to life. The only time it came on was when there was breaking news for the republics. They both turned, ready to see the latest announcement.

The Santa Fe Cloning Laboratory Corporation would like to announce an amazing breakthrough. We have developed an inoculation that repairs damaged and abnormal cells. Just think about it. No more diseases. No more illness. Reverse the signs of aging. We're calling it Project Scarlet.

With Scarlet running through your veins, your life will never be the same.

Have your credits ready to sign up now.

"What does that mean?" Red asked.

Morgan's brow furrowed. "If I understand them correctly, it could mean an end to the Others."

"A cure? Are you saying they've developed a cure?" Red squealed in delight. Maybe she wouldn't have to learn how to control the change after all if the Scarlet vaccine worked. She could go back to the tactical team. The people of Nuria wouldn't have to hide any longer. "That's wonderful," she said. "Don't you think?"

Morgan's expression became unreadable. "There have been vaccines that made the same kind of promises before. None of them have worked."

"You sound like you're speaking from experience."

"I am," he muttered.

"Oh," she said, deflated. "But it's still possible."

"Anything is possible," he said, looking more and more unhappy.

A woman's face flashed on the screen. She had warm brown hair and laughing green eyes. Her image slid to the left and a child's face popped onto the screen beside her. The child reminded Red of someone, but she couldn't place whom. It was obvious that he was somehow related to the woman. He had the same coloring. Red reached for the remote and turned the volume up.

Santa Fe Cloning Laboratory Corporation would also like to announce its two latest clone models. The Sarah-3000, the woman's face enlarged on the screen, *will be released as a pleasure model starting in the spring.* Sarah's face faded and the boy's smiling image took center screen. *And Joshua-200, who will be a nice addition to any home. He can be used as laborer or you can make him part of the family. Just think what it would be like, having an eight-year-old child for life. We are taking preorders now.*

What would they think of next? Red shook her head and looked at Morgan. The color had drained from his face and his features were twisted in agony.

"What's wrong?"

He didn't respond, only pointed to the screen with trembling fingers.

"Morgan, what's wrong?" Red shook him to get his attention. He didn't move. "You're starting to scare me," she said.

He turned to her, his amber eyes full of pain, before looking back at the viewer in disbelief. "It can't be. It's not possible."

"I don't understand. You look like you've seen a ghost." Red's chest clenched, strangling her breath. She looked back at the screen at the woman and child. A shiver ran down her spine. "Do you know those clones?" she asked. *Please say no. Please say no.* But she knew from the look on his face that he did.

"Not ghosts." Morgan's tormented eyes met hers once more. He was looking at her, but Red was pretty sure he couldn't see her. His gaze was so distant. "It's worse than that. Much worse."

"What could be worse?" she asked. Her mind filled with various scenarios. All bad.

"That's my wife and child."

chapter four

Punching her would've hurt less. Red couldn't breathe. The air in the room refused to enter her lungs. She forced herself to her feet and stumbled away, her body protesting her movements. She dropped into a metal chair, hearing the echo of Morgan's words in her mind. It couldn't be. He'd said he loved her. Begged her not to leave him. Swore he'd never leave her. She'd heard him last night and this morning. There had to be some kind of mistake.

Blood roared through her veins until the world around her bled to crimson. Red hadn't realized Morgan had moved until he touched her. She jumped, pulling away from him.

"Don't—don't." She held out her hands to keep him at bay and blinked rapidly to get the world to come back into sharp focus.

"Gina." He reached for her once again and she growled in warning.

"I said don't touch me." Red pulled her legs into her chest, hugged them close, and began to rock. "How could you? After everything we've been through." How could he not tell her about a wife? Hell, he'd had a child. A son. Those things were important. The kind of things you shared with someone you loved. Maybe he didn't love her as much as he'd claimed. She hated even thinking it, but why else would he have kept something so important a secret?

Morgan ran a hand through his hair and began to pace. "You have to understand it was a long time ago. Another lifetime."

"Oh, God, you left her?" Would he do the same to her when he grew tired of her?

He spun on her. "No, never," he said, continuing to pace. "It wasn't like that."

"What was it like then?" Her eyes narrowed on him. "Why didn't you tell me? Why didn't anyone mention this before?"

He stopped and looked at her, letting her see the torment that clawed at his insides. "Not many people know. Like I said, it was a lifetime ago—*literally*. Long before I came to Nuria."

"Why did you leave them?" Red's stomach soured and she fought to keep from throwing up. How could the man that she loved abandon his family? She had made a mistake. A huge mistake. She never should've come to Nuria. Never should've allowed herself to fall in love with Morgan. Her gut had warned her in the beginning and she'd ignored it. Maybe it wasn't too late to go back to IPTT.

Morgan dropped to his knees before her and pressed his hands to the sides of the chair, effectively caging her in. "I told you, I *didn't* leave them. I would've never left them." His voice choked with emotion. "They died a long time ago. In a bombing. So you see, they left me."

"God, I'm sorry," she said. "I know what it's like to lose your family. The pain never goes away. One minute everything is moving along nicely, then the next, the world shakes, knocking our feet out from under us. I'm trying to understand. This is just a lot to take in." Red's thoughts jumbled into a blur of shock and panic.

"I never meant to hurt you," he said softly.

Red knew he meant every word, but that didn't stop the pain. "Why do you think they're back now?" she asked.

Morgan let his head fall forward until his hair brushed

her shins. Soft wisps caressed her arms and she clutched her legs tighter. If she didn't, Red knew she'd reach out and pull him closer. And she just couldn't do that right now. She was too confused. Too upset. Too hurt. Damn him.

"I don't know, but I have to stop this." He pushed back onto his feet and stood.

Red frowned. "What do you mean?"

"I can't allow them to turn Sarah into a whore. She deserves better than that."

The love he infused into Sarah's name scorched Red, leaving her raw. "How do you plan to do that?"

Morgan met her gaze. "I'm going to go to the Santa Fe Cloning Lab to reason with them. If need be, I'll get a job there, so I can find out what's going on. I can be very persuasive when I have to be. If they don't listen, I'll find the cells and destroy them."

"You can't do that. It would cost the corporation millions. They'll arrest you and put you away for life."

"I don't care!" he snapped.

"I do," she whispered. He was going to risk everything they'd built together for a ghost. It was there in his amber eyes. Red wanted to be supportive. She really did. She understood the need to protect one's family, but there had to be some other way to stop them that didn't require sacrificing his freedom and their future. Her distress must have shown on her face.

"You don't understand. I can't let them do that to Sarah and Joshua. I can't." He shook his head. "There's no way I can sit back and do nothing. They are . . . they *were* my family. My world."

"I understand more than you think." The slip he made was a little one, but it might as well have been a death knell. A wall dropped down between them. Red couldn't see it, but she could sense its presence. And it was more impenetrable than maglev armor. "What about Nuria? We're in the middle of trying to build a tactical team to protect them and Others around the world. What we're attempting to do is greater than the genetic material of two people. We need you." *I need you.*

"They have you." Morgan gave her a small smile. "You can continue to build the team. You're already off to a good start. I plan to leave you in charge while I'm gone. Maggie will be your second in command. She knows everything about running Nuria and the Sheriff's station. The deputies love and respect her. They'd do anything for Maggie, so if you need help, ask her. She'll be more than happy to pick up the reins."

Now he was dumping that responsibility into her lap. He didn't ask. He just assumed she'd take over running the town. "They might listen to Maggie, but they're not going to listen to me. I'm an outsider. The only reason they accept me at all is because of you." Red hated the desperation she heard in her voice. Next she'd be begging him to stay.

"That's not true," he said.

"It is. You don't see it." Most people just tolerated her presence. What would happen when the person standing between them left?

Morgan's gaze softened. "You are the strongest person I know. If anyone can hold this town together, you can."

He was wrong. She wasn't strong. At least not in the way needed to keep this town ticking until he returned. His will alone did that.

"What about us?" Tears blurred her vision as she swallowed back a sob. "I-I need you." It hurt her to admit it, but he needed to hear it. "I can't do this on my own."

Morgan pulled her to her feet. Red tried to resist, but there wasn't much fight left in her. It had seeped out the second he'd said the words "wife and child." It didn't matter that they were dead. They were back now. The fact they were clones wouldn't mean a lot once Morgan laid eyes on them.

Red knew that was the case, since she would give anything to see her family again and have them back in her life.

"You know I love you. And I wouldn't be leaving if it wasn't important," he said. "I have to do this. I hope someday you understand. I'd do the same, if it were you in that laboratory."

She nodded, but couldn't speak the words. She *did* understand, but that didn't stop the pain. Nor did it stop her from wanting him to stay.

"I need you to be strong while I'm gone," he said, brushing her cheek with his knuckles.

Red felt the warmth of his skin beneath his shirt. She leaned forward and inhaled, taking his clean scent into her lungs. "When are you going to leave?"

Morgan loosened his hold so he could look into her eyes. "As soon as I've informed my staff. I'm not going to tell them everything because I don't want anyone to interfere. This is my decision, and mine alone. I'll be back as soon as I can," he said, then kissed her good-bye.

Red watched him walk out of her life. Her insides were on fire, or at least that's what it felt like. How could this have happened? She wanted desperately to prevent Morgan from leaving, but didn't know how. What could she say? If you want us to work, you'll stay? It was the truth, but hardly compelling enough to change Morgan's mind at this point. Nothing was strong enough.

Not even their love.

Morgan's emotions were in turmoil as he walked away from Gina. It felt as if he were being ripped in half, but there was no turning back. The faces of Sarah and Joshua flashed in his mind. The pain of their deaths hit him like a blow again, doubling him over.

He remembered that day like it was yesterday. They'd

sent his unit out to scout the area for rebel forces. He'd left Joshua and Sarah at the house he'd built for them. An agreement had been reached between the factions to avoid further civilian casualties. It was supposed to be safe in town. *They* were supposed to be safe.

He'd only been gone five hours when the air sirens filled the sky, deafening the birds squawking in the trees nearby. There were no other targets in the area, or so Morgan had been told. No one had known about the ammunition storage units hidden in town. Not even him.

His heart had nearly exploded in his chest as he raced back to the small Colorado town nestled in the mountains. By the time Morgan reached the valley, the town had been leveled.

It took him five minutes to orient himself. With all the street signs and buildings reduced to rubble, everything looked the same. If it wasn't for the fresh blood flowing into the roads, he wouldn't have known he was in the right place. Bodies were strewn about the alleys and sidewalks where people had been strolling only moments before.

Mangled, ripped, charred, and shredded. The lifeless corpses looked more like mannequins than real people. At least it was easier to think of them that way. A few minutes later, Morgan found his house and immediately began digging.

There was a chance they'd survived. Or so he'd told himself over the hours it took for him to uncover his family. He'd found Joshua first, his small body crushed beneath the collapsed wood beams. His little face was bloody and pale and his blue eyes were lifeless. Morgan roared in impotent rage as he clutched his dead son to his chest and wept for the first time in his adult life.

He'd taken off his jacket and gently placed Joshua on it, then continued digging, his knuckles bloody from the repeated knocking. Exhausted and numb, he'd found Sarah two hours later. She wore a faded pair of jeans and a shirt he'd given her for her last birthday. She'd complained about the expense, but he'd caught the glee in her lovely eyes. Sarah had worn the shirt every chance she got.

Scratches covered her fingers and face. He picked up her hand, marveling at the dainty size before pressing a kiss to her cool palm, then gently holding it to his chest. Her long nails were broken and bleeding, which told him Sarah had at least survived the initial attack and attempted to dig herself out. If only he'd gotten there sooner she might have lived.

Morgan had scooped her up. "I'm so sorry," he murmured into her soft hair. It still smelled feminine and light despite being covered in debris. Part of him had died that day with his family. A part of him he thought he'd never recover. Until he'd met Gina. She'd showed him what he'd been missing. Made him want to love again, even though the prospect terrified him. Morgan knew he wouldn't survive another loss of that magnitude, yet he couldn't stop himself. The decision had been made for him.

And now he was about to leave Gina to go in search of a past Morgan thought he'd buried long ago.

The cage was dark and musty, a windowless prison that could be easily forgotten. The chains holding the man had rusted, but not enough to weaken them. His brown hair was dirty and reeked of sweat, blood, fear, and desperation. Sores covered his wrists and scratches dotted his pale skin where he'd tried to break his restraints. Fresh feces and urine splattered the floor in a massive pile of human suffering. A cloud of ammonia floated in the air, choking off any chance of a deep breath.

How long had the man been down here? Roark Montgomery couldn't quite recall as he stood with his arms crossed, staring at the pitiful thing in disgust. His eyes watered from the stench, but he wasn't about to clean it until he got what he'd come for.

Roark had had him picked up after he'd been spotted wandering in the desert. An *unknown* without papers or family. The fact the man wasn't registered with any of the republics made it so very easy. The man had come here from no-man's-land to have a better life—or so he'd said when he first arrived. Roark eyed him. That hadn't worked out so well for him, but it was perfect for what Roark had in mind.

"Are you ready to get out of here?" he asked.

The man didn't move, not even a twitch from his limp limbs. Roark stepped forward and kicked the cage. The sound reverberated in the room, then quickly dampened due to its underground location. He hated coming down here, but the place served its purpose.

"I said, are you ready to get out of here? If you're too far gone, then just say so and I'll find another."

The man's head rolled to one side as he fought to raise it. "Yes." He coughed. "I'm ready," he croaked out from behind split, dried lips.

Roark smiled. "I thought as much."

The man tilted his chin up until he could look at Roark. One eye was sealed shut from the beatings, but the other glared with the fire of hatred, letting him know that despite the man's diminished capacity there was still some fight left in him.

"I have a job for you," Roark said, meeting his gaze. "If you do this right, you'll never see me again."

The man licked his lips. "And if I don't?"

Roark's eyes narrowed. "Then you can rot down here, for all I care. Your choice. There are plenty more where you came from."

The man's head slumped forward in defeat, then he forced it up once more. "What do you want me to do?"

"That's more like it." Roark's grin returned. "I need you to take a little trip."

The man frowned. "Where?"

"After being in this place, does it really matter?" Roark asked, astonished at his gall.

"No, I guess not."

"Now listen carefully." Roark filled the man in on the details of what he wanted him to do. "When you're done, wait in the valley to the north. Do you understand the instructions I've given you?"

"Yes. Find the woman," the man said. "I'm free to do as I please afterward. Right?"

"Of course," Roark said. "That was our deal."

The man stared at him, searching for signs of deception. He wouldn't find any. Roark made sure. He'd had fifteen years in politics, giving him plenty of time to perfect the art of lying. The man finally nodded in agreement.

"Good," Roark said. "My assistant will be down in a moment to get you cleaned up. Do try to behave yourself. He's not nearly as patient as I am." With that Roark left. The elevator carried him from the bowels of the basement up to his office on the fifth floor, which overlooked the west side of the Republic of Missouri's biodome.

He found his assistant, Michael Travers, waiting in the hall for his return. He was a meek man with pale skin and slick black hair that moved like a second skin on his head. His lips were overly full, almost feminine, and tended to smack when he talked. Deep down, Roark despised the man, but he'd always done good work. Until now.

Lately, he'd changed. Michael had taken to asking more questions than was necessary when Roark gave him an assignment. He talked back often. And there was something else in his dark eyes that hadn't been there before—defiance. Roark didn't like it one bit, but until he found a suitable replacement, he was stuck with the man.

"What do you want?" Roark asked.

"I've finished all the reports and sent them to their respective departments. The officers are waiting in that room," Michael said, pointing to a door on the right. "Is there anything else you'd like me to do before I bring them in?"

"As a matter of fact, I have a little errand for you to run."

Michael frowned. "An errand? But I thought you wanted me to stick around for the interviews."

"There's been a change of plans," Roark snapped. "I have a package down in the basement, room number seven. Get it cleaned and patched up. Regenerate it, if necessary. I want it in top shape by the time it leaves here. Once that's done, I'd like you to drop it off outside of Nuria."

"Why Nuria?" Michael asked.

"Because it's the closest town to the boundary fence." Roark's gaze narrowed. "And because I asked you to." He blew out a frustrated breath. "Your insubordination is getting tiresome. One of these days you'll go too far. Now do as you are told."

"Yes, sir," he said, scurrying off.

Roark waited until he was out of sight, then stepped into his office. With Michael out of the way, he could begin phase three of his plan.

chapter five

Metal chairs elbowed each other for space in the small, cramped room. A lone fluorescent bulb flickered endlessly, threatening to plunge the area into oppressive darkness. Hot air filled with influ-gas seeped in through an antiquated air-filtration system. The gas held neither scent nor taste as it drifted onto the two occupants waiting to be summoned.

Roark Montgomery steepled his fingers under his chin and leaned closer to the monitor. The petite, shaggy red-headed female sat a chair away from the steely eyed, blond bruiser. Their crossed legs faced away from each other. You didn't have to be a body language expert to know that there was no love lost between them. Roark tilted the screen and zoomed in.

The man reminded him a little of himself twenty years ago. Same ambition, same skill as a tactical team member. The only difference was Roark had always thought for himself, which was something he couldn't say about this man. Pity.

By now the gas would be permeating their skin, filling their pores, landing on their tongues if they spoke. In a few more minutes, they'd grow sluggish and forget why they were here. Eventually they'd pass out and then he'd start the subliminal messages. It was important that his voice be the first thing they heard.

Any interruptions could ruin all his hard work and shatter the connection he planned to forge with these two people. That's why Roark had sent his assistant out to take care of the package. He was becoming more and more unpredictable and Roark couldn't afford to screw this up.

Roark stared at the screen. The woman had started to perspire. The man wouldn't be far behind. He had to time things right. Roark needed to make sure that Lieutenant Bannon Richards and Private Catherine Meyers were under completely or the subliminal implantation wouldn't be successful.

As it was, his suggestions would only last a month or two. The influ-gas wasn't made for long-term use. It had a tendency to kill the subjects if they were dosed too often.

Not that Roark was worried about killing either of these International Police Tactical Team members. By the time they finished carrying out his plans, the tactical team would do that for him. Roark grinned. There would be no more mistakes. He was done trusting outside help. From now on, he'd force cooperation through any means necessary.

Roark saw Catherine's lips move and decided to turn up the volume so he could hear what she had to say.

"Why do you think he called us here?" she asked. "I mean I've heard of the guy. Who hasn't? He's practically a hero. But it's not like our paths have ever crossed. There's no way he could've known about me. I'm nobody at headquarters."

Bannon turned his buzz-cut blond head toward her. The vein in his neck bulged and his blue eyes narrowed to icy slits. "You're right. You are a nobody." His gaze raked her, confirming his words. "I have no idea why he wanted *you* here. You haven't even finished training yet." He shrugged. "Maybe he needs a charity case for his next campaign stop. As for what I'm doing here, I suspect he contacted me for a job."

"What kind of job?" she asked, perking up. "Do you know the politician personally?"

His lip curled into a sneer. "Yeah, we go way back," Bannon said, the lie slipping easily from his mouth.

Roark laughed, the sound rusty from disuse. Bannon really was a bastard. He shook his head. No wonder he liked him. Maybe if he handled the job he wanted him to do, he'd save him from IPTT's wrath and find him a permanent position within his office.

Catherine fidgeted and pulled at the collar of her black tactical team uniform. "Is it hot in here to you?" she asked, fanning herself with a scrap of synth-paper that had been left on the metal table by her seat.

Bannon ran a beefy hand over his forehead and came away with wetness. "Now that you mention it." As if realizing what he'd been doing, he glared at her. "What's the matter, can't take the heat?"

Catherine snorted. "Just trying to make small talk to pass the time while we wait."

"Well don't bother," Bannon said, then shook his head and swayed before grabbing the arm of his chair. "I'm not interested in hearing your thoughts, Private. In fact, I'm not interested in hearing you at all, so button it up."

She crossed her arms over her well-endowed chest. "Is that an order?"

"Yes," he snapped. "That's an order."

Sweat glistened like dew drops on the big man's skin. His short haircut was no defense against the ovenlike heat of the small room. Roark had made sure it was hotter in the room than it was outside. Heat intensified the gas's potency and now it was starting to take effect. Soon he could begin to reprogram them.

"I don't feel so well," Catherine said, clutching her stomach and groaning loudly. "Maybe I should ask Roark's assistant if I can reschedule. I don't want to walk into his office and toss my lunch on his shoes."

"Women," Bannon said in disgust. "You're all the same. I

still don't understand why they allow you on the tactical team."

Catherine glowered. "With all due respect, sir, you can fuck off." She turned and faced away from him, her crossed leg bobbing angrily.

"That'll go in your personnel fi—" Bannon slumped forward, his large body folding in on itself until his knuckles dragged the floor. Roark frowned as he watched the man's lips puff out like a fish. He glanced back at the woman. Normally the gas affected smaller individuals first. Other than the sweat on her brow and the dampness at her temples, Catherine seemed strangely alert.

She glanced over her shoulder and her eyes widened. "Hey, are you okay?" she asked. Bannon's only answer was a loud snore. "Terrific," she muttered. "We come all the way down here from tactical team headquarters and you decide to take a nap. Jerk. Lieutenant, wake up." Catherine stood to go check on him and collapsed to her knees. "What the hell?" She swayed a few seconds, then tumbled onto the floor.

"That's better," Roark said. For a moment he'd been worried she wasn't going to go under. She must have a high tolerance for drugs. Roark made a mental note for next time. He shook his head and laughed. There wouldn't be— couldn't be—a next time.

If all went as planned, Lieutenant Bannon Richards and Private Catherine Meyers would be dead within a month, and all trace of his interference would die with them.

He'd considered asking for Bannon Richards's assistance, but in the end decided he couldn't trust him to not tell the tactical team commander his plans. Bannon was rigid when it came to the rules, which was one of the reasons Roark had chosen him.

Unfortunately, his need to follow the letter of the law was also the reason he needed to be drugged. Roark had decided to call in Catherine Meyers at the last second, not for her skill or experience, but because she'd make the perfect fall guy and be none the wiser.

Roark pressed a button on his desk. The influ-gas turned off and fresh air began to pump into the room. He flicked a switch that allowed him to speak over the intercom. "Wake up, children." Now that he'd spoken, they'd listen to whatever he had to say.

The scientist who'd invented influ-gas had called it auditory synaptic bonding. Roark called it brilliant. To the outside observer, they'd be functioning normally. Only he would know the truth. One word from him and they'd do exactly what he wanted. No questions asked.

Bannon and Catherine stirred, their eyes glassy and unfocused. "I want you both to listen carefully. I have a job for you to do. I know you've heard about the new tactical team forming in Nuria. We can't allow that to happen. It will be very bad if they succeed. They'd try to eliminate the IPTT. Do you understand?"

They nodded and their expressions changed to anger.

"I want you to stop the formation of that team by any means necessary. I will notify you when to begin. You must not act until you hear the word . . ." Roark thought for a minute. The word "scarlet" popped into his head and he smiled at the irony. "The code word is scarlet. Understood?"

They swayed, then acknowledged him.

"Now I want you to stand and walk to the door."

Both soldiers hobbled to their feet. Roark rose from behind his desk and hit a button near his compunit. The door to his office opened. He walked to a nearby mirror to take in his appearance one last time before greeting his guests. His blue suit looked good against his dark hair. Only the gray at his temples hinted at his true age.

Roark straightened his striped silk tie, catching a glimpse of his mutilated hand. A hand missing three fingers courtesy of that bitch, Gina Santiago. He'd purposely avoided regeneration in order to have a reminder of her treachery.

She was about to learn the hard way that you don't mess with Roark Stonewall Montgomery. If she wanted a war, he'd give her one. He took a deep breath then walked out into the hall. It was now or never.

A panel to his right was hidden from the casual observer. Roark laid his hand on the spot above it. The panel slid open, exposing antique guns resting silently on a rack.

The International Police Tactical Team had disposed of most weapons after the war. What they didn't destroy, they kept for themselves. It was rare for anyone outside of law enforcement to have a decent weapon, much less the collection he housed here. Roark ran his hands reverently over the guns, their smooth wooden stocks satin-soft under his callused fingertips. They didn't make them like they used to.

Roark pulled out a tan custom-made laser sniper rifle before sealing the door once more. He tucked the gun in the crook of his arm and carried the weapon down the hall. He pressed his hand to a panel outside the room. A scanner read his fingerprints and the grooves in his palm. The door unlocked a second later, freeing his invited guests. The tactical team members stood in front of him staring in confusion.

Roark focused on the team member nearest him. "I need you to take this," he said, shoving the gun forward.

The soldier reached for the rifle. The weight pulled to the right and they nearly dropped the gun.

"Be careful."

"Sorry, sir. It's just heavier than I expected. Nothing like the IPTT-issued laser rifles."

"It's been custom made. I expect it back in the same condition." Roark went immediately into giving instructions. "Wait for it to charge. Look through the sight and squeeze the trigger. Then once that's done, I'd like you to approach the target and slash its throat. Do you think you can handle that?"

He received a curt nod.

"Good," Roark said. "I want you to shoot anyone found around the area of Nuria. They should be considered suspect

and in collusion with the enemy. They must be eliminated.
That includes any new trainees on the Nurian Tactical Team
that stand out. Your first target will be waiting north of Nuria
in the valley in two days' time. Is that clear?"

"Yes, sir."

Roark glanced at the second soldier. "I'd like you to gather
intel on their numbers. We cannot allow Gina Santiago and
Morgan Hunter to succeed in forming a new tactical team. It
would be a threat to the security of all the republics if the
Others were allowed to survive. Feel free to dispose of them
if you get the opportunity. That's an order."

"Understood, sir," the soldier said.

"Remember the code word?" Roark asked.

They both murmured, "Scarlet."

Catherine swayed.

The drug was beginning to wear off on her. *That was fast,*
Roark thought. She must have an unusually high metabolism.

He smiled and reached for her hand to shake it. The movement woke her out of the trance. Roark immediately did the
same to Bannon. "I'm sorry it's taken me so long to see you.
I had trouble with a package that needed to be sent out.
Please come with me and we'll discuss why I called."

Both frowned and looked around in confusion.

"Is there something wrong?" Roark asked.

"No, sir," they said in unison.

"We just—" Catherine stopped. "Sorry, I guess I fell
asleep."

Roark hid his smile. "I'm not surprised. I kept you waiting for a while. Sorry about the heat. I'll have Travers fix
that air unit the second he returns."

Catherine ran a hand through her wet hair, sending red
strands every direction. "Thank you, sir."

"Is that all?" Roark asked.

"Yes, sir," Catherine said.

"Splendid. Please follow me." Roark turned and headed

down the hall without looking to see if they'd follow. A moment later they stepped into his office, none the wiser. The space was far bigger than the one they'd just left and the light pouring in through the windows caused both team members to blink rapidly.

The air in here was fresh and lightly scented with lemon. Roark inhaled deeply and watched the two team members follow suit. "Glorious day, isn't it?" he asked.

"Yes, sir," they said.

Catherine and Bannon glanced out the window. Roark looked, too. He gazed at the Republic of Missouri's vast fields and dried-up riverbeds. He looked beyond the biodome at the dead forests and gnarled bushes. Inside the dome everything was green and wondrous, much like the planet used to be before the last war. Only a portion of what they were viewing was real. The rest was artificial.

Outside was a different story. Sand took the place of fertile fields. Dust storms were as common as the radioactive sunshine, which now glowed 360 days of the year thanks to ozone depletion, the last world war, and climate change. Nothing lived for long on the outside without a steady stream of supplies and immunization against radioactive poisons. Not even the Others, and they'd been engineered to survive.

Bannon rolled his thick neck, popping the joints. The noise brought Roark out of his musings. He glanced at the two soldiers covertly, then moved behind his large desk and sat. There were two metal seats opposite him, but he didn't ask either officer to sit. He thought it best they stand until their haziness passed. Roark pressed a black button to his right and the door to his office closed with an audible hiss. "Thank you for coming on such short notice."

"Anytime, sir," Bannon said, stepping away from the window to stand at attention in front of him.

Catherine shook her head and pressed a hand to her temple. She followed behind, her movements sluggish.

"Am I keeping you awake, Private Meyers?" Roark asked.

"No, sir. Sorry, sir. I just have a bit of a headache."

Roark ignored her statement. By the time they left, they'd both have migraines. "I wanted to check to see if you'd be available for security duties. I'm thinking about doing a tour of the republics and could use a couple of experienced team members to guard my back."

"Yes, sir. Anytime you want," Bannon said. "I have to clear it first, but I don't think that would be a problem. I have a lot of time saved up."

"Good, Lieutenant."

"I'm sorry, sir," Catherine said, interrupting the men. "But I'll have to also check with the commander to see if I can get the time off. To be honest, I doubt he'll grant it. I only have seven days saved."

"I understand, Private Meyers. I wouldn't need much of your time. A few days here and there are all. Your job with the tactical team would obviously be your first priority. You know how much I respect the team and what they stand for."

"Yes, sir. I've read about your service record. It's impressive." Catherine squeezed her neck and winced. "But let me make sure I understand your offer. You want *me* to work security for you?"

"Yes, Private. I do."

"No disrespect intended, sir, but why did you pick me? I mean it's not like I'm a senior officer. I've only been on the team for a few months. How did you even hear about me? I haven't exactly made a name for myself at headquarters."

"Don't question the politician," Bannon hissed, shifting the bundle in his arms. "He's going to be our next great leader."

Roark smiled. "It's okay, Lieutenant. Private Meyers has every right to ask. To answer your question, I think it's best to have an experienced officer along with a new recruit. Shows the people that I can relate to all walks of life, not just the ones influential enough to contribute to my campaign. Not to mention you're one of the few women on the tactical team now that Gina Santiago no longer works for IPTT."

Bannon tensed. Roark noted it, but didn't say anything. He'd obviously hit a nerve. He was convinced more than ever he'd made the right decision when he chose to gas them. Catherine was too smart for her own good and Bannon obviously had some emotional connection to the target. Whether it was positive or negative remained to be seen. Either way it might work out to Roark's advantage later.

"Do you really think you can unite the republics and convince them to allow you to lead?" Catherine asked. "They seem pretty happy as self-governing entities. I've never known anyone who'd willingly give up power. What you're talking about could start a war." She tilted her chin to look him in the eye. The slight movement caused her to rock forward. She quickly stepped back into place.

"Sometimes it takes conflict to bring about change," he said, picturing the new world order. All the republics united under one pureblood banner with him at the top, running the show. "But hopefully it won't come to that. Hopefully the republics will see reason. I can be very convincing, if I do say so myself." And when that failed, he had no problem resorting to violence. Roark leveled his gaze on her. "If I didn't believe I could unite the republics, then you wouldn't be here."

chapter six

Red stared at the compunit screen, unable to focus. Her stomach twisted into angry knots. It didn't help that everyone in town was giving her dirty looks as if she was somehow responsible for Morgan leaving. He had been gone for a week—a week that felt more like an eternity—and she hadn't heard a word from him.

Leaving her in charge had been a mistake. She'd known it when he told her his plans. She didn't know a thing about the day-to-day operations of a town. Give her a tactical team and she knew what to do, but running a town required diplomacy and tact. Hell, everything she lacked. Not to mention it had caused trouble in the sheriff's station.

The animosity was like a living entity, pressing in from all around, waiting to devour her. Red didn't have to look up to confirm her suspicions. She could feel the eyes of the deputies upon her. They were angry that one of them hadn't been appointed to lead. Even Maggie seemed resentful to have been relegated to second in command. It was the same when she walked around town.

No matter where she went, Nurians watched, waiting for her to slip up. It had been like that for a week and wasn't showing signs of stopping. She'd done her best to ease the tension by assuring them that Morgan would return shortly.

They hadn't bought it. The truth was, Red had no idea when he'd return, but it couldn't be soon enough.

Just the thought of Morgan brought fresh pain flooding in. She knew he'd made it to the Santa Fe Cloning Laboratory because they'd sent notice of his application to the sheriff's station. That had started tongues wagging and they hadn't stopped since.

Someone cleared his throat.

Red glanced at the interviewee, startled that she'd forgotten all about him, and wishing she was anywhere else but here working. His soft brown eyes stared back at her with compassion. "I'm sorry. Name?" she asked.

"Juan Sanchez," he said.

He had a kind face and a peaceful demeanor. His black hair was cut short, nearly shaved at the sides, but the hard angles did little to sharpen his sensual features. His light brown skin glowed with vitality.

Just being around him made the tension ease in her shoulders and neck. Red knew that gentleness didn't always denote an unlikely candidate, but it did stack the odds against him. They were looking for warriors, not ambassadors of peace. Juan watched her closely, but she could read nothing in his expression.

"Former occupation?"

He smiled. "Educator."

That fits, Red thought. "That's a good occupation. One that would pay far more than tactical work. Why change jobs?"

Juan shrugged. "Education is becoming more and more automated. Pretty soon teachers like me will be obsolete. At least this way I can make a difference in people's lives."

She typed in his answer on the application. "Fair enough," she said. "Birthplace?"

"The Republic of the Floridian Islands."

Red brows rose. "Like Demery Wilson, you're a long way from home, Mr. Sanchez."

"I could say the same about you, Ms. Santiago." His mocha eyes glittered as his smile returned.

Red's gaze narrowed and her attention sharpened. "How did you know my name?"

"I'm psychic," he said. "And you're easy to read. Especially when you're in so much pain. Besides, everyone in here has been staring at you like you're an outsider. I thought it was my presence that had garnered so much attention, but then I realized they weren't looking at me."

She glanced around to see if anyone had overheard his comment. At her notice, the men looked away.

"I'm sorry you're hurting," he said, leaning a little closer. "You're a stronger leader than you realize. And someday, you will be a great one."

Stunned, Red sat back. "You don't know what you're talking about," she snapped. "Now stay out of my head."

"As you wish." Juan inclined his head. "I was only trying to be of assistance."

"Well, stop it. No one asked for your help." She masked her fear with anger.

He remained blissfully unruffled by her outburst. "I doubt very much you would ask for help. Even if you needed it."

Red opened her mouth to refute his words, but he cut her off before she could.

"He's okay for now, but I don't know how much longer that will remain true. Unseen danger nears," Juan said, then shook his head. "So much pain. So much loss. He's traveled far, but he won't find what he's looking for."

She frowned. "Who?" It was difficult to keep up with his various methods of communication.

"Morgan. That is the name of the man that you love. Correct?"

Red's heart jumped in her chest. She wanted to ask how he knew. Hell, she wanted to ask him a million questions, but this was not the time or the place to ask them. "That's none of your business," she said defensively.

He laughed. "Sorry if I hit a nerve."

"You didn't."

"If you say so." His expression grew solemn. "If you ever need to talk, just call. I'll hear you whether it's by vidcom, navcom, or other less obvious means of communication." He stood to leave.

"Mr. Sanchez," Red called out, stopping him.

"Yes?"

"Report to training tomorrow morning."

He grinned and gave her a brisk nod, then strode to the door.

"And Mr. Sanchez."

"Yes?" He looked back over his shoulder.

"Thank you," Red said, then quickly dismissed him.

"Anytime, Ms. Santiago. Anytime."

Morgan sat in the personnel office of Santa Fe Cloning Laboratory, bouncing his knee. He'd submitted his application a week ago. They should've had time to run his information and approve him for the open security position by now.

He'd been lucky. The job had just opened up two weeks ago and several candidates had already applied. Fortunately, none seemed as well suited for the position as he was, or so he thought. So why weren't they offering him the job?

His mind drifted to Gina. God, he missed her. He missed the smell of her hair first thing in the morning. The feel of her skin when he caressed it. The sound of her soft moans when he entered her. Her boisterous laugh. The way she never backed down from a fight. The fire in her hazel eyes. He missed everything about her.

He closed his eyes and pictured her sitting in his office on the first day they'd met. She'd been a handful, with her black hair and long legs. She'd strode into his office like she owned the place and demanded his cooperation with her murder investigation. He couldn't have known then the murderer she sought would turn out to be his cousin, Kane. Or that her appearance would turn his world upside down and inside out.

He loved her. There was no question in his mind about that. But his feelings for her didn't squelch the doubt that seemed determined to linger. Was he truly committed to their relationship? He thought the answer was a resounding yes, but if that were the case, why had it been so easy to leave? The pain in Morgan's chest increased. He pressed a palm against his ribs and rubbed to ease the tension.

"Mr. Hunter," a voice behind him called out, wrenching Morgan out of his disturbing thoughts.

"Yes." He dropped his hand and turned to face the personnel officer.

"Sorry it took so long. We had a satellite malfunction and your credentials didn't arrive until today," the man said, taking a seat behind his expansive desk. He removed his glasses and looked at Morgan. "May I ask why you'd want to leave a position of command for one of subordination?"

Morgan met the man's beady gaze. Like most republic clerical employees, the man wore a drab brown suit that enhanced the color of his sallow skin. He'd combed his hair over to disguise the balding patch on his head. If anything, the move drew more attention to the man's pale crown. Morgan forced his eyes back to the man's face before he answered. "I was looking for a change. Wanted to work someplace more civilized." He ground the words out, even though it irked him to do so.

"Yes, quite," said the man, whose name he'd already forgotten. "Most unpleasant being that close to the boundary, I suspect. Never been there myself," he said, putting his large-framed glasses back on. The move magnified his eyes, making them go from beady to absurdly large. "I hear that you can see the boundary fence glowing in the dark from Nuria."

"Yes, you can." Morgan thought about the green glow

that flanked one side of Nuria. He hated the segregation the fence stood for, but had grown rather fond of the color.

The man shuddered. "No wonder you want out."

Morgan nodded. "Yes, it's horrible. Can't imagine ever going back." As each word fell from his lips, Morgan felt something wrench inside of him. Gina's smile flashed in his mind. The thought of never seeing her again seemed unbearable. He had to stay strong. Morgan pictured Sarah and Joshua. They were the only things that kept him in his seat and not rushing out the door. They were the past. Gina was the present. But Morgan knew he couldn't leave until he saw this through. He had to find Sarah's and Joshua's cell samples quick, so he could get back home.

"Do you have any questions?" the man asked, straightening his tie.

"No. I've read the literature about your company. I know you're doing cutting-edge work here. It's one of the reasons I came here and not one of the other biotech labs."

The man smiled and sat up straighter. "Yes, we're quite proud of all we've accomplished. Have you seen the latest clones about to be put into production? I imagine the Sarah-3000 model will sell quite nicely. We haven't had a pleasure model of that caliber for five years."

Morgan's hands clutched the side of his chair as he fought to keep from reaching over the desk and pummeling the man into the ground. "I'm sure it'll be quite a success," he said, vowing to wipe all record of Sarah out of their system.

"Would you like one?" the man asked, grinning at him lasciviously.

"No, thank you," Morgan grit out, ignoring the temptation. He'd loved the original. A copy would pale in comparison.

"I'm sure a strapping guy like you doesn't need a pleasure clone. You probably have the real thing waiting for you at home in your rest pad. As for me," the man grinned, "I can't wait to get my hands on her."

Morgan could barely breathe as his wolf clawed its way through his internal organs in an effort to reach the surface. It wanted to rip the man's throat out. Feast upon his rotten flesh. And he had no doubt it would indeed taste rotten. His pores stank of the excesses he tried to hide. It was difficult not to gag in his presence. Morgan released the chair and brought his trembling hands to his lap.

"What about the position?" he asked, his voice raspy from his effort to control himself.

"Well, seeing as though you're our most qualified applicant and you've signed the confidentiality agreement, I'd like to offer you the job if you're still interested."

"I am," Morgan said.

"Good." The man rose and stuck out his hand. Morgan shook his sweaty palm, but he had to will his fingers to release the man's hand before he crushed it. "You can start tomorrow."

Morgan smiled, his lips so tight he thought they'd crack. "Thank you. I'll be here bright and early."

"Wonderful." The man glanced at the door. "There are more reports to file. Just step into the waiting area and Gloria will take down all the necessary information. Once again, welcome aboard."

"Glad to be here," Morgan said, feeling anything but happy. He left without a backward glance.

The second Morgan closed the door behind him, the man's smile dropped and he tapped his vidcom. His hands flew over the keys as he punched in a familiar number. He drummed his fingers on his desk as he waited. Several beeps followed and the vidcom connected. The man listened, waiting for an answer.

"Talk," the voice on the line barked, but a picture did not appear.

"It's done. He just left," he said, then pressed a button to disconnect.

* * *

Situated in Nuria on the corner of Pine Street was a food dispensing station that resembled a twentieth-century movie theater. Faded walls held posters advertising various films that had long since faded from memory. Metal doors marked the entrance, muting the sound of the dinner crowd.

Red walked inside. Her stomach had been growling for an hour and she was ready to chew her own arm off if she didn't get food within the next thirty minutes. The interviews had taken longer than she'd expected, but at least she'd found two more recruits she hoped would work out. She still hadn't heard from Morgan. Juan had said he was okay, but she wasn't sure if she could trust the psychic. That particular gift wasn't known for being the most accurate, according to the reports she'd read.

The din of voices abruptly stopped when she came into view, the food all but forgotten on the diners' plates. All eyes were upon Red as she scanned the eatery for an empty table. She noted one in the back and made her way there.

The room was arranged in tight squares to accommodate dozens of stainless-steel tables. Seating could be added with a touch of a button, thanks to the hydraulics under the floor. A minicompunit sat on every table, listing the day's menu. Red sat down and scanned the list. The sound in the room hadn't gone back up to its previous volume, so she could hear whispers from nearby tables.

"When is Morgan coming back?" one woman asked.

"I heard she ran him off, so she could take over," said another.

Red closed her eyes and balled her hands into fists to keep from standing up and screaming at them. She didn't want this job, had never asked for it. If she hadn't made a promise to Morgan before he left, she'd have been out of here the second he told her his plans.

"Is anyone sitting here?" said a familiar voice.

Red opened her eyes and looked up at Raphael Vega. He smiled and inclined his head.

"Please," she said, indicating the empty chair across from her. It was a relief to see a friendly face.

"Is everything all right?" he asked.

For a vampire his age, Raphael wasn't bad looking, if you could get past his translucent skin and black penetrating eyes. But it wasn't his striking looks that drew people to him. It was his charisma. He exuded charm and an easy grace that made whomever he was talking to feel like they were the most important person in the world. That ability had gotten him invited into plenty of rest pads around town. Or so Red had heard.

When they'd met, Raphael had hissed at her. It was the first honest reaction she'd received from someone in Nuria. The rest of the population had been too busy covering their asses. They'd become friends after he'd saved Morgan's life by sharing his blood. Something she'd found out later didn't occur often because of the link it created between Raphael and his recipient.

"I've been better," she said.

Raphael looked at the patrons. Most looked away. A few gave him an invitation he'd probably take them up on later. "I have been out of town, visiting my brother, Michael. I dropped in to see Morgan when I returned, but they said he was gone. What did they mean by that? What's going on?"

Red stared at him, trying to decide how much to share. In the end, she decided she needed to confide in someone and since Raphael was close to Morgan's real age and probably knew about his past, he might as well be the one.

"Morgan went after his wife and child," she whispered.

Raphael sat utterly still, his expression unchanged. Without a hint of what he was about to do, he turned and hissed at the tables around them, baring his fangs. "Move!" he shouted.

Red jumped in surprise. The people nearby rose instantly, gathered their food, and made their way to the door. Everyone else went back to eating.

"I figured a little privacy was called for," he said. "Now please say that again. I couldn't possibly have heard you correctly."

Red sighed. "Yes, you did. Your hearing is better than any wolf's."

His face filled with genuine concern. "Tell me what happened. Leave nothing out."

"We were watching a viewer announcement last week about the release of the new clone models. Two pictures popped up on the screen and Morgan went pale. As pale as you," she said, pointing at his face. "I asked him what was wrong and he didn't answer." Red swallowed hard to keep the lump in her throat from choking her.

"Please continue." His dark eyes burned with unspoken emotion.

"I asked him if he knew those clones and he said they were his wife and child. I didn't even know he was married." Red's voice cracked and Raphael reached across the table and squeezed her hand.

"He was, but it was a lifetime ago."

"So he said. Did you know them?" Red asked.

Raphael hesitated, then met her gaze. "Not as well as I would've liked. They were killed shortly after I met them. I'm sure Morgan told you that he's much older than he appears."

Red nodded. "Yes, he mentioned something about the war."

"Yes, the *originals,* such as Morgan and me, have been around from the beginning. Being around that long is a blessing and a curse. If you're fortunate, you meet someone who will accept your differences. With that fortune comes pain, because you also get to bury those same people." His eyes grew distant as the memories crowded them. "Sarah was one of those people. Morgan met her during the war and they married. Joshua came shortly thereafter. They were killed eight years later in a bombing that obliterated the town they were living in. After their deaths, Morgan threw himself into fighting and never looked back."

"Until now," Red said.

"What did this broadcast say?" Raphael asked. "I do not understand why Morgan would leave at such a tenuous time."

"It said the Santa Fe Cloning Lab would be taking pre-orders for the latest pleasure model and showed Sarah's picture. Then they flashed a picture of Joshua up on the screen. He's to be used as labor or an addition to the family. I can't imagine the grief seeing my dead child's face digitally broadcast all over the world would cause."

"I understand why that got Morgan's attention. But I find it odd they'd both come up at the same time. Corporations through the years have purposely avoided familial blood when making clones. It could be an innocent mistake, but the chances of that occurring randomly are astronomical."

"I was thinking the same—"

"You bitch!"

Red's head snapped around at the same time as Raphael's. A man stood in the doorway of the food dispensing station glaring at her. He wore an ill-fitting brown suit with an open-collar shirt. His dark hair was cut short, framing a weather-beaten face that appeared slightly bruised. His brown eyes burned with desperation. Everyone froze, waiting for some-one to make a move.

"Do you know that man?" Raphael asked, releasing her hand.

Red examined him closely. "I've never seen him before in my life. Is he an Other?"

Raphael inhaled. "It's difficult to tell with the food, but no, I don't think so. He's a pureblood."

Red stood at the same time as Raphael. She shot him a glance.

"What are you doing?" she asked.

"Confronting him, of course," he said as if that were patently obvious.

"It's all right." She motioned for him to sit. "I'll handle this. Remember, it's my job."

He inclined his head and sat, newfound appreciation gleaming in his eyes. "As you wish."

"Look at me," the man shouted and stepped forward. "You ruined my life when you left me. How could you, Gina?"

Red flinched at the casual use of her name. "How could I what? Who are you?"

"You've forgotten me already? Did our time together mean nothing to you?" He laughed, pain evident in the sound. "I heard about your affair with Morgan Hunter and I don't care. I forgive you."

Shock silenced the food dispensing station.

Her eyes widened. Who was this guy? What was he doing in Nuria? She was positive she'd never seen him before, but that didn't stop a blush from spreading over her face. She didn't need this. Not with everything else. "Listen, mister, I think you have me confused with someone else," Red said, ignoring everyone around her.

He closed the distance between them. She could see his fingers tremble as he reached for her and the uneasy waver in his gaze. Red's hand moved to the laser pistol Morgan had given her.

"There's only one Gina Santiago," he said. "I should know, I've made love to you often enough."

"What?"

Gasps peppered the room. Red could see stunned faces in her peripheral vision. She'd been shown little respect before this man's arrival. This would take weeks to straighten out, and that was only if she could convince everyone this man was a liar. They wouldn't be able to smell it for themselves with the food masking his odor. They wouldn't want to, even if they could. It was easier to believe the worst. She hadn't smelled his lies until she'd gotten close to him. And there was no doubt he was lying. The proof oozed out of his pores. This had gone too far. Whomever this man was, it was time for him to leave.

"You're coming home with me now." The man grabbed her. His grip firmed, pinching her skin. He was stronger than she'd anticipated.

Red didn't think. She reacted. Her pistol was out of its holster before the next breath left her lungs and shoved deep between his ribs.

"I don't know who you are or what game you're playing, but I'm giving you one chance, and one chance only to leave town." She dug the weapon in deeper and he winced in pain.

"Gina, please," he pleaded.

"Stop calling me that. You have no right. You don't know me. The fact that you're calling me Gina is proof. And I sure as hell don't know you. I rarely forget a face, especially one I'm about to blow off."

He whimpered like a wounded animal. "How can you say that?"

"Get out," she hissed, pressing her thumb on the scanner in the handle of her pistol. The gun began to charge. In a second, it would be ready to fire.

The man swallowed hard and released her. "There's no need for violence. I'll go, but I haven't forgotten the promise you made."

What was he talking about? "What promise?" she asked, knowing she wasn't going to like his answer.

"That you'd love me, and only me, forever."

"Get the hell out of here. You're insane."

The voices around them rose. Exclamations of continued shock and disappointment roared through the crowd. Red heard more than one "told you so" muttered and the click of several comlinks. She ignored them all, keeping her eyes trained on the man she knew she'd never met until this moment.

He left reluctantly, looking back over his shoulder more than once.

When the door shut behind him, she strolled back to her table where Raphael was waiting.

"Interesting . . . Who was that?"

"No idea." She shook her head. "I've never seen him before today."

"You sure he's not from your IPTT days?" he asked.

"Positive. Most of those people ended up dead."

"That was quite a show he put on," Raphael said, sitting back to look at her. "Most convincing."

"Yes, it was," Red agreed, glancing back at the door. "Too bad no one but me could smell the fear and lies in his sweat." Red holstered her gun and sat back down, then ran her hands over her face. "Now the question is, who benefits from his performance?"

chapter seven

Night descended upon the Northern Hemisphere, but did little to relieve the heat. The sun might not be out, but it was still hot enough to make the mountains sweat. The cooling unit in my maglev shuttle had little to no effect. Sweat trickled down my neck, prickling my flesh until my uniform stuck to my body like a blanket soaked in honey. I glanced out the window at the training facility for the new Nurian Tactical Team.

It had started out as nothing more than a few makeshift shanties with an obstacle course made up of old tires, thick chains, and rough mats thrown into the center. All that remained was rubble and twisted metal, thanks to my laser pistol. It would take weeks before they could replace what I'd destroyed.

I'd been out here for five hours patrolling for unregistered individuals or—as IPTT members referred to them—*unknowns,* when I'd spotted the training grounds. Something told me not to pass up the opportunity, some little voice whispering "scarlet" in my mind. I didn't know what that word meant, but I knew what I had to do.

So I'd circled around to make sure they didn't have anyone guarding the area, then got to work. Destroying the place only took a matter of minutes and a few well-angled shots. They were in for quite a surprise when they showed up tomorrow. I laughed. The cruel sound reverberated in the enclosed space.

Hitting a button in the shuttle, I scanned the area. Beyond a few rodents, there weren't many signs of life. Pity, since I was in the mood for a confrontation. A little hand-to-hand combat would take care of the adrenaline coursing through my veins. I hit the scanner again. Not a blip showed on the screen.

The unknowns had gotten as good at hiding from us as we'd gotten at hunting them. I glanced at the power gauges. The shuttle would be good for another ten hours, but I didn't plan on being out here for that long.

The desert plays funny tricks on your eyes, even in the dark with night vision in place. After a while, you start seeing things like biodomes in the distance, when there was nothing there but endless dunes of shadowed sand. I'd been to this place before, but not at night. I don't normally go on patrol, but today I found myself out here searching for something. Searching for I don't know what.

Boulders the size of my maglev shuttle surrounded the barren valley. At its widest, the valley was two and a half miles, but it stretched on into the horizon and out of sensor view.

Powering up took the work of seconds. I made a wide arc with the shuttle, tipping it around. That's when I picked up the heat sensor blip. There was one. Maybe two. It was hard to tell from this range. I'd know for sure when I got nearer. Excitement filled me, energizing my mind. The predator within me snapped to attention and my muscles tensed. Had I finally found an unknown?

Stopping a half mile out, I hiked the rest of the way in. I didn't want the sound to scare away my prey. Luckily, thanks to the rocky terrain, there were plenty of places to hide. Plenty of places to see without being seen. I could be upon the unknowns before they had a chance to scatter.

My gloves felt snug as I slipped them on and slung the rifle over my shoulder. Running wasn't a problem on the flats, but I had to slow as I neared the rocks. I was drenched by the time I hit the first boulder. My muscles burned, but I pushed on.

Times like these made me realize I kind of liked being on patrol. It was a nice change from my regular assignments. I have many duties to perform at headquarters that leave me little time for fieldwork. Especially with Gina Santiago gone. Maybe I'd request a permanent change when I got back.

The climb up the boulders was rough going. If I hadn't had my gloves, my hands would be shredded. I squeezed my body through narrow openings, careful to not scrape my skin in my quest for higher ground. At a ridge just below the top, I crouched down and took out my binoculars with built-in infrared. The man in the valley below was dressed in an ill-fitting dark suit that allowed him to blend in with the bone-dry background.

Where were the other unknowns? I watched for signs of movement. There were none. Not even the man had moved from his present position. It was as if he was waiting for something. I hit a button on my navcom to pinpoint my co-ordinates. Twelve miles outside of Nuria in the Republic of Arizona, which meant the boundary fence wasn't very far away. Exactly where I needed to be.

I scanned the horizon and caught a glimpse of a green glow in the distance. This unknown hadn't made it very far. If it had been me, I would've been halfway to the Republic of Ontario by now.

My navcom beeped as a message arrived. Pressing a button, I waited for it to pop up on the screen. The message consisted of one word—*scarlet*.

My head swam and I grabbed onto a nearby rock to steady myself. I reached for my canteen and took a swig of water, but that didn't seem to help. My brain still felt like a bowl of undercooked synth-noodles. I shook my head and the world tilted. Wouldn't be trying that again.

You must stop the tactical team by any means necessary. Anyone found in the area of Nuria is suspect and must be eliminated. Your first target will be waiting . . .

The words filled my head, leaving no room for argument. The voice sounded familiar, but I couldn't quite place it. Never one to disobey an order, I gave a slight nod of acknowledgment to the disembodied voice and continued my mission. My muscles strained as I climbed higher. I ignored my discomfort, for I knew what I had to do: protect the International Police Tactical Team at any cost.

I couldn't allow this upstart group to gain power. They wanted to destroy the only organization I'd ever believed in. If that meant sabotaging their training facilities and eliminating their sympathizers, then so be it.

A lazy breeze kicked up the sand in the vast valley below, sending it swirling in all directions. The boulders surrounding me worked to dampen my scent, cocooning my presence. The man would never know I was here unless I wanted him to. I didn't.

From my vantage point, I could see him looking around expectantly. For me? Doubtful. I considered drawing out the encounter, but rejected the idea, preferring instead to get in and out before anyone noticed the shuttle.

I lifted the laser sniper rifle and looked through the scope until I could see the gun sight. The weight surprised me again and the gun dipped forward. I nearly dropped it onto the rocks. I was so used to the newer lightweight laser rifles the weapon felt clumsy in my capable hands. I removed one glove and laid it on the rock beside me.

Steadying my grip, I hoisted the rifle once more and notched it against my shoulder to prevent kickback. I twisted the scope and the man gradually came into view. Sweat poured off his face, whether from nerves or the heat, I couldn't tell. He was smiling, almost giddy.

I scanned the area one more time to make sure I hadn't missed anyone while the rifle charged. There was no doubt he was alone. I took a deep breath and let it out slowly, my finger resting gently on the trigger. The man threw his head back and laughed. There was definitely something wrong with him.

The merciful thing would be to put him out of his misery. My finger caressed the trigger. The hot metal teased my skin, threatening to burn if I held it there too long.

It would be so easy to end his suffering. My body shook as I fought the urge to squeeze off a round. I gasped, my lungs filling with hot desert air. Killing him was *not* why I was here. My eyes slammed closed, then opened again. I shook my head to clear it.

Killing him was *exactly* why I was here.

I forced the sight back onto the fatigued man and found him with the crosshairs once more and waited, counting my breaths as I allowed the rifle to become one with my hands. There was an art to hitting a target this far out. Everything had to be taken into consideration, wind movement, distance, target location, weapon velocity, and position. All were factors that would make the difference between a hit or a miss.

Chuckling, the brown-haired man stood and brushed his hands off on his pants. He was obviously done waiting. We both were. I pulled the trigger and then quickly pressed the recharge button in order to fire again. Blood sprayed out his back as the shot went clean through.

The man's laughter ceased, leaving only the wind to howl out his pain. I watched him fall to his knees, a look of surprise upon his face. He glanced down at the front of his sweat-soaked shirt and grimaced as crimson spread across his chest, staining the fabric. Now everything he was wearing looked brown.

The man keeled face forward onto the desert floor as death embraced him.

There was no one to mourn for him. No one to come rushing forward to press a finger to his carotid artery, hoping to find a pulse. It was too late for that anyway. I had one more thing to do, then it would be time for me to go.

I stepped deeper into the shadows, allowing them to swallow me. If anyone had been around, they wouldn't have been able to see me slip away. The darkness made sure of that.

I gathered the rifle, my glove, and my duffel bag. The maglev shuttle I'd borrowed was parked behind the hill a half mile away. It would be a long drive back to IPTT headquarters, but the road I'd come in on would keep me out of sight.

Back in Nuria people were safely in their rest pads. I wished I could wait around and see their faces when they discovered the body, but that wasn't part of my assignment. The job was to get in, neutralize the threat, and get out. I pride myself on my ability to follow orders even when I can't recall why that's important.

I packed the rifle into a case. No one would bat an eye back at headquarters if I walked in carrying this weapon. Lots of team members carried sniper rifles in their shuttles and on their person. I hoisted the weapon over my shoulder and hiked down the hill. It didn't take long to reach the man. I put my glove back on and flipped him over. His eyes were wide with surprise. He definitely hadn't seen it coming.

The odd-shaped blade slipped easily from the strap on my calf. I held it up, twisting it in the darkness. The blade looked more like metal teeth than a knife. I shrugged. Who was I to question orders?

I slashed, cutting the man's throat. Blood welled, but didn't flow. I flipped him back over. Done with the job, I made a quick dash to my vehicle. It only took a moment to open the shuttle door and toss the gun behind the seat. I slid behind the wheel and started the engine with a press of my palm.

The shuttle purred to life. "Let's get out of here," I murmured. I hit the pedal and felt the maglev power slam me back against the seat, pressing my body into the memory foam. One click of a button and the window opened with a hiss. The warm desert air smacked my face, leaving a fine powder of dust behind.

The air felt good against my suddenly muddled head. I looked around, more than a little confused. A blip on the dashboard showed me where I was and gave a projection of how long it would take me to get back to IPTT. I punched in the coordinates and gave the area one last look.

I couldn't remember how I'd gotten here or why I'd come. The only thing I knew for sure was that it was imperative I get out of here. Urgency ate at me, fraying my nerves, causing my lungs to constrict. I panted as something close to fear trickled over my skull, leaving my short hair standing on end.

I drove faster than I'd ever driven before. The shuttle swerved, tilting wildly as I took a corner too sharp. It screeched, sending shivers down my spine. Somehow I managed to keep it on the road and out of the sandy ditch.

I glanced in the rear viewing screen. There was no one behind me. At least no one I could see. The vast desert spread for miles and miles in all directions. It looked empty. But I knew they were there. Lurking in the darkness. Soon they'd be coming like a force of nature. Scouring the land. Looking for clues to my identity. There were none. I also knew something else.

I'd just gone from being the hunter, to the hunted.

chapter eight

R ed stood in the middle of the valley near the edge of the dead woods. Her clothes sat at her feet, folded into a neat pile, while she allowed the warm desert air to bathe her skin. It was strange being out there without Morgan's support. It was strange being in Nuria, period, without him. If she tried, she could almost feel him lurking in the woods. She glanced toward the dead forest. Nothing moved. *Stop playing mind games with yourself,* she chastised, then got back to the task at hand.

She'd finally shaken the earlier encounter with the odd man at the food dispensing station. She still didn't know who he was, but she was glad that he'd gone without further incident. The last thing she needed was more trouble.

Red shook out her arms and legs, then inhaled deeply, allowing her muscles to loosen. She needed this change. Needed desperately to feel the wolf emerge. It was the only thing in her control at the moment, so why wasn't it cooperating?

"Don't you desert me, too," she murmured. "I need you now more than ever."

Red pictured its canines and felt a blast of white-hot power shimmer beneath her skin. *Come to me,* she willed as it playfully nipped at her consciousness before scurrying off. She growled in frustration.

"Get back here, damn you," she shouted, dropping to her knees. Tears that she hadn't been able to shed in town flowed freely. Her shoulders shook as she cried out of frustration, pain, and loneliness. She glanced at the sky through blurry eyes and tried to imagine Morgan doing the same.

"Where are you?" she asked, her gaze following a shooting star. "I need you."

Raphael Vega stood in the woods, watching Red fight the change. He could sense the struggle inside of her, feel her need and her fear in equal measures. He stared at her naked form, taking in her small breasts and long legs. Hunger rose in his veins, beating at his temples. His fangs extended along with his shaft. What he wouldn't give for just one taste of her.

He knew it was wrong to look upon her that way. Morgan was his friend, despite their differences over the years. But the wolf inside of her was growing in strength. Soon he wouldn't be the only male fighting its call. It might've started already. She was ripe for the taking. Forbidden fruit. Sweetness scented her skin. His mouth watered and his fangs began to ache.

Raphael thought of the man in the food dispensing station today. Morgan had picked a hell of a time to leave his mate. She was vulnerable. Particularly now, standing naked for the world to see.

His gaze caressed her length, following the thrust of her upturned nipples and the slope of her concave stomach. She had firm thighs. The kind of thighs that would grip a man tight when he entered her. He'd seen her legs plenty of times clad in uniform issue pants, but bare, they took on a whole new light. He followed the long line up to the soft curls that hid her moist center.

Raphael ran his tongue over his teeth as his hunger increased. How he longed to bury his face there until she forgot all about Morgan and her previous lovers; until it was his name and his name only that she cried out during completion. The urge to seduce and take rode Raphael hard. She was so near.

What would she do if he stepped out of the woods? With Morgan having abandoned her for a ghost, would she welcome him with open arms and legs? Raphael's lips quirked and he laughed to himself. Knowing Red, she'd shoot him on sight. That was only one of the things that made her a perfect mate for his friend. There were many others.

He allowed himself to take one last longing glance, then turned away to adjust the discomfort in his pants. He needed to get out of here before he did something supremely stupid like act upon his primal urges.

Raphael doubted his old friend would be understanding when it came to Red. He'd never seen the alpha wolf so entranced. But even knowing that didn't stop Raphael from longing for the woman he should never have—*could* never have. The fact that his attraction to the she-wolf went far deeper than lust was all the more reason to stay away from her. He couldn't afford an emotional complication. At least that's what he told himself all the way back to town.

Once she'd pulled herself together and got over feeling sorry for herself, Red stood in the middle of the valley for another hour chasing a wolf that refused to be caught. She'd tried bribing it, coaxing it, pleading with it, and threatening it. Thus far, no tactic had worked. She stared down at the one lone claw protruding out of her right hand. The same claw that came out every time she'd tried to make the change.

Why couldn't the rest of them be as cooperative as this one?

"Is that the best you can do?" she shouted and kicked the ground, sending dirt flying into the air. The wolf inside her ignored the outburst.

She waited for her body to repair the damage, then gathered her clothes. It was getting late and she wasn't accomplishing anything tonight other than losing sleep. She thought about Morgan and wondered, not for the first time, if he was still alive. Would the lab notify them if he'd died or would they just recycle his body and be done with it?

Her heart thudded painfully in her chest. He had to be okay. She would accept nothing less. She dressed slowly, dreading her return to Nuria. Things in town were getting worse. The people wanted a leader—a leader who was one of them. That left her out of the running, even though Morgan said otherwise. How long would they continue to listen to her before they rebelled?

Red decided at the rate she was going, it wouldn't be too much longer. She'd heard the rumbles and the whispers circulating like a dust storm over the valley. They wanted Morgan back. Failing that, they wanted a new alpha in his place. They'd have a fight on their hands before she'd allow the latter to happen. There wasn't anyone she knew of beyond Raphael who was strong enough to be considered a potential alpha, and there was no way the Nurians would pick a vamp to lead. It didn't really matter. She doubted very much Raphael would want the job.

She yanked on her clothes and shoved her feet into her boots. She was lacing them up when a crack sounded in the valley. Red squinted as something blue flashed a half mile or so away. She stared for a few seconds, but it didn't come again. Probably just heat lightning, she thought as she stood. It was always threatening to rain, but rarely did. And when the sky did let loose, it was best not to be out in the downpour. The acid burned skin and flesh right off bones.

She drove back into town. It was late and there didn't seem to be anyone around, for which she was grateful. Red stopped at the sheriff's station to make sure there hadn't been any calls from Morgan. There hadn't, according to the vidcom on Maggie's desk. The sinking feeling that started in the valley now threatened to drag her under completely. She flipped off the lights and stepped out the door, nearly colliding with Maggie Sheppard and Jim Thornton.

Maggie dropped Jim's hand when she saw that it was Red. "What are you doing here so late?" she asked.

Red glanced at the couple. Jim's eyes twinkled and his thick lips split into a wide smile.

"I just got back and thought I'd check to make sure all was quiet," Red said, shutting the door.

"Back from where?" Maggie asked.

"The valley." Red pointed over her shoulder.

"Was anyone with you?"

What was with all the questions? Red's eyes narrowed. "No, why do you ask?"

Maggie shrugged. "Thought I saw Raphael Vega heading out that way earlier."

Red kept her expression neutral. She hadn't seen Raphael, not that she would've if he didn't want to be seen. She recalled the sensation of being watched. Had she imagined it?

She was just being paranoid. Feeding off Maggie's suspicions. Raphael hadn't followed her. He was probably off visiting one of the women that lived on the fringes of town. "What are you insinuating?"

Maggie shrugged. "Just that you and Raphael seem a lot cozier now that Morgan's no longer in the picture."

"I had lunch with the man. He's my friend." *My only friend,* Red thought. "I haven't seen him tonight. And for the record, Morgan isn't out of the picture. He'll be back soon. You should probably keep that in mind."

"Unlike some people, I never forgot." Maggie lifted a brow and sniffed haughtily. "What you do with your time is your business."

"You're right. I suggest you remember that the next time you accuse me of wrong doing." Red's hackles rose.

"I'm sure Morgan will be interested to know who you've been spending time with in his absence. As I recall, Raphael was the reason for his last major breakup."

Red's gaze narrowed as the wolf inside her snapped its

jaws. "Are you threatening me?" she asked, her voice dropping an octave to a guttural growl. "Because I think he'd be just as surprised by *your* actions." Appointing you to second in command was done as a courtesy. It doesn't give you the right to usurp my authority or to question my judgment."

Jim stepped forward and pulled Maggie back. "Calm down, no one is accusing you of anything," he said. "Are you, Magpie?"

Maggie's eyes widened and she blushed. "I told you never to call me that in public," she hissed.

Jim kissed her on the side of the head and Maggie's expression softened. "We'd better get going," he said. "Nice to see you, Red. Have a good night."

"Yeah, you, too, Jim." Red strode back to the share space, cursing under her breath. Maggie had some nerve to all but accuse her of cheating on Morgan. She might be attracted to Raphael—there weren't many women who were immune to his charms—but she'd never act upon her attraction. *Would she?* No, definitely not. But if she did, it was her business. She wasn't the one who'd left.

Red opened the door to the share space and found three of the recruits drinking at the bar. Takeo Yakamura, Demery Wilson, and Juan Sanchez looked up as she entered. "Gentlemen," she said in way of greeting. Olson and Jones must've been staying at a different sharespace.

"Care to join us?" Takeo asked.

"You do know your training is scheduled tomorrow bright and early, right?"

"Yes," Demery said, grinning past the dreadlocks that had fallen into his face. "That's why we're drinking tonight, mon. Care for some synth-rum?" He laughed and drank the shot in front of him, slamming the cup down when he was done.

Red considered the offer. She really shouldn't drink with the recruits. It would make it harder to gain their respect, but after the day she'd had, she could really use a drink. "What else do you have besides rum?"

Takeo lifted the synth-scotch, so she could see the bottle. It certainly wasn't the good stuff, but in Nuria, you couldn't be too picky.

"Sure, why not," she said with a shrug.

The men split, giving her space between them. Takeo grabbed another bottle, then made quick work of the top before sliding it over to her. His expression was unreadable as Red clutched the bottle and wiped off the top. She tipped it back and took three very long swallows before placing it back on the bar.

All three men were watching her, waiting for God only knows what to happen. "Boys," she said. "I was a tactical team officer for years. If you're expecting me to spit this crap out or gasp over the taste, then you're going to be waiting awhile. My guess is that I could drink you all under the table."

All three men burst out laughing and raised their bottles in salute. They drank amiably for the next two hours, until Red called it a night. "See you tomorrow, gentlemen, and don't expect me to take it easy on you just because we've put back a few."

Juan's eyes glittered in speculation. "Need company?" he asked.

Red's brows shot to her hairline. "No, I think I can handle getting to my rest pad on my own."

Demery and Takeo hit him in the arms, bouncing the man back and forth between them. "She shot you down, mon," Demery said, chuckling.

Takeo didn't laugh. He met Red's gaze evenly. She didn't miss the longing in his eyes or the calculation. Red shook her head in warning. He grinned, flashing fangs that were larger than any she'd ever seen. A wave of awareness struck and Red suppressed a shiver.

She kept her eyes on Takeo as she walked up the stairs. It had been a mistake to drink with them. It gave them ideas that she didn't want rattling around in their heads. Red thought about Maggie's accusation. She hadn't done anything wrong.

It wasn't her fault more men seemed to take notice of her now that Morgan was gone. She rubbed her forehead. Did it have something to do with Morgan leaving, or was something else behind their change of behavior?

Red glanced down at her appearance. Her breasts were still small, her legs were still long, and her stomach was still flat, thanks to her irregular eating habits. She sniffed. Her scent had changed a little. Grown sweeter perhaps, but it was still nothing particularly remarkable as far as she was concerned. To her, she looked and felt the same as she always did. Yet no one had seemed to notice her before. The wolf inside of her swished its tail, sending delicious tremors up her spine.

"It's a little late to show yourself now," she muttered.

Red pressed her palm on the panel outside of her door.

"Credits running low," a computerized voice intoned.

Great. Her shoulders slumped as the door slid open. That warning meant she had a week, maybe two if she was lucky, before she'd be creditless and locked out of her room.

"Morgan, you'd better be back by then," she warned as she shut the door behind her.

chapter nine

The vidcom lit up at five in the morning. Red blinked, momentarily blinded by the bright light. "Who is it?" she asked, her voice sleep hazed.

"You are a sight for sore eyes," Morgan said.

Red came awake in an instant and threw the covers off. She stumbled forward to stand in front of the screen. Morgan's eyes were bloodshot and he had several days' growth shadowing his jaw. His dark hair protruded and his skin had lost much of its bronze color. She barely recognized him.

"It's so good to see you. Are you okay? Where are you?" she asked, touching the screen. "You don't look like you've been eating or sleeping."

He touched the screen where her hand rested. Red could almost feel the warmth of his skin brushing hers.

"I know I don't look it, but I'm fine," he said, gazing at her. "I've been working security for the Santa Fe Cloning Lab. I have to go in later today. How are things with you?"

Red bit her lip. She debated whether to lie, but she didn't have the energy. "Things here aren't working out. People are unhappy with your decision to leave me in charge. Really unhappy. They think I've driven you off. There's talk of appointing a new alpha. Although goodness knows where they'll get one."

Morgan's eyes grew frosty and a rumble tore from his chest. "That would be a mistake."

"I know that, and you know that, but they need a leader and you're not here."

"But you are. And I left you in charge," he said, as if that should solve all the problems.

"I know, but a lot of people don't agree with your decision." She wasn't about to tell him that Maggie seemed to be leading the charge to have her run out of town. Power had clearly gone to her head. She was acting like she was the new sheriff. Red didn't tell him because Morgan would never believe it. Hell, *she* barely believed it. She'd always been so mild mannered when Morgan was around and had gone out of her way to make Red feel welcome.

Morgan scrubbed a hand over his face. "I'll be back as soon as I can. I have to have time to locate . . . You have to give me more time. Can you hold the town together until I get back?"

Gee, he wasn't asking for much. What did he expect her to do? Lock them up until they agreed to accept her as their new leader? She blinked back tears. There was no way she was going to cry in front of him. "This isn't a tactical team unit, this is a town. They aren't going to drop everything and listen to orders. I'm doing the best I can. It's hard, since you didn't tell them about Sarah and Joshua. I won't be able to put them off for long. They don't understand what's happening. All they know is that their alpha left them vulnerable." Heck, she didn't understand what was happening and she knew why he'd left. Red let out a frustrated breath that smelled like last night's synth-scotch. Her nose crinkled and she groaned.

"It can't be that bad," he said. "I haven't been gone long."

He wasn't listening or maybe he didn't want to hear what she had to say. "Morgan, like it or not, I am still considered an outsider by most. The fact that I can't control my change only makes it worse. They don't trust me. And to be honest, at least when it comes to the wolf, I can't blame them."

His expression drooped, making him appear even more exhausted. "I take it that means you haven't had any luck with transforming since I left? I thought maybe I'd been holding you back."

Red pulled her hand away from the screen and planted it on her hip. "Don't you think I would've told you?"

"Sorry," he said. "It's just been a long week."

"You're telling me," she said, as the comlink by the bed beeped. Red frowned. "Hang on a sec. Someone's trying to contact me."

She grabbed the device, pushing the button on the side to activate the two-way communication. "Red here," she said.

"It's Maggie." Red glanced at the time. Only five minutes had passed since Morgan called. There was only one reason Maggie would be contacting her this early—to convey bad news. "We've found a body." And there it was.

"I'll be there in fifteen," Red said, then flicked the switch disconnecting the call. She turned back to Morgan.

"Is everything all right?" he asked, concern evident in his voice.

"Nothing I can't handle," she lied. "But I do have to go." Red stared at the face she knew like the back of her hand. She loved this man more than she'd ever loved anyone, and she had no idea if she'd ever see him again. What he planned was dangerous and beyond foolish, but there was no way she could talk him out of it. This was something he had to do.

"I'll call again when I have a chance," he said, reaching for the screen once more.

Red placed her hand on top of his and choked down a sob. "Be careful. I want you back in one piece."

He smiled. "I'll be back as soon as I can. Do your best to keep them in line."

"I will."

"I love you," he said, passion burning in his amber eyes.

Red sniffled. "I love you, too. Got to go." She disconnected the call before she humiliated herself by begging him to come home.

The sheriff's station was abuzz by the time Red reached it twenty minutes later. Maggie sat at her desk, commanding the chaos. For a little woman, she did a terrific job juggling the troops. The three recruits she'd been drinking with waited quietly in the corner.

"Head out to the obstacle course. I'll catch up with you as soon as I can," she said, handing them the coordinates.

The men nodded and took off.

"Now what do we have?" Red asked Maggie.

"Dead male found out in the valley," she said, staring at the report in front of her. She traced a finger over a map and then back again. Her eyes widened.

"What?" Red asked.

"The body looks to be near the location you frequent," she said, not bothering to hide the accusation in her voice. "You got in pretty late last night."

Red replayed the evening in her mind. She was sure she hadn't forgotten anything, but that didn't prevent doubt from rearing it's ugly head. She'd shifted multiple times without ever being aware it had occurred. What if this was one of those times? She recalled her bloody claw. Had there been more? She wouldn't know until she examined the body. "I have nothing to hide."

"We'll see." She cocked her head. "Sure you didn't come across anyone while you were out there?"

"Positive." Red's jaw clenched. "I was out there *alone*. Didn't realize I needed an audience to vouch for me."

"No crowd, but as I recall, you do need a spotter since you're not aware of when you shift. Without someone to bear witness, how do you know you didn't succeed?" she asked.

The station grew quiet as everyone awaited her answer.

Red's mouth open and closed. She'd been alone. Could she be certain she'd failed? She looked into Maggie's assessing eyes. The coldness she saw chilled her. It didn't matter what she believed. Red needed to convince the people listening that she could lead. And the only way that would happen was if she stood firm on her answers. "I would've remembered," she said loud enough for all to hear.

Maggie's lips pursed. "Well since you don't have anyone to vouch for you, then I guess we'll just have to take your word for it."

"Yeah, I guess you will."

Red's body vibrated with barely leashed anger as she drove to the scene. Not even Morgan's call could help her sour mood. How dare Maggie accuse her? She didn't even know who'd been killed. And even if it turned out to be someone she knew, she didn't have anything to do with this death.

Or at least Red didn't think she did. Had she shape-shifted without knowing it? No. She'd woken up in the same condition she'd gone to bed in. That never happened when she changed during the night. *What if she'd changed before she left the valley?* Red couldn't be sure. Fear lingered in the back of her mind. *Please don't let him be ripped apart.*

Jim Thornton had already been called and was on his way. He might even arrive before she had a chance to look at the scene. He was professional enough not to touch anything, or at least he had been when Morgan was around. These days, she didn't know for sure what he'd do.

The desert sand blurred in her peripheral, swirling into a mix of tan and red. The temperature was already on the rise, and it would turn into a scorcher by midday.

The road stretched on for miles. Red stared out the window at the endless wasteland, letting it shift before her eyes. The knot in her stomach had grown to the size of a laser cannon blast. What were the chances that a body would be found in the same area she trained in? Sure, she trained there every night and knew the place like the back of her hand. And yes, she'd dreamed about the site before, but she hadn't dreamed about it last night.

She reached a nondescript ridge and pulled over to the side of the road, cutting the engine on the hydrogen car. According to the coordinates, this was where the body would be found.

Red climbed out of the vehicle and grabbed her canteen. It didn't take long to scale the small hill. From the rise, she could see the valley below. She stared at the spot in the distance where she'd been standing last night when the change refused to embrace her.

It was a bitter reminder of her failure—or so she'd thought at the time.

The body was lying on the ground seventy-five feet from the boulders. Red slipped her laser pistol out of her holster and ducked behind a nearby rock. She pulled out her binoculars and scanned the hills. There didn't appear to be any movement, but that didn't mean anything. She hit a button on the side of the viewer and the heat-sensing mechanism kicked in. The only thing she was able to pick up was the heat in the rocks. That was good. Maybe the death had been by natural causes or exposure.

Red kept that positive thought in mind as she walked over to where the body lay. The dark-haired corpse was face-down, but she could tell it was a man from his size. A brown suit rumpled around his outstretched limbs. Something about him seemed familiar, even though she couldn't see his face. Red moved in for a closer look, scanning the area for DNA traces as she went.

Blood stained a ten-foot radius, telling her that an artery had been hit. *At least he went fast,* she thought. She took out a drop of glove seal from the pouch on her holster and put it on her hands. Ten seconds later, her hands were protected with a thin polymer that would allow her to touch the body without leaving trace behind.

At first glance, his injuries appeared to be from a laser blast. Relief flooded her. Thank goodness this was a normal murder. Not that it made a lot of difference to the victim, but it made her job easier. She could turn the case over to the International Police Tactical Team.

Red couldn't tell if the blast was from close range and wouldn't be able to until Jim arrived. The scanner in her hand beeped. She looked at the screen. There had to be a mistake. She looked around mentally retracing her steps. She hadn't touched the body until her hands were sealed. Red turned the scanner off and restarted it. She did another slow sweep of the area, but came up with the same reading.

Why was her DNA on the body?

Red reached down and turned the man over. An ugly slash bisected his throat. She grimaced. Thanks to the dirt he'd fallen in, dried blood caked the wound. His eyes had clouded, turning milky as death descended, and his body was already starting to desiccate in the hot desert air.

She was lucky the predators hadn't gotten to him. If they had, cause of death would've been difficult to determine. She reached down to open his mouth and a cockroach crawled out from between his lips. Red shrieked and jerked back.

"Damn, I hate those things," she said, toeing it away with her boot. She took a shot of the victim's face with her nav-com. She looked at the image to make sure it was clear and frowned. He seemed familiar. She glanced back at the body. Where had she seen him before?

Red stepped closer so she could get a better look at his face. "Oh no," she said, retreating a few feet away. It was the man from the food dispensing station. The one who'd hassled her yesterday.

No, no, no, this couldn't be happening. Her lungs squeezed, cutting off her breath. She looked around as panic set in. For a split second, Red considered hiding the body. It wouldn't take much effort. She could slip it between the boulders and dispose of it later. She could say it had been a false report. The Nurians would never know. But Red would.

She couldn't break the law. She'd spent her life upholding it. It wasn't as if she had anything to do with his death. She glanced over at the rotting corpse. At least she didn't think so. Red looked at his neck and thought about the claw she could produce. It was sharp. Razor sharp. Certainly sharp enough to cause that kind of injury. And from its appearance, the wound was consistent. It could've been caused by a claw or a knife. Maybe even teeth. Was the blood spray from the neck wound or the gunshot? Did it really matter?

Her stomach lurched. She was going to be sick.

How would she convince Maggie that she wasn't involved? Convince the new recruits? Heck, how would she convince the people of Nuria when she wasn't entirely convinced herself? They already distrusted her. What would they do when a body was hauled back to town? She knew she hadn't shot the man. Was absolutely certain. But the other wound . . .

This was bad. Really bad.

Before she could decide her next move, Jim Thornton arrived on scene and sealed her fate.

chapter ten

From a distance, Nuria looked quaint and historic. It wasn't until people neared the town that they noticed the broken windows and the boarded-up businesses that made up the outskirts.

Red ignored all that as she drove straight to the dissecting lab. Jim would have the body laid out on a stainless steel gurney by now, ready to be examined. The dissecting lab was located five blocks from the center of town and a block away from the sheriff's station. The concrete-and-lead-lined building didn't look like much from the outside, but it was the most efficient dissecting and recycling center in the southwest quadrant.

Disinfectant filled the air as Red strolled into the lab. Stainless steel gurneys dotted the room. Lights hung above each gurney, illuminating the dismembered bodies. Cabinets lined one wall, while disposal chutes took up another. Large drains pocked the floor, ready to catch fluids from the dissecting process. Nothing was wasted on this dead world. Humans made up 70 percent of the liquid mulch used for growing plants in hydroponic chambers. In the end, everyone got juiced.

Burials were considered antiquated and had been done away with years ago. On a planet where human and animal survival hinged on the ability to recycle, burials were wasteful. Mourning the dead occurred behind closed doors, not over a hole in the ground.

Red grabbed protective gloves and an apron. She didn't bother with the headgear, since she had no intention of standing near the table when Jim started cutting. The scent of rot hit her as she neared the table. It seemed strong despite the disinfectant wafting through the air.

Jim looked up as she finished putting on the protective clothing, his brown eyes exuding compassion. "I've just started my initial examination. How are you holding up?"

"I'm fine," Red said.

Jim arched a brow. "Really?"

So he was back to being her friend. At least for a little while. Red sighed. "As good as can be expected. This isn't going to help my situation," she said, nodding at the body. "I'll have to notify IPTT."

"Actually, you won't." He paused, the laser cutter in his hand poised above the dead man's bare chest.

"I can't let a body go unreported," she said. She'd like to, but Red knew in her heart she couldn't break the law.

"You can with this one." He pointed at the body. "From what I can tell, he's an unknown," Jim said. "He doesn't have a chip and there are no signs that one has been removed. His prints aren't on file. Neither is his DNA. As far as the republics are concerned, he doesn't exist."

That didn't make any sense. Why would an unknown stroll into town? They avoided anyplace that could identify them as unregistered. Red looked at the table and frowned. "If he's an unknown, I won't have to report the incident to IPTT, but there's another problem."

"What?" Jim looked at the dead man as if he'd somehow missed something in his initial exam.

"He's the man who hassled me yesterday at the food dispensing station."

Jim's brows furrowed over his thick glasses. "I heard about that. Quite the news. Wasn't he shouting something about you abandoning him?"

Red snorted. "Yeah, which is a neat trick, considering I've never laid eyes on the guy."

"That doesn't make sense. Why would an unknown do that?" Jim asked, wiping a beefy hand on his dissecting apron. "You sure that you've never seen him before?"

Not you, too, she thought. Something in his expression changed. It was so subtle that Red almost missed it. He was still the same old Jim Thornton, but now there was suspicion in his gaze. So much for being her friend.

"Do you have anything else to tell me about the body? Anything that would point to the individual responsible?" she asked, ignoring Jim's question. She'd already given him her answer. If he didn't believe her, then that was his problem.

Jim coughed. "Just making small talk."

"Well don't," Red snapped.

His chin dropped a notch, whether in disappointment or anger, Red couldn't tell and didn't care. She had a job to do. The sooner she had the answers she needed, the sooner she could get back to work.

"As you wish," Jim said. "The man was shot in the chest from at least a couple hundred yards away. The burn pattern looks like a rifle blast, but I can't be sure since it's not like any I've seen before."

"Sniper?" Not many people could make that kind of shot. A handful at best.

"Perhaps, but that's not the important issue." Jim fiddled with his glasses, before pulling them off to clean them. "The only people who own weapons capable of doing this are International Police Tactical Team members or *ex*-IPTT members. Didn't you bring some of your weapons with you when you left IPTT?"

"Yes, and they're all accounted for, including the pistol

Morgan gave me." She patted the gun on her hip. "If you're going to accuse me of something, Jim, then just come right out and do it. Otherwise, stop wasting my time."

He colored. "I was simply stating my medical determination."

"You've stated it. Now move on." Red leaned over the body on the gurney. "Is there anything else that stands out about this killing?" she asked.

"Besides the fact he was in town asking after you?" he retorted.

"Yeah, other than that." Red's lips thinned. "Have you seen any other strangers in town?"

Jim scratched his head. "Well, there are a lot of new recruits floating about. I don't know all their faces," he said.

Red thought about the interviews she'd conducted. None of the men had sniper skills in their background other than possibly Demery Wilson, but he didn't seem a likely candidate. He and the other recruits hadn't been aware of the altercation at the food dispensing station. This left the Nurian people. Several had been present when she drew her weapon on the unknown. Were they dealing with someone on the inside again?

"I don't think it was any of the new recruits, but I'll look into it," she said.

"Whoever did it wanted to ensure he was dead," Jim said, twisting the corpse's neck around to get a better look at the cut. "They slashed his throat to be sure."

So he'd been shot first. That didn't mean she hadn't sliced his throat, but at least she didn't kill him. Red hid her relief. "Seems like overkill to me."

Jim nodded in agreement. "I've detected no foreign DNA besides your own. How did it get on the body, by the way?" He kept the question neutral, but Red didn't miss the speculation in his brown eyes.

"He grabbed me in the food dispensing station yesterday. I shoved my pistol into his ribs. It must have occurred then."

"Seems like an awful lot of trouble for a stranger to go through. Especially an unknown. He took a chance by coming into town."

"I agree."

"What did he have to gain?" Jim asked.

"No idea," Red said. "But I intend to find out."

He stared at her. "You know I have to put this in my report."

"I know." Her name coming up in any kind of official death report would dampen her chances of getting hired at the sheriff's station. Red pulled off her gloves and tossed them into a nearby recycling bin, along with her apron. "I'm going to head back to the station to file an incident report. Let me know when you've finished with your examination. At this point, even minor details may be able to tell us what he was doing out there and who would want him dead." She'd certainly wanted him to get the hell out of town, but she hadn't wanted the man dead. Obviously, there had to be someone out there who did. If they were still in town, she'd find them.

Red strode out of the dissecting lab. If this guy had been a regular unknown, then the case would be open and shut. The fact that he'd ventured into town and sought her out meant there was more behind his appearance than wandering into civilization. He'd been sent here, and there was only one person she could think of who'd do such a thing. *Roark Montgomery.* The question was, why?

Red walked down the sidewalk to the sheriff's station. From the looks she was getting, word had already spread about the body. Jim had probably contacted Maggie on his way into town. Nuria would be buzzing by this evening. She looked straight ahead and ignored the townspeople's fearful gazes.

She heard someone say her name as she neared the front door of the station. Red stopped to listen.

"Do you think she did it?" someone said.

"Seems likely," Maggie answered.

"Doesn't make sense," Juan Sanchez interjected.

What was he doing back so early? They should still be out in the valley training. Had someone ordered them to return without her permission?

Maggie cleared her throat. "You aren't a member of this sheriff's station and you aren't a tactical team member yet. Just because you uncovered sabotage at the training area doesn't mean you know anything about crime solving."

Sabotage? What was happening?

"I may not be versed in investigative techniques, but I do know a little something about motive. People have to have a reason for killing," he said. "A man showing up and causing trouble isn't enough."

"You weren't there when he confronted her," Maggie countered. "Word is he made a big scene at the food dispensing station. Practically begged her to come back to him. And how does she repay him? By shooting him in the chest and cutting his throat. I'm telling you, she and her wolf are out of control. She's going to bring death to Nuria."

Red's heart sank a little further with every word uttered. They thought she was a murderer. She'd killed plenty of people, so to a certain degree that was true, but she hadn't murdered this man. It wouldn't be the first time Roark had someone else doing his dirty work. Like it or not, she had to investigate.

"Morgan, where are you when I need you?" she whispered.

Morgan stared down the massive corridor in the central building of the Santa Fe Cloning Laboratory. Hundreds of doors lined the walls, each one secured and labeled in a language comprehensible to scientists alone. He'd already searched two outlying buildings and come up empty. How in the world was he going to find Sarah and Joshua?

He stepped forward and stood at attention, something he hadn't done since his days in the old military. The position felt odd, but strangely familiar. "Morgan Hunter reporting for duty, sir."

A squat man with a wide forehead turned his green gaze on Morgan. Rows of monitors surrounded him in a cocoon of static images. He sat in the center, pressing buttons rapid fire. Morgan couldn't tell what the buttons did from his vantage point, but the man seemed happy with what he saw.

"You the new guy?" he asked, using his flat tongue to flick at the debris stuck in his yellowed teeth from his last meal.

Morgan straightened and stood a little taller. "Yes, sir," he said, giving his uniform a last tug into place.

"Heard all about you. Nice to finally meet you." The man gave him a leisurely perusal that caused the hair on the back of Morgan's neck to stand on end. He'd received that kind of look from women on several occasions, but never a man. The man's gaze followed the line of his body back up to his face, his interest clear.

Morgan wasn't sure how to react so he stood stock still and kept his expression neutral. Apparently, that wasn't the response the man was hoping for because he dropped his gaze.

"You'll be on patrol with Smith here." He pointed to his right without looking.

A blond, fresh-faced guard stepped forward and gave him a curt nod, then extended his hand. Morgan shook it.

"Listen to everything he tells you and we'll get along just fine," he said, then swirled back to face his monitors.

Morgan started to leave.

"By the way," the man called out, stopping him. Morgan's heart raced in his chest. He knew there was no way anyone should suspect him, but being in this facility so far from Nuria and Gina made him nervous. Even if no one else realized what he was up to yet, Morgan knew.

"Yes," he said, glancing over his shoulder.

"My name is Coleman Parker, but everyone calls me 'the Eye of God.' " He waved his hands at the monitors. "If you need anything, anything at all, call me."

"Thank you. I'll keep that in mind," Morgan said, then followed Smith down the hall.

When they were out of visual range and earshot, Smith stopped him. "Don't mind Coleman," he said. "He's really harmless."

"It's not going to be a problem. I've met his type before." Love was love as far as Morgan was concerned. People had to find it where they could.

"He's actually okay to work for. The guy before him was a real ass. Made an easy job hard. By the way, you can call me Pete."

Morgan smiled. "Okay, Pete it is. My name's Morgan Hunter. Everyone calls me Morgan."

Pete grinned and started walking again. "This job is a little confusing in the beginning. We have access to some of the doors, but not all unless there's a fire, in which case the doors automatically unlock so everyone can get out before they seal once more. But that's not likely. Someone like Coleman is always on guard, watching for anything out of the ordinary. The sweepers would get to any sort of blaze and contain it before it got out of control."

"Sweepers?"

"They're our automated fire control and maintenance system. They're three feet high and made of rolling steel. Get out of the way if you see them speeding down the hall."

"Why?" Morgan asked.

"They're not known for their braking abilities." Pete chuckled. "I found that out the hard way when I first started." He pulled up his pants leg so Morgan could see the gnarled scar on his shin.

"Looks painful," Morgan said.

"It hurt like a son of a bitch."

Morgan laughed. "Thanks for the tip." He filed the information away. "What about our patrol route?" he asked. "Do we make our way around the entire facility?"

Pete shook his head. "No, we don't go near the fields or crops. Something about contamination."

Crops didn't refer to plants. It was what they called the new clones. Morgan had read up on the subject after he'd put his application in. It was still hard to think about the growing of clones as crops, but he supposed it made it easier for the scientists involved. Kept the emotion out of production. That way if a bad "crop" was developed, they could destroy them without any guilt.

"But what if something happens in the development lab? Surely they want us to be able to address the problem." Morgan's mind worked overtime as he tried to figure out how to gain access to the cloning cell storage area. There had to be a way in. He hadn't gone to all this trouble to be deterred now.

"For security purposes, development is broken up into several labs." Pete frowned, his pale brows nearly opaque against his skin. "Besides, there haven't been any problems like that within this facility. A few wackos have tried to force their way in through the front gates, but they were quickly neutralized. I wasn't here when it happened. It was before my time. They've beefed up security since then. You'd have to be suicidal to try to break into this place. Even if you made it in, we wouldn't let you leave." He elbowed Morgan playfully.

"Yep, they'd be sorry once we got a hold of them." Morgan had never considered this a suicide mission. Dangerous and difficult, yes. Suicidal, no. What if he'd been wrong? What if this was impossible and he was wasting his time? He thought about Gina. He thought of never seeing her again, touching her, smelling her skin.

Emotion welled within him and he forced it down, closing himself off to that tender place that left him feeling vulnerable. He couldn't afford to be distracted. Not when he was so close to finding his family.

"So how long have you worked here?" he asked.

Pete bit his lip as he considered the question. "It'll be four years in March."

Morgan blinked.

"What's the matter?" Pete asked.

"From the way you were talking, I figured you'd been here longer. Much longer," he said.

Pete ducked his head and looked around sheepishly. "This place has a high turnaround rate. Don't know why. It's an easy job. A hell of a lot easier than shoveling pig shit," he said. "I guess the pressure gets to people. Doesn't bother me though," he added quickly.

"What pressure?" Morgan asked, watching a couple of scientists walk by. They didn't even look up from their conversation. He made another mental note and then turned his attention back to Pete.

"You're always being watched. Doesn't matter what your job is here. They like to know what all their people are doing at all times. Makes some people a little paranoid."

Morgan looked around. "I don't see any vids."

Pete smiled. "You wouldn't. That's the whole point." He winked, then pointed to a couple of obscure dots on the wall that looked like rivets. "Coleman can watch us wherever we go. Those screens at the front of the facility aren't for show. They're the real deal. The Santa Fe Cloning Lab has sunk a lot of money into security. Terrorists aren't the only ones who want in here. Their competitors are just as relentless— maybe more so. They tried bribing me once, but I told them to take a hike."

"I imagine this is a pretty tough market."

He nodded. "Tougher than people realize. If they come out with the next popular clone, it could set the company up for years. If they lose the race to produce the next hot thing, well, then we're both out of a job. Along with a thousand other people. Cloning is a cutthroat business."

Morgan scratched his chin, which had already started to

shadow despite the shave he'd given himself a few hours earlier. "I can see how that wouldn't be a good thing," he said. "Don't want to be out of a job before I've had a chance to start."

"Me either." Pete shook his head. "I need my job too much to allow anyone to take it away from me." His soft features hardened, making him appear older.

"So tell me about this place. It's not like the other two buildings," Morgan said.

Pete perked up, his dark mood vanishing in an instant. "It's set up a bit like a tree, if their branches grew straight up and out to the sides. There's one main hall and we're standing in it. Eight other halls branch off from this main one. Product assembly is off to the left and development is on the right."

"Seems like a lot of ground to cover for two guys," Morgan said, knowing he'd seen at least three other teams.

"Oh it isn't just the two of us. There are six other teams covering the grounds at all times."

"Are there any A.I. defenses in place?" he asked.

"I'm sure there are," Pete said, looking around. "But they don't tell us about them. Guess they consider us under the pay grade for that kind of information."

Morgan had no doubt they did. Unfortunately, he needed the information in order to slip past security. His gaze landed on the hidden vids. He knew just the man to ask. "So where do we start?"

"This way," Pete said, leading them in the opposite direction of the area Morgan wanted to explore.

Red had a headache from listening to the speculation circling the office. There were many, many theories and very few facts. How could she fight this and expect to win? The talk continued on and on. Finally, she'd had enough. She walked into the sheriff's station and the conversation stopped cold. "Don't quit on my account," she said. "It was just starting to get interesting."

The recruits stood upon her approach. "Reporting problems at the training facility, Commander," Juan said.

"I heard. I'll deal with the sabotage later. I'm sure you've all been apprised of the latest situation," she said, looking at Maggie, who had the grace to turn away. "So I won't need to repeat it other than to say I plan to investigate this death aggressively. No one gets killed on my watch. Not even an unknown." She glared around the room before meeting their wary gazes. "If you're ready to learn," she said, addressing the remaining five new recruits, "then I suggest you gear up. We'll be heading out into the desert in less than," Red glanced at her watch, "two minutes."

"Yes, ma'am," Juan said, saluting her before turning sharply and striding to the back of the station with Takeo, Jones, Olson, and Demery tight on his heels.

chapter eleven

It had taken two weeks tracking various shipping arrivals for Morgan to figure out that both the cloned cells and Project Scarlet were being stored in area 47F. Fifty-two people were allocated for the project as far as he could tell. From the schedules he'd glimpsed at the Eye of God's station, they worked nearly around the clock.

There was only one hour that seemed to be unstaffed, and that was when the deliveries were made at 2:00 P.M. Everyone left their positions and helped to unload, including the guards, since the items were environmentally sensitive.

Morgan decided that was when he'd strike.

Placing two video looping devices on the Eye of God's monitoring system would've been hard had Morgan not flirted blatantly with Coleman. By the time he'd finished, Coleman had shared information Morgan had no doubt would be labeled top secret. If he really worked here, he'd bust the man for it. But Coleman acted on the belief that he had a chance of getting Morgan into bed, which was exactly what Morgan had intended. He hated using the man, but he'd had no choice. Time was running out.

The next phase of his plan would be harder. Morgan and Pete began their shift as usual, walking the circuit, checking doors, and observing personnel badges. They were on their way to the loading docks when Morgan told his partner that he heard something. It was a simple ploy that should've worked easily.

Unfortunately, convincing Pete that he'd heard a noise in one of the labs proved more difficult than Morgan had anticipated. Pete was green to the security business despite his four years of experience, which meant he'd never really seen any action. The idea of actually checking out a potentially dangerous situation didn't sit well with the young security officer.

If Morgan hadn't stepped through the door, insisting he'd heard a noise, he doubted that Pete would've followed.

Morgan had spent his weeks on the job casing the areas. He now knew that lab 34 contained all the ingredients needed to make a quick flash bomb. It wouldn't do a tremendous amount of damage, but it would fill the place with dense black smoke, giving Morgan plenty of time to slip out undetected. But he needed to act now before the first vid-loop ended and the Eye of God saw what he was really doing.

"You go that way and I'll go this way," Morgan said, indicating to the right and to the left.

Pete's eyes widened and he shook his head, refusing to move. "I think maybe we should stick together."

"It'll be okay. Holler if you encounter anyone who shouldn't be here."

The young guard nodded, then slowly stepped to the right. He looked back several times to assure himself that Morgan was still there. Any other time, Morgan would cut the poor guy a break, but not today. It had taken far longer than he'd anticipated narrowing down Joshua's and Sarah's location. He'd expected to be back in Nuria by now. Back with Gina.

He forced his mind on the job at hand. If this mission was successful, he'd be able to turn in his notice and leave tomorrow. The thought of being in Gina's arms by tomorrow night caused Morgan's heart to thump hard and his body to tighten in anticipation. He shook his head to clear it. *Finish the job first. You're not out of here yet,* he thought.

Beakers filled with various chemicals lined rows and rows of tables. Sterile white sheets divided the work areas, creating faux cubicles and the perfect place to hide. The vids would show an empty room, thanks to the looping device. Morgan glanced back. Pete was farther away now, but still watching him. He had to make this convincing or they'd arrest him for sabotage.

"Hey, you there! Stop!" he shouted and jumped behind the nearest sheet where the chemicals he needed were located.

Pete's head shot up and he broke into a run. Morgan quickly mixed the chemicals needed for the flash bomb, then rushed back out. "Run," he said to Pete. "I think he has a bomb."

The young security officer's eyes widened and he skidded to a halt. Fortunately, it didn't take him long to recover. He raced for the open door that led to the hallway without waiting for Morgan. "What happened?"

Morgan caught up with him easily. He gasped, making it sound like he was out of breath. "I'd just rounded the corner at the far end when I saw movement. I didn't catch the person's face because I was too busy concentrating on what they were doing."

A boom sounded, shaking the wall closest to them. Black smoke billowed out, choking the air with its noxious fumes.

"What the hell?" Pete exclaimed, starting to run back into the room.

Morgan stopped him. "Are you nuts? I told you it looked like he had a bomb. We don't know what he used to make it. Looked pretty toxic to me. We need to call the sweepers in."

Pete glanced down the hall. "They should be coming. I don't understand what's taking them so long. Coleman doesn't miss anything."

"I'll go this way and look for them. You head back down

to Coleman and make sure he's notified the other security teams to be on the lookout for a lone male suspect," Morgan said.

Pete started to move, but stopped. "We aren't supposed to split up. It's company policy."

More smoke belched out from the open door, filling the hall with a thick haze. Morgan glanced at it, trying to judge how much time he had left before the sweepers arrived to clean up his mess. He turned back to his partner.

"We don't have time to argue about this. I don't want this guy to get away. I'm sure a capture would look good in both our files."

Pete's eyes lit at the possibility of a commendation. "Okay," he said hesitantly. "But I'll be right back."

"I'll be right here." Morgan hoped that wasn't a lie.

Morgan waited for the smoke to thicken before he sprinted to area 47F. His security badge wouldn't open the door, but the fire would. Morgan fought the urge to open the panel and bypass the security system. He glanced up the hall and saw the doors begin to open. Soon people would be pouring out of the rooms.

"Come on, come on, come on. What's taking so long?" A second later the door slid open . . . and Morgan stepped into an empty room.

It had been two weeks without any leads. Recruits were canceling their interviews left and right now that word had gotten out about the stranger's suspicious death. Several others had quit. Red still hadn't managed to find any clues to uncover the person responsible for shooting the unknown. It didn't help that Jim Thornton hadn't ruled out a claw as a weapon for slitting the man's throat.

Everyone in Nuria knew Red was capable of shifting in her sleep. They also knew that all she'd been able to intentionally produce thus far was a single claw. That was enough of a weapon to slice the unknown. The fact that he'd probably been shot with an IPTT weapon only solidified her guilt in the town's eyes.

She glanced around at the five remaining recruits gathered at the water trader bar. Takeo Yakamura, Demery Wilson, Juan Sanchez, Randall Jones, and Keith Olson stared at her expectantly. She was grateful that Yakamura, Wilson, and Sanchez had decided to stay, since they held the most potential. Unfortunately Jones and Olson had started to buy into the talk around town. She could see it in their eyes. Red knew if she didn't find the killer soon, they'd be the next to walk.

"So, gentlemen, what do we have so far?" she asked.

Takeo looked at the other men, then began to speak. "Not much in the way of forensics."

"What does that tell us?" Red asked.

"It tells us that whoever killed the unknown didn't want to get caught," Demery said.

Red stood. "I think it's safe to say that they didn't want to get caught. They went to a lot of trouble to cover their tracks. Anything else stand out?"

The men's faces scrunched in concentration. "The location seems odd," Juan said.

"Why?" she asked. "It's not far from the boundary fence or Nuria."

He flipped through the navcom pictures, looking at the crime scene. "It's too obvious."

"What do you mean?" Demery asked, rubbing a gloved hand over his arm to scratch an itch. The sun would be down soon and he'd be able to remove the protective suit.

Takeo let out a long breath as if this whole line of conversation was boring him. "He means that of all the places the guy could've been killed, the killer picked the one place they knew you'd be tied to, Commander."

Red kept her body relaxed despite the tension coiling in-side of her. She'd come to the same conclusion. The fact most of Nuria ignored the obvious only made her angrier. And hurt. She may be an outsider, but they should know her well enough to know that if she was going to kill some-one, she'd at least make sure the crime wasn't linked to her. They also wouldn't have found a body, had she murdered the man.

The killer had all but stood up and shouted, *look at me, look what I've done*. That was not the mark of a professional assassin. And it certainly wasn't the mark of someone with more than ten years of tactical team service under her belt.

"Does anyone think the killer is still in town?" Red asked.

Jones and Olson looked away, refusing to meet her gaze. They'd given her their answer. Fortunately, Wilson, Yaka-mura, and Sanchez had no such qualms.

"I know you didn't do it," Juan said with a half-shrug. "Doesn't matter what anyone else says." His dark gaze shot to Olson and Jones. "As to your question, no, I don't think the killer stuck around after they killed the unknown. I know I wouldn't have, if I'd just shot someone and slit their throat."

"Yeah, it would be stupid to hang around," Takeo added. "They're probably long gone."

Demery stared for a moment, then said, "Commander, can I have a word with you alone?" The white suit he wore didn't hamper his movements as he stepped away from the bar and strode out the door of the water trader space.

Red followed, curious. "What do you want to talk about, Wilson?" she asked.

He turned and smiled, his dark skin parting to show gleaming white fangs. "I thought I'd make you an offer."

Red arched a brow. "And what exactly would that be?"

"I thought maybe you'd like me to use my 'gift' to locate the killer."

Red had considered asking him earlier in the week, but had thought better of it, since there was a chance he'd be psychically detected when he was off remote viewing.

"I don't want you to get hurt," she said.

His grin widened, showing off dimples. "I've been a bounty hunter for the past fifteen years, Commander. The chances of me getting hurt or even detected are slim."

She stared at him, trying to gauge his sincerity. It was hard to do through his protective mask. She knew he wanted to help, but it was wrong to put a new recruit in danger for any reason. There would be plenty of time later where his life would be on the line. It didn't need to be at the beginning of training.

"I-I'm not sure that's such a good idea," she said.

His smile wavered. "We've been chasing a ghost for two weeks. You've already taken a lot of heat for something you didn't do."

"How do you know I'm innocent?" she asked.

Demery's grin returned full force. "If Sanchez says that you didn't have anything to do with it, then I believe him. He knows things about me no man should know. He truly has a gift. Besides," he elbowed her teasingly, "you don't seem the type to waste your time on revenge."

"Thanks for the vote of confidence." She smirked.

"Any time."

Red looked up and down the street to ensure their privacy. "If I agree to let you do this, what do you need me to do?"

Demery's eyes twinkled behind the faceplate. "Would you buy that I need you to get naked while I'm doing my deep-breathing exercises?"

Red laughed. "No."

"It was worth a try." Demery chuckled. "But if you're not going to get naked, then I guess the answer would be nothing. I just need a quiet place to clear my mind, so I can get in the altered state necessary to do remote viewing."

"Do you want to do it in your room?"

"That would be fine."

"When do you want to start?" she asked, feeling a prickle on the back of her neck.

"Now is as good a time as any," he said, staring at something over her shoulder. "I'll let you know what I find."

"Thanks," Red said, looking behind her. Even though her vision was good, she didn't see anything lurking in the shadows.

Demery touched her arm and she jumped. "Sorry, Commander, didn't mean to scare you. But I think Raphael wants to see you." He nodded to a spot across the street. "I still can't believe he can walk in the light." Envy and awe filled his voice. "Must be nice."

Red tensed. "Yeah, he's different all right." How had she missed Raphael's approach? It was humiliating. She was supposed to lead these men. How could she do that if she couldn't detect a lone vampire? "I should've known it was him. I would've been able to scent the others."

Demery laughed. "The only reason I detected him was because we have something in common."

Her brow crinkled. "What's that? Fangs? A blood fetish?"

"No." He looked at her and all humor fled his face. "You," he said softly, then walked back into the depot.

Morgan's mind reeled as he stared at the empty lab. It wasn't possible. He'd seen the shipping orders. Watched the vehicles arrive to unload their shipments. Project Scarlet and his family should be here.

He stepped through the door and his booted feet echoed in the emptiness. Morgan scanned the room, even checking the area near the ceiling. Nothing but a white void stared back. He heard the alarms as the sweepers arrived to battle his diversion. He couldn't afford to stay any longer. The muscles in his chest tightened as he stared in disbelief. Something was wrong, seriously wrong.

Muffled footsteps sounded from nearby. Morgan had a split second to move. It was either that or risk discovery. He leapt up, shifting into his wolf form on the way. His claws latched onto a beam high above his head, sinking into the metal with a scraping clank. Pain shot through his hands and arms, but Morgan didn't utter a sound as two security guards he'd never seen before poked their heads into the room. They looked around quickly. Without spotting anyone, they shut the door.

Morgan waited, his claws straining under his weight. A few more seconds passed. When no one returned, he forced them to retract and he dropped to the ground, sweat dripping down his forehead. That was close. He took a shuddering breath and forced the wolf back inside.

By the time Morgan returned to the scene of the bombing, the sweepers had managed to clean up the fire. Smoke still wafted in the air, but it wasn't nearly as black as it had been earlier. Pete's uniform was disheveled and his face was gray.

"Are you okay?" Morgan asked.

"We got a call that someone broke into area 47F when you were gone." He hadn't come right out and accused Morgan of the crime, but something in his eyes told Morgan that Pete suspected him.

"I know. I heard," he lied. "I went there to check it out, but no one was there. One of the workers must have tripped the alarm."

Pete stared at him hard. "We didn't find the person who set the bomb. The sweepers said it was sabotage."

"That doesn't make sense." Morgan frowned. "I didn't think there was anything in this lab of any importance," he said.

"There isn't, but it's obvious the saboteur didn't know that." Pete's shoulders relaxed.

Morgan knew Pete had realized if he was behind the sabotage he would've picked a real target.

"I'm about ready to call it a day," Pete said, wiping the grime from his face.

"Me, too," Morgan said, clapping him on the shoulder. "How about I buy you a drink?"

"Sounds good to me."

The two men walked down the hall to Coleman's desk. The Eye of God was pressing several buttons and scowling.

"What's the matter?" Morgan asked, edging closer to the spot where he'd planted the video loops.

Coleman didn't look up. "This damn thing doesn't seem to be working right. I don't understand the problem. I've run two different diagnostics and they've come up with nothing."

"Would you like me to take a look at it?" Morgan asked, brushing the man's leg as he slipped past him.

There was a sharp intake of breath behind him as Morgan bent over and pretended to analyze the circuits and wires. "I think I found the problem," he said, jiggling a few circuit boards for effect. "It's here," Morgan said, pulling out a charred wire, while palming the video loops with his other hand. "I'm surprised you didn't smell it."

"What?" Coleman's eyes slid from Morgan's ass to the burnt wire in his hand. "Yes, that could do it," he said unapologetically.

"You may want to get someone down here to run another systems check for you," Morgan suggested. "That is, once they replace the wires."

Coleman swallowed hard as Morgan slipped slowly past him again. Morgan could smell his arousal. It filled the air like a tangy spice. He was sure that if he looked down the man would be erect. A twinge of guilt hit, but Morgan brushed it aside.

"I'll get right on it," Coleman said, caressing him with his gaze.

"You do that." Morgan winked at him and followed Pete out of the building.

Pete stopped him when they'd made it to his hydro car. "I didn't think you were interested in Coleman that way," he said.

Morgan met his gaze. "I'm not, but it makes our job easier if he thinks I am."

"How so?" Pete asked.

"Coleman takes care of our schedules. One wrong word and he can have us working the night shift."

Pete grimaced. "I never thought about it that way before. Heck, if I had, I would've probably tried flirting with him myself. Though I doubt I'd have been as convincing as you. Had me worried there for a minute, partner." He laughed.

"Why?" Morgan asked, knowing it would put Pete on the spot.

"Because . . . well . . ." Pete blushed from the tips of his ears straight down his neck.

Morgan snorted, unable to keep a straight face any longer. "Don't worry," he said. "You're not my type."

chapter twelve

Red strolled across the street to the alley. Now that the sun had dipped behind the buildings, the shadows were deep. "You can come out now. I know you're in there."

A cool breath caressed her ear. "Are you sure?" he purred, stepping out of striking range.

Red jumped. "I was." A minute ago. "What are you doing spying on me?"

Raphael's brow arched. "I wasn't spying on you."

"Were you standing in the shadows, watching me and Demery talk?"

"Yes."

"Were you listening to our conversation?" she asked.

"Yes," he said.

Red cocked her hip and settled her hand on it. "I don't know what you call it, but I call that spying."

Raphael's lips twitched and he gave a slight shrug. "Observing is the not the same as spying."

"If you say so."

"I didn't come here to argue semantics, I came here to see if you'd found your killer yet."

Her shoulders drooped. "No. I'm sure you would've heard about it if we had. The consensus is that the person left when the job was done."

"Logical conclusion, since there haven't been any strangers in town other than your accuser. Of course," he paused, "it could always be one of the new recruits."

"Jim Thornton suggested the same thing." Red glanced over her shoulder. Fear prickled her senses. She'd considered an enemy within the town. It had happened before with Morgan's cousin Kane to devastating effect, but she hadn't wanted to suspect the recruits.

Yet she couldn't deny there was no safer place for a murderer to be than right under her nose. She thought about each candidate. Some of these men were dangerous, no doubt. They could easily kill someone without leaving a trace. But were they behind the murder? She didn't think so.

"I've vetted them. Their backgrounds check out," she said.

Raphael cocked his head. "Backgrounds can be manipulated. You of all people should know that."

She sighed. Yes, Red knew firsthand how easy it was to change someone's past. Most of hers had been a complete fabrication, thanks to her grandfather's overprotective nature. "I still don't think it's any of my men. They've all been too determined to catch the killer, even the ones who suspect I'm behind the murder."

"And who exactly would they be?" His voice dripped with menace.

Red balked. "Knock it off. I can handle them. I don't need you going all alpha on me." Her stomach took that moment to growl, ruining her confident stance.

"When was the last time you ate?" he asked, giving her a closer perusal. "Your cheeks are sunken and you have dark circles under your eyes. You should take better care of yourself."

Red snorted. "Thanks, Mom. I'll keep that in mind."

Raphael scowled. "I am not your mother, but I *am* concerned about your well-being." He reached for her hand, clasping it in his cold one. "Now let's get you something to eat."

She didn't bother to pull away. It was nice being around someone who didn't look at her with suspicion. Someone who was willing to listen to her vent. Red allowed Raphael to walk her down the street to the food dispensing station. There were few people out, but the ones who were eyed them with something close to contempt.

"They think I'm cheating on Morgan with you," she said. "Maggie practically accused us of having a clandestine meeting in the valley. Can you believe it?"

Raphael didn't respond.

His silence caused her to chatter on. "I told them the idea was ridiculous." Even as she said the words, she felt the warmth of his touch shimmering up her arm and through her body. He'd been cool moments ago, but no longer.

He stopped, meeting her eyes a second before his molten gaze dropped to her mouth. "You're right. How could they imagine anything so *outrageous?*"

Red's pulse kicked up a notch as Raphael wet his bottom lip. The moisture glistening there had her undivided attention. His thumb brushed the back of her knuckles in a gentle caress. The move was innocent, but the look that followed was not. Red felt the touch all the way to her toes. Her breath caught in her lungs. She cleared her throat. "We'd better get going."

Raphael's mouth quirked. "Of course. You must be positively ravenous by now."

She was pretty sure he wasn't talking about food. Red reluctantly pulled her hand away. She'd needed another human's touch—even if that human happened to be a vampire. She put some distance between them. The fact that she was tempted by his unspoken offer scared her. Morgan had only been gone a few weeks. What did that say about their relationship? What did that say about *her*?

Red had never been a fickle woman. She'd always known what she wanted and whom. So what if she'd never been in a relationship until now. That shouldn't change things. Maybe it was because of the responsibility that had been heaped upon her shoulders. The added stress had clearly muddled her thoughts. Made her feel attraction where there was none. That had to be it. It had nothing to do with Raphael. She glanced back at his pale face and a fresh wave of heat swept over her.

"Are you coming?" she asked, moving down the sidewalk without waiting for him. Retreating was cowardly. Red realized that, but it seemed like the safest move.

He caught up with her in a couple of long strides and grabbed her hand once more. Red tugged, but he didn't release her. Fine, if he wanted to hold her hand while they walked, then that was his business. It meant nothing as long as she didn't participate.

It didn't take long to reach the food dispensing station. Red dropped Raphael's hand when they reached the door. They'd already created enough talk around town without walking in as a couple.

Raphael didn't say anything, but he did look at her with a curious expression. He stepped forward and opened the door, waiting for her to enter before following her inside. He moved up beside her and scanned the space for an empty table.

"There's one," he said, making his way across the room.

The talk in the eatery turned to muted whispers as speculation spread.

Red's head rose and she looked down at everyone as she made her way toward the back. Raphael was waiting next to the table with a chair pulled out for her. She took her seat and waited for him to follow suit.

They ordered, a synth-steak for Red, synth-blood for Raphael. He waited for the server to put their water down on the table and walk away before he spoke.

"How long has it been since you heard from Morgan?"

Red glanced around and lowered her voice. "It's been

weeks. The last time we spoke, he'd just gotten hired at the lab. I've been watching the news reports, but so far, not a peep." She nervously stroked the pistol strapped to her leg.

He watched her, his dark eyes penetrating. "He should've been back by now. You are vulnerable with him away."

"I'm hardly defenseless." Red patted the weapon.

"That is not the kind of vulnerability I'm referring to. Can you not sense the wolf brushing your skin, yearning for release?"

Red felt the blood drain from her face. "How did you?"

"It gives off a scent. Even if *you* can't smell it, others can." Raphael inhaled and closed his eyes. "The scent is alluring and hard to resist."

Was that why the men had been looking at her differently? Red raised her arm and sniffed. She didn't smell any different that she could tell. Her eyes widened. "Is that why you—" She broke off.

He shook his head. "No. I admit I can smell the change in you, but that is not the only reason I enjoy your company." He had the grace to look away when she blushed.

"That's not why Morgan's attracted to me, is it?" Red had to ask. She didn't want to, but she needed to know. If all he saw in her was the wolf or some sweet aroma, then she'd leave tomorrow and not look back.

Raphael peered at her beneath long dark lashes. "Morgan rarely acts upon his feral instincts. If they came out around you, then it means his feelings are strong. His heart is in the right place, even if his head appears to be off course."

"Do you think he'll return?" she asked softly. "I don't know what I'm going to do if he doesn't come back. The town is on the verge of rebellion and I don't have enough pull with the townspeople to stop it. No one trusts a wolf that's out of control. They think I killed that man."

"Did you?"

The question slapped her across the face, sobering her.

"No!" Her voice rose, then her gaze dropped. Red stared down at her hands. "I would've remembered, and if not, there would've been some kind of proof in my room. I checked my guns. They haven't been fired recently."

"Do not worry, I don't believe you're involved," he said after a moment.

Her head shot up.

Raphael smiled. "Too many odd things are happening. I've sent a message to Michael to find out what Roark's been up to lately, but I haven't heard back from him. It has me worried."

"Do you think Roark's done something to your brother?" she asked.

"Doubtful. Michael, as you know, is very powerful. It would be hard to harm him."

"Hard is not impossible." Red frowned. "I wouldn't put anything past Roark."

"Neither would I," Raphael said as their food arrived. "Now let's try for more pleasant conversation or we'll end up with indigestion." He winked.

Red tried not to watch as he took his first sip of synth-blood, but it was impossible. Curiosity got the best of her. She had to admit Raphael made the whole blood-drinking thing look frankly sexual as he allowed the liquid to rest in his mouth before swallowing deep. He licked his bottom lip afterward to catch any wayward droplets, then grinned at her with his fangs extended.

"Sorry about the fangs," he said, after catching her staring. "They react to blood in the same way a man would react to a beautiful naked woman lying on his rest pad."

"Huh?"

"The blood makes my fangs hard."

Red's eyes widened and warmth spread over her face and down her neck.

Raphael threw his head back and laughed. The hearty

sound reverberated through her, causing her nipples to pucker. She casually crossed her arms, but not before he noticed. His lashes lowered over his eyes and his mouth took on a seductive bent.

She reached for her water and took a big gulp before digging into her steak. "This is good, too," she said with her mouth full.

He leaned closer until only she could hear him speak. "There is nothing wrong with being attracted to me."

Red met his gaze. "Yes, there is. Can't you see that? I shouldn't feel anything other than friendship for you. I love Morgan."

Raphael flinched, but held his ground. "I know you do." Sadness enveloped him, but he quickly doused it. "What we'd experience together, should you allow it, wouldn't be love," he lied easily, his heart threatening to burst from his tired old chest. How long had it been since he'd truly felt anything other than desire for a woman?

Raphael tried to remember past the transformation. A ghost from a lifetime ago flashed in his mind, her red hair had shone copper in the sunlight and freckles dotted her pale cheeks. Beth Ann's photo had gotten him through some of his darkest moments. He squelched the memory before the pain struck a blow to his soul.

Red was unlike anyone he'd ever encountered, and yet so like the woman he'd lost years ago. And like Beth Ann, she belonged to another. Raphael could accept that—almost. But that didn't stop him from wanting to be near her. Spend time with her. Kiss her. Make love to her. He'd vowed to himself he wouldn't seduce her. No matter how much it pained him to resist those urges.

Despite longing for Red, Raphael did care about Morgan. He considered the man a friend. Sure, he'd slept with one of Morgan's women, but that had been a long time ago and she hadn't deserved the alpha's attention. Or so he'd thought at the time, when he'd seduced Morgan's fiancée, Karen Martin. She'd left town after Morgan broke off their engagement. The whole ordeal had nearly cost them their friendship.

If he seduced Red, saving his friendship with Morgan would be the least of his concerns. Morgan would kill him. There was no doubt in his mind. It would be a fight to the death between two alphas.

At the same time, Raphael couldn't deny the feelings he had when he was around her. Red made him feel alive. More so than he'd felt in decades. She was a tempting bloom in the middle of his soul's barren wasteland. He only wished to experience her fragrance once—or twice—before he allowed another man to whisk her away.

A fresh flask of water was placed on the table. Red turned her head to acknowledge the server and Raphael saw Morgan's mark on her neck—a painful reminder that she'd already been claimed. He lifted his glass of synth-blood and wished, not for the first time, that it was Red's blood he was about to taste. She smelled so delicious. So tempting. So feminine. The stronger her wolf grew, the more attractive she became. He wondered what she'd do now that she knew the truth.

The rest of the meal went quicker than he'd intended. The rumors and insinuations bantered about at the nearby tables buzzed in his head until he thought he'd go mad. Red set her fork down and looked around.

"I'd better get back in case Morgan tries to contact me."

"Of course." Raphael rose from his seat and walked around the table to pull her chair out. "Allow me to walk you back to the share space."

She stared at him, then looked around at the patrons. Her gaze hardened. He had no doubt she was considering turning down his offer. Finally she nodded. "Sure, why not?"

Raphael relaxed as they strolled outside. The streets were

nearly vacant as the dark thickened, descending on Nuria, working its way into every crevice.

He reached for Red's hand, but she dodged him. He let her. It was probably best that he not touch her right now, since the blood was still coursing through his veins, heightening his senses. Making him hunger for more than she'd be willing to give. He felt his cock harden and shifted to make it less apparent.

They reached the water trader space in short order. Red started to walk in, but Raphael stopped her. Before he knew what he was going to do, he pulled her into his arms and kissed her. Her lips were warm and pliant; there was no tension as she melted into his body and gripped his shoulders lightly. He sunk into the kiss, parting her lips to taste her deeply.

In his fervor, a fang nicked the inside of her mouth and blood flooded the moist cavern. The coppery goodness powered his hunger, tightening every muscle in his body. He groaned as the sweet taste of her slid over his tongue, making him dizzy with desire. Raphael pulled her closer, bunching her clothes in his fists. His erection brushed her stomach and he felt her quiver. He had to have her. Damn his good intentions to hell.

"No!" Red wrenched her bleeding mouth away and struggled out of his grasp.

Red held out an arm to keep Raphael at bay, or perhaps she needed the distance to stop herself from touching him. She couldn't believe she'd allowed him to kiss her. Her tongue darted out and she tasted blood. Red's hands were shaking as she touched her lips. She glanced down. Her fingers came away covered in crimson.

"I-I'm sorry," she said, trying to slow her racing heart. "I shouldn't have allowed that to happen. I don't know what came over me."

"Gina," he said, reaching for her.

"No!" She stepped back. "Don't call me that. The only people who call me by that name are Morgan and my grandfather."

Hurt flashed across his face, but he masked it quickly. "My apologies for overstepping. It will not happen again." His words were clipped.

Red softened. She hadn't meant to cause him any pain, but they couldn't do this to Morgan. "I'm not saying I didn't enjoy the kiss, Raphael. I did. Maybe too much. But I *love* Morgan. I guess I just missed being held more than I realized." Her resolve hardened, along with her voice. "I hope you understand."

His hand dropped away and he pushed his fingers through his hair, pulling it out of its queue. "Again, I apologize," he said. "I had no right to touch you in that manner. Please forgive me."

Red tried to smile, but her lips trembled. "There's nothing to forgive. We're still friends, right?"

He nodded. "Of course. Friends."

Red could hear the disappointment in his voice. "I really *am* sorry. Perhaps if we'd met sooner," she added, knowing she was only making things worse. She'd never been in this position before and wasn't quite sure how to handle it. She'd made a royal mistake by giving in to her attraction. What would Morgan say when he found out? Had she just ruined the best thing that had ever happened to her?

Raphael ran a finger over her furrowed brow and smiled. "Relax, she-wolf. You were destined to be Morgan's mate. Fate would not have saved you for me."

"How do you know?"

"I've never been that fortunate," he said, but his eyes were back to twinkling mischievously.

She stepped forward and grabbed his hand. "There is someone out there for you. Someone who will capture your heart and refuse to give it back. I can feel it."

"Now you speak of fairy tales," he said, losing some of his bravado.

"No, I speak the truth," Red said, giving his hand a squeeze before releasing him to step inside. "Thank you for dinner . . . and everything else."

"My pleasure." He inclined his head and strode into the night.

It was late by the time Morgan returned to the share space he'd rented. He'd stayed out longer than he'd intended with Pete. He punched in the number that he knew would connect him to Gina. She answered on the fourth beep, out of breath as if she were running to catch the call. He glanced at the time. He thought for sure she'd be asleep. His sharp gaze took in her appearance. Her hair was disheveled and her lips looked kiss swollen. Morgan's chest clenched.

"I thought I was going to wake you, but I see you're still dressed," he said. "Did I interrupt something?"

Gina blushed. "No, nothing. Dinner just ran longer than I'd expected."

"Were you alone?" he asked the question mildly, feeling anything but. Morgan watched her closely. Since he couldn't smell her, he'd have to rely on visual cues to determine if she was lying.

"I was with Raphael," she murmured.

Was that guilt he detected in her voice? Morgan's body tensed with rage as memories from the past flooded him. He'd been engaged to Karen Martin for almost a year when he found her in a rest pad with Raphael Vega. She'd been groaning and scratching at his back, half crazed and out of her mind while he fucked her. It had taken everything in Morgan's being to walk away without killing them both.

In the end, he'd realized that Raphael had done him a favor. He needed a mate who would be loyal, even when he wasn't around. Karen was not that woman, but he'd thought Gina was. Now he wasn't so sure.

He pictured Raphael and Gina lying together. His vision clouded and his body began to shake. The wolf snapped at his haunches and snarled. Claws sprang from his fingertips. Morgan tasted blood as his teeth were ejected, replaced by long incisors made for ripping flesh off the bone. She was his mate. How dare that vamp lay a fang on her. He'd kill them. He'd kill them both if he smelled Raphael on her body. His nostrils flared as Morgan fought for control.

Gina pressed her palm to a panel on the wall and light flooded the room. The rest pad behind her came into view. It was still made, the blankets military tight. Morgan's shoulders relaxed a little and he was able to push the wolf back inside.

"When are you coming home?" she asked, ignoring the obvious changes in his appearance. "I miss you so much."

He took a deep breath. "I haven't been able to find the cells. Something weird is going on here."

"What do you mean?" Gina leaned closer to the screen.

Morgan had been so distracted by her swollen lips and tousled hair that he hadn't noticed the dark circles under her eyes or the fact that she looked like she'd lost weight. Gina wasn't holding up any better than he was. Guilt deflated the last of his anger. "I went to the place where they were supposed to be storing the cells and the new Scarlet vaccine."

"And?"

"There was nothing there."

She frowned. "What do you mean there was nothing there? They didn't have the cells?"

"I mean the space was empty. There was absolutely nothing in the locked room."

"Then why keep it locked?" she asked.

"That's what I've been wondering," he said. "It doesn't make sense."

"Maybe they moved them," she suggested.

Morgan shook his head. "No. I've been tracking the shipments and following the arrivals. That lab should've been bursting with cryonic chambers, cell-storage facilities, and work spaces for the scientists. But there was nothing there. Not even a scrap of synth-paper. The warehouse was spotless like the room had never been used."

"I don't understand," she said. "If the lab hasn't been moved, then where is it?"

"I don't know. It should've been there." He scrubbed a hand over his face.

"What are you going to do?" She crossed her arms, bracing for his answer.

"The only thing I can do—follow the employees." He blew out a heavy breath. "There's supposed to be fifty people working in there, collecting pay credits. I intend to find them."

Gina shook her head. "How are you going to do that?"

Morgan growled and pulled at his disheveled hair. "I'll go room to room if I have to."

"That's not a plan. It's suicide." Gina grew quiet, her expression distant. "Maybe it's time for you to come home. You can regroup while you come up with another plan."

Morgan met her gaze. God, how he missed her. He wanted nothing more than to return to Nuria and hold her in his arms, but he couldn't. Not until he found out what had happened to Sarah and Joshua and the missing employees. He knew there was a very good chance he'd lose her if it took much longer. He'd seen that look on a few occasions, and it always came before good-bye. But he'd come too far. Risked too much to turn back now. "I can't. Not yet anyway. Just give me a few more days. That's all I ask," he pleaded.

"You've said that before."

"I mean it this time. If I haven't found the cells by the end of the week, then I'll put in notice and head straight back to Nuria."

She swallowed hard and tears shimmered in her hazel eyes. "Please hurry. I'm not sure how much longer I can take being here all alone."

Her words echoed in his mind. Morgan bit the inside of his mouth to counter the pain he felt. She was lonely—he could hear it in her voice. See it in the lines etching her beautiful face. And he was in no position to ease her. How long before she sought out another to comfort her? He pictured Raphael biding his time and the wolf's hackles rose. "I understand," he said, forcing his voice to remain calm. "I'll be home soon."

She gave him a watery smile.

"I love you, Gina." If only he could reach through the screen and pull her into his arms. Morgan ached at the sight of her. How he'd made it this long without her, he'd never know.

"I love you, too," she whispered.

"I'll call again as soon as I can."

Her bottom lip trembled. "Don't let it take another week."

"I'll do my best, but I can't make you any promises."

She looked away and made a quick swipe at her face. Morgan looked down to give her some privacy. "I have to go now. I need some sleep," he said gruffly.

"Yeah, me, too," she said. "I'll talk to you soon."

"Have a good night," he said, staring at her for a minute more.

She laughed to herself. "Too late for that, but thanks."

Morgan disconnected the feed. He'd considered asking Gina what she meant by her comment, but he didn't think he could stand to hear the truth. Urgency spurred him on. He had to find the cells soon or there might not be anything to go home to.

chapter thirteen

Roark Montgomery sat behind his desk and hit the buzzer that would summon Michael Travers into his office. He tried to wait patiently, when he felt anything but. He stared at the communiqué he'd intercepted from Raphael Vega. It had been addressed to Michael, but didn't say much. Even so, the fact that it arrived right after the death of the unknown made him uneasy. It could be coincidence, but Roark wasn't willing to take that chance. He thought it best to keep the note.

His gaze dropped to a synth-document on his desk. He'd read the unknown report from the dissecting lab in Nuria. It hadn't said much. No details on how the man had died. He'd hoped for more, but all he'd really wanted to know was if the man was dead. He was. Mission accomplished. Roark grinned. Things were falling into place nicely.

Michael Travers entered the room on scurrying feet. The man didn't seem to have a normal walk; everything had to be overexaggerated and disjointed. Almost as if he'd forgotten how to move properly. Maybe he'd never learned as a child.

"Sir, you wanted to see me?" he asked, ducking his head in a curt bob like a good lackey.

"Yes," Roark said, suppressing the need to yell. Every

time he was around Travers he had the overwhelming urge to beat him senseless. It had taken great restraint not to act upon those impulses. The truth was, he'd yet to find anyone else who'd do the questionable work Travers performed. If he had, he would've been gone long ago. Something about the man made him nervous. And it had nothing to do with the ease with which he could kill. Roark studied him. There was just something "off" about the man. "I have another package for you to deliver."

Travers' pasty face paled further. "Is it in the same condition as the last one?" he asked.

Roark arched a brow. "Does it matter?"

"No. I just wanted to know if I'd have to heal it before I sent it off."

Roark relaxed slightly. At least he wasn't asking too many questions this time around. "This one is *fresher,* so all you need to do is drop it off in the same spot as the last package."

"Will I find it in the same location?" he asked, shuddering slightly.

"Unless I say otherwise." Roark pulled at the sleeves of his jacket. He was already growing weary of this conversation.

"When do you need it done?" Michael asked.

"I was thinking that now was as good a time as any. That is, if your schedule is clear. I'd hate to interfere with any of your plans." Sarcasm dripped from his words, leaving a sting of acid behind.

"I'll get right on it." Michael nodded, swaying on his miserable feet.

"What are you waiting for?" Roark bellowed. "Go!" Did he have to do everything for himself? Why was it so hard to find competent help? He was trying to make the world a better place and all around him were rejects who couldn't tie their boots without help. They would be the first to go once he came into power and rid the planet of the Others.

There was no room in the world he imagined for people like Michael Travers.

Michael flushed and shuffled out into the hall. He was in such a hurry to leave he forgot to close the door behind him.

"Aren't you forgetting something?" Roark called after him.

He looked back and his eyes widened before he rushed forward and quickly shut the door. "Sorry, sir. It won't happen again," he said.

Michael strolled down the corridor to the door that led below ground. He needed to find out what Roark was up to. He hadn't heard anything from his brother Raphael since his recent visit, but that didn't mean there weren't problems in Nuria.

He debated whether to contact him. And say what? That he suspected Roark was up to something? That was nothing new. His boss was always up to something. There was a time when he knew what most of that was, but those days were long gone. Ever since Roark was shot by Gina Santiago in Nuria, he'd shut Michael out.

Fear marched over his skin. Did Roark suspect his involvement? No, if that were the case he'd be dead already. Roark wasn't one to put off an execution. But something had changed. His boss was becoming more and more secretive, and it made Michael nervous.

Why the sudden need to drop human packages off outside of Nuria? As far as Michael could tell there wasn't anything special about the packages. He'd probed the mind of the last one and had only gotten jumbled images due to the man's fear. If the next one was anything like the last, he'd get nothing.

What purpose did they serve? He could think of none. The last one had been an unknown, which meant he didn't exist in the republics' identification system, so killing him wouldn't matter. The IPTT authorities wouldn't recognize his death. Neither would the people of Nuria. Which probably was why he hadn't heard from his brother. Yet Roark didn't do things without a reason, which meant Michael was missing something—something very important. Perhaps this new package would hold the answers that he needed.

Michael walked down the stairs, descending deeper and deeper into the bowels of the building. The walls were musty and stank of depravity. The odor tickled his nose until he sneezed. It was only when he'd dropped two more floors that he heard the steady thud of a strong heartbeat. His ears perked up. Michael could almost hear the blood rushing through the man's veins. His stomach growled.

A clean scent greeted him. Roark was right, this package was in much better shape than the last one. *He mustn't be an unknown,* he thought. A drifter, maybe. Michael's stomach gurgled again and his fangs extended. He shouldn't have skipped lunch.

Michael entered the room and saw the man chained to the wall. His firm muscles struggled against the bindings at his wrists. His tawny head jerked up when Michael purposely made his footfalls heavy.

"Who are you?" the man asked, pulling at the chains.

Michael didn't immediately answer. He was too busy tamping down his hunger. The man yanked at the restraints, rattling them in their links.

"I asked you a question." The man's face was flushed with anger . . . *and blood.* Its sweet scent drifted over the filth, temporarily blocking the stench from his nose.

Michael licked his lips and casually glanced over his shoulder. They were alone. The area had been built before the introduction of vid-feeds. That's why his boss used this place to carry out his cruelty. No witnesses. He listened to be sure, but could hear nothing over the man's struggles and his roaring stomach. Roark would never know if he took one little sip. What could it hurt? The man's gaze was locked on him when Michael turned back.

"Remain calm and I will get you out of here," Michael said, catching the man's eyes with his and telekinetically pinning him in place.

The angry lines on the man's face eased and his jaw slackened. The muscles in his arms relaxed, causing his body to hang from the chains. Michael walked forward slowly, his gaze never leaving the man. He opened the cage and not so gently pulled the man's head over to the side, exposing the vein throbbing in his neck. The man whimpered, but couldn't pull away.

Michael wet his lips, his mouth all but watering at the thought of the first taste. He lowered his head until his lips brushed the man's throat. The skin was moist from sweat and slightly salty to the taste. Michael licked, enjoying the jump of muscles as he cleaned off a spot to bite. The cries grew louder. "Shush," he said, then opened his mouth wide and sunk his fangs in deep.

Rich, hot, coppery blood exploded in his mouth, showering him with much-needed nutrition. Michael closed his eyes and began to suck hard, greedy for what the man unwillingly gave him. He'd avoided the carotid artery because he didn't want the man to bleed out. It had been so long since he'd fed from anything but a bottle. Michael groaned as his body flared to life. There was nothing like going to the source when it came to quenching one's hunger.

The man hung helplessly in his arms, cradled against his chest in an inhuman embrace. Michael's head swam as the intoxication hit. It wouldn't last more than a few seconds, but he enjoyed it all the same. The man's heart stuttered. Damn it! It was too soon. He'd just started enjoying himself. But stuttering was only the first sign. The man would die if he didn't stop.

Michael reluctantly released him. He swiped his tongue over the wounds to speed his healing, then straightened and wiped his mouth with the back of his hand. Blood glistened on his flushed knuckles. He quickly licked it off. *Waste not,* he thought with a laugh.

Roark sat in his seat staring at the monitor for the hidden camera he'd planted in his interrogation room. Fear warred with revulsion. His mind refused to believe what he was seeing. He couldn't be. All this time, all these years, he'd had an Other under his nose and never even knew it. How could Michael have gotten away with the lie for so long?

His palms began to sweat as he recalled all the assassination missions he'd sent the man on. Michael Travers had enough information floating in his head to make his life hell.

Hell? What was he thinking? He'd be ruined if this got out. His political career would end with a whimper instead of a roar. Well he'd have none of it. He'd worked too hard. Roark wiped at his forehead and his hand came away wet. What was he going to do?

How long had his assistant been spying on him? Roark had no doubt the man was a spy. He'd changed after their last mission together and now he knew why. He didn't want to think about all the years he'd allowed Travers into his inner circle. Roark shuddered, his mind working overtime to figure out a solution to this sudden and very grave problem.

His knee-jerk reaction was to kill him. Burn his body somewhere in the desert where no one would ever find him. Unfortunately, Travers had been around long enough that people would note his disappearance. There had to be some way to get rid of him without drawing the wrong kind of attention. Roark thought hard. So far Michael had followed orders, and would probably continue to do so to keep his cover.

He decided to go ahead and let Michael deliver the package as planned. If he changed his mind, there was a good chance Michael would suspect something. The last thing Roark wanted was to have his own assassin after him—at least not until he was ready for him. He ran his hands over his pant legs to dry them and took a deep breath. He'd made a huge mistake. The fact that he was caught so off guard didn't sit well with Roark.

He reached for the vidcom and punched in a number. He waited for the line to connect. "We have a problem. A very big problem. I may need help," he said, then disconnected.

The sun beat at the curtains, crashing into the room like an unwanted party guest. Red cracked an eye and winced. It couldn't be morning already. Guilt had kept her up most of the night. How could she have let Raphael kiss her? Morgan had only been gone a short while. Yes, she'd needed a friend. And yes, she'd missed human contact. Both of which had been scarce since Morgan's departure. But that didn't mean she should act upon those feelings with the first guy who took an interest in her.

She sighed and turned over, giving the sun her back. Raphael hadn't been the only man to show interest, but he had been only one she'd been tempted by. She closed her eyes, but after a few minutes gave up on going back to sleep. Red ran her hands through her long, black hair, pushing it off her face so she wouldn't bump into a wall as she stumbled to the chemical shower.

She pressed a button and a heavy lemon scent came out a second before she stepped under the penetrating spray. Hopefully the new scent would overpower the smell of her wolf. She let the shower beat down upon her head as she mustered the courage to face another opposition-filled day.

Please don't let anyone know about the kiss. She sent the silent prayer into the ether and started planning her day.

The new trainees were coming along nicely. If she could get a few more, they'd officially have a full team. There wouldn't be any extras, but it would be a good start. Of course, that wouldn't happen if people kept quitting. Red knew she was the cause. Or at least their beliefs about her were the cause of their change of heart. The dead body didn't help.

Even though she'd made each recruit sign a "no-quit" contract, she'd let the men go. Red didn't want men who weren't here willingly. It was hard enough to patrol with people who knew the dangers and accepted them freely. She couldn't have reluctant members guarding her men's backs or guarding her back.

Red pressed a button and the shower turned off. She wrinkled her nose as another burst of lemon filled the air. She eyed the shower with disgust. *These scents really should be adjustable,* she thought, grabbing a towel.

Within minutes Red was armed and dressed, ready to head out the door. She glanced at the vidcom. Even though Morgan had called last night, it felt like years since they spoke. This whole relationship business was more difficult than she imagined. She wanted to be understanding. Really she did. But how long should a girl wait?

Red placed her palm on the door and it slid open. She heard voices down in the bar area as people submitted their water orders. She plodded down the stairs, catching sight of Takeo, Juan, and Demery. Demery was wearing his white protective suit. Jones and Olson were noticeably absent. The other two men looked up when she came into view, almost as if they'd been waiting for her. Red hoped they didn't plan to quit, too. They were the best of the lot.

"There she is," Takeo said, elbowing Demery, who swung his masked face around to smile at her.

"Can I help you, gentlemen?" she asked.

"We were worried about you. We know the investigation isn't going well, but we're still invested in seeing it through," Takeo said. "Under the circumstances, we thought you'd like to know that."

"Where are Jones and Olson?" she asked.

"They're waiting at the sheriff's station for us," Juan said.

Red gave them a nod. "Then let's not keep them any longer."

The four of them walked down the street. Demery got a few strange looks, but mainly the people kept their attention trained on Red. Most had the decency to save their gossiping until they passed. A few didn't bother with such courtesy. They started murmuring when they saw her.

"I bet she's sleeping with all of them. Maggie said that she's seen her with Raphael. It's only a matter of time before he gets into her rest pad—if he hasn't already. You know how he is when it comes to the sheriff's women. Take, take, take. The man's insatiable." The last was said breathlessly.

"Poor Morgan," one of the people said as they approached.

"Heard she killed that unknown," another answered. "Jim said the findings were inconclusive, but I bet that was because he was trying to protect us. No need for Nuria to be taken down because of one wolf's indiscretions."

By the time they reached the sheriff's station, Red's ears were burning and she was seething. So the whole town thought she was a murdering whore. It didn't help that guilt assailed her when Raphael's name was mentioned. She'd felt her face heating on more than one occasion. Red knew that only made her look guilty. Takeo, Juan, and Demery hadn't said a word, but she'd felt the tension coursing through the men as they listened to the slander.

Red decided it was time to put an end to this nonsense. She'd have to have a talk with Maggie. She had been trying to avoid her, but the woman seemed to be behind the bulk of the rumors floating around town. It hurt Red more than she cared to admit. Maggie had been so kind to her when she first hit Nuria. This sudden about-face was hard to bear. Red needed to find out what she'd done to her and make amends, if that was possible. Maybe then she would receive some support.

Maggie smirked as Red and the team walked into the station. Her eyes lit on the men, then fell accusingly onto Red. *Why didn't the woman just call her a slut and get it over with?* Red stiffened. A productive talk was looking less and less likely. After last night, she was too tired to fight. She shook her head and walked to her desk. For some reason, Maggie was out to get her and wouldn't be happy until she was gone.

The rest of the morning passed uneventfully. The new recruits were busy in a back room, studying military tactics and unknown-apprehension vids. Red had sent the men out to repair the training facility, but it would take awhile to scavenge the materials. She stood, stretching her back before walking over to check on the recruits.

Takeo and Demery were sparring as they took turns playing an unknown. Demery's body moved smoothly in the white protective suit as Takeo came at him. All fire and grace, Takeo's chimera rippled beneath his skin as he feigned another attack. Demery pivoted, using a backhanded punch. He'd aimed where Takeo's head should've been, but was too slow, despite his blurring speed.

"I'm going to get you one of these times," Demery said, laughing.

Takeo grinned and his golden eyes glittered with anticipation. Red cleared her throat and the men straightened like naughty children caught playing ball in the house. "I'm going to step out to the food dispensing station for some lunch. Can I get you guys anything?"

The men shook their heads. "It's hard to fight on a full stomach," Takeo said, letting her know they planned to get right back to it after she left.

Red snorted. "Finish watching the apprehension vids first," she said, turning to leave. "Oh, and try not to break anything."

She heard laughter behind her and couldn't help but smile. The grin faded when her gaze landed on Maggie. Not that she had to report to the woman, but Red thought it best she let her know where she'd be if there was a problem. She was still trying to work up the nerve to have that talk with her.

Okay, so she'd been putting it off. Red really wasn't looking forward to the upcoming screaming match she knew would ensue. Maybe once her stomach was full she'd feel different.

"I'm going for lunch. If there's a problem, give me a call on my navcom."

Maggie stared at her. "Meeting anyone in particular?"

"No," Red said, facing her. "Are you?"

Maggie blushed and looked away.

Red set out toward the food dispensing station. The day was warm, as usual. The air shimmered over the protective tarp road in watery waves. She could see Pine Street ahead, and was already scanning the mental menu in her mind. Synth-chicken or beef? She was so preoccupied she didn't see the man come out of the alley until he was upon her.

"Please," he said. "You have to help me." He tugged at her arm.

Red jerked out of his grasp, stunned that he'd gotten so close without her being aware of his presence. "What's wrong?" she asked, eyeing him suspiciously.

Tall and evenly built, the man wore traditional boundary clothing, tan fatigues. His tawny hair was styled neatly, a sharp contrast to his rough, work-hewn hands. Sunshades covered his eyes. He seemed fine other than being a little agitated.

"We must hurry," he said, attempting to grab her again. She stayed out of reach.

"What seems to be the problem?" Red asked, glancing around.

A few people passed by, giving her and the stranger curious looks. The last thing she wanted was more speculation. Red stepped off the walkway into the mouth of the alley. Lead pipes were stacked along the side, narrowing an already small space. Barrels that at one time held fuel gaped openmouthed, long dried out from the sun. Tattered clothes had been tossed haphazardly onto the heap, turning it into a refuge for trash. Nothing moved. Not even the wind.

Red lowered her voice. "Are you hurt?" She gave him a once-over, but detected no visible injury.

He shook his head, sending strands of tawny hair onto his forehead. "No, but my friend is."

"I'll call it in," she said, feeling the familiar adrenaline rush she got anytime she was on active duty.

"No, please." He stilled her hand. "There's no time. He won't make it unless we move him now and get him to the emergency care center." The man pointed down the alley, but Red didn't immediately spot anyone else.

She looked again. "Where is he?"

"He's behind those pipes. I propped him up against the wall. I think his leg is broken and he might have a head injury."

Red's gaze narrowed and her hand moved to her pistol. "How did it happen?"

"I'll explain on the way. Can we please hurry?" The man seemed on the verge of panic.

"Sure, right after I call it in." Red pressed a button on her navcom and sent the code for medical emergency. Maggie would receive the message and send backup.

She looked down the road and spotted the top of the care center roof. It wasn't far away. A couple of blocks, tops. If all the man had was a broken leg and a possible head injury, then it might be quicker for them to haul him there. Maybe if she was seen helping the stranger when backup arrived, Maggie and the people of Nuria would think better of her.

"Okay," Red said, stepping deeper into the alley. "Show me where he is."

The man smiled. "Thank you. I really appreciate this. You have no idea what it means to me."

He led her down the alley toward the unoccupied buildings at the back. Neatly painted siding gave way to broken windows and pockmarked walls. They neared the stack of pipes.

"A little farther," the man said. "He's just on the other side."

Red picked up her pace. Something about the alley made her decidedly uncomfortable. She'd avoided these spaces since arriving in Nuria. They reminded her that despite the polish on the main road, the town continued to decay. It was only a matter of time before the rest of Nuria followed suit and became a notation in the history books, like the city of Phoenix.

Red rounded the corner, expecting to see someone propped against the wall, but there was no one there. "Where is he?" she asked, looking around. From this far down the alley, she didn't have a clear view of the main street, which meant her backup wouldn't be able to see her. Red stepped back. "What's going on?"

The man gave her a sad smile. "Sorry about this," he said. "But I have no choice."

"Sorry about what?" She rounded on him, thinking he was about to attack. Her limbs loosened and she widened her legs until she was in a fighting stance. She'd only shoot him as a last resort.

"For this," he said, running full tilt toward the old brick wall.

Red watched in shock as the man didn't put a hand up to prevent the collision. He hit the wall so hard she actually heard something crack inside of him, then he bounced back, blood running down his forehead and out his broken nose. His sunshades were shattered, hanging loosely from one ear.

He cried out in pain, then repeated his actions, this time hitting the wall with his shoulder. Something crunched and he crumpled a little under the agony.

Red cringed. "Stop it! What's wrong with you?"

"Help! Help! Someone help me!" he shouted.

She stopped, concerned it might not be smart to get too close. He was obviously insane, despite his earlier lucidity. What if he was sick? That thought led to a more disturbing one. Was he contagious? Red couldn't seem to move as she watched his bizarre behavior play out like a training vid identifying what to look for in the mentally ill. She'd never seen a crazy person before. Normally once an abnormality was detected in pregnancy it was "corrected" before the baby was born.

The man continued to scream like he was surrounded by wolves, until several people on the main drag heard him. They rushed into the alley, swarming in response.

"You need help," Red said. "The kind of help that the emergency care center cannot provide." She looked at the people, heading down the alley toward them. The group had grown in number. None appeared to be from the sheriff's station.

"Keep her away from me. Please keep her away." He cowered, holding up one hand in defense. The one that was attached to the shoulder he'd hit lay limp at his side.

Red turned to the crowd. "He did this to himself. I think there's something wrong with him. We need to contact the emergency care center and have him sedated."

"She's lying," he countered, stepping forward, only to shrink back again when Red looked at him. "Someone please take me to the sheriff's station. I need to file a complaint. She's out of control. She tried to kill me."

Her eyes widened. "I did no such thing," Red said.

"Look at me," the man turned to the crowd. "Who are you going to believe? If you all hadn't arrived when you did, she would've finished the job."

Red gaped, then quickly recovered. "You lying son of a bitch."

"Stay away from him," a man said, putting his body between Red and the injured man.

"I told you I didn't touch him," she said. "He asked me to come down here. He said his friend was injured. I called for backup."

"Then where are they?" he asked.

That was a good question. Red planned to find out. "They should've been here by now," she said.

"You said he had a friend. Where is he?"

"I didn't say he had a friend," she ground out. "He did." Red pointed at the injured man.

"There's no one here now but the two of you," another man said.

"That's my point," Red said. "He lied about having a friend."

"Seems like there's a lot of that going around these days," someone in the crowd said. "Didn't you say that other fella was lying, too?"

"I heard tell she threatened to shoot the man at the food dispensing station," said a woman. "And look what happened to him."

Red met their wary gazes. Most looked away, but several stared back, her guilt clearly written in their eyes. "Look," she said. "There's not a mark on me. Don't you think if I'd beaten him this badly my knuckles would be bruised?"

"Not if you used a pipe," the injured man said.

"I didn't touch him," Red said.

"Then you'll have no problem coming to the sheriff's station with us."

chapter fourteen

Horrified, Red turned on the injured man. The reason for his apology suddenly became clear. He was setting her up so formal charges could be brought against her. She watched the Nurian help the injured man off the pile of pipes.

"It's okay," he said. "We'll take you to the sheriff's station right away."

The condemnation Red saw around her scalded her insides, leaving her raw. She'd done nothing but try to look out for these people. Yet they were so quick to judge her guilty. And now she'd have to fight formal charges because she'd tried to help a stranger in need. Red's head slumped. This was getting ridiculous. She was thwarted at every turn.

The crowd filed out of the alley. Some of the people were shocked by her supposed actions. Most seemed unsurprised. Red wasn't sure which hurt more. The people walked the man down the street. A blood trail followed their progress. What would her grandfather think when he received the charges? Would he believe them? Would he have her arrested? Would he even have a choice? She had no doubt he'd be humiliated. She was embarrassed to have fallen for such a weak ploy.

Bloodied and bruised, the man who'd set her up looked

over his shoulders. For a moment, Red saw genuine remorse in his green eyes. It was gone so quickly she convinced herself that she'd been mistaken.

He moaned and allowed his legs to give out. The man beside him caught him under the arm and hoisted him back up. "We're almost there," he said. "One of the deputies will take your statement."

"Please don't let her hurt me anymore," the man pleaded. His voice cracked as he put on the performance of his life.

They entered the sheriff's station a couple of minutes later. Maggie gasped when the man came into view. "What happened?"

"He'd like to file assault charges against Red," the man holding him up said.

Maggie's gaze widened even further as she sought Red out. "What have you done?" she cried, rushing forward to pull a chair over for the man to sit on.

"I didn't do anything other than send in a call for backup," Red said.

Maggie flushed. "It must have gotten lost. I have no record of receiving such a call." She busied herself, refusing to meet Red's gaze.

A touch of a button would be all it would take to drop a distress call. Unfortunately, there was no way to prove it, if Maggie purged her system. Red had no doubt that if Maggie had gone to the trouble to ignore the call, then she would definitely cover her actions.

The man collapsed into the seat as if he could no longer support his weight. "What's your name, sir?" Maggie asked.

"John," he coughed out. "John Green."

Hearing the uproar, the recruits came out of the back room. Takeo, Demery, and Juan stopped dead in their tracks. Randall and Keith continued forward for a better look.

"I'd like to file a formal brutality complaint against that officer," the man said, pointing at Red.

"She's not officially an officer here yet," Maggie said, giving Red a look that said *and you never will be*.

"Doesn't change anything," he said, hiding his surprise. "I still want to file a formal complaint."

The recruits nearest the scene gasped and looked at each other. "Told you," Randall said to Keith. "She's a menace. How can she expect to lead a team, when she can't even keep this town ticking without resorting to violence?"

Red felt his words like a blow. She flinched, but forced her chin up. She wouldn't look guilty, no matter what they said. She hadn't done anything wrong.

"I'm finished," Keith said. "Consider this my resignation. There's just too much shit going on with you and this place." He pushed past the crowd and left.

"Count me out, too," Randall said, looking back at the other recruits. "If you're smart, you guys will leave before she drags you down with her. That's what you get for putting a woman in charge."

Takeo, Juan, and Demery still hadn't moved, but they appeared to be taking in the whole scene. Would they be next? Red vowed not to stop them if they decided to go. The departing recruits were right about one thing, if any of them chose to stay, their reputations might be damaged by being affiliated with her.

"They're leaving," Maggie spat. "And it's all your fault. If you were able to *control* yourself, we wouldn't be going through this now. Someone call a medic before Mr. Green bleeds to death in the station."

Red shivered at the accusation. Maggie believed that her out-of-control wolf was responsible for this man's injuries. Red looked at the faces in the crowd. Some were familiar to her, while many others weren't. The one thing they had in common was they all looked convinced that she'd done it.

She stepped forward and reached for John Green. One of the townspeople blocked her way, stopping her.

"Oh no you don't," the man said. "You're not getting another go at him."

"Fine!" Red snapped, taking a step back. "Tell them the truth," she growled at Green as he slumped in the seat. The bleeding had started to clot, so his face didn't look quite as hideous as it had moments ago.

"I don't know what you mean," he said innocently.

"You ran into that wall." Red's voice rose with each syllable. "I've never seen anything so insane."

"Figures you'd say something like that. What did I ever do to you?" He whimpered like a wounded animal.

Red balled her fists and felt her entire body tense with anger. "I don't know what you're up to, but you won't get away with this," she said. "I'll see to it."

His eyes widened in fright. "She has it out for me. Someone protect me." Green tried to move out of the chair, but the man behind him held his shoulders down.

"You're safe now. We won't let her hurt you anymore. Will we?" he asked the crowd.

The murmurs grew in fervor.

"I know what it looks like, but I didn't touch him!" Red shouted.

People backed away, clearing a small area around her. The fear was easy to see, and even easier to smell. It stank like bitter synth-beans. She wrinkled her nose. How could she convince them she was innocent, when all signs pointed to her guilt? Red looked up and saw the three remaining recruits staring at her.

"If you want to leave, then go now," she snapped. "I won't hold it against you. I don't want anyone around who doesn't want to be here."

The men looked at each other and seemed to come to an unspoken understanding. Takeo stepped forward. "We're not going anywhere. It's just starting to get interesting around here. Besides, I think you need our help now more than ever."

Red looked at them and hoped the gratitude she felt showed on her face. She gave them a curt nod and strode off to Morgan's office. She hadn't been inside of it since he'd left. She hadn't wanted the empty reminder. Now she desperately needed to be around the familiar. Red pressed her palm on the door and it opened. Everything inside was exactly as he'd left it—neat, compact, and stringently organized. She stepped inside, noting the jacket hanging on the back of his chair.

Maggie began her report. Red listened in dismay as the chances of regaining her career went down the recycling drain. She pressed a button and the door shut, closing the world out. Why was this happening to her? All she'd wanted to do was come to Nuria and see where her relationship with Morgan led. She hoped by doing so that she'd also find a place to fit in. She'd been such a fool. Nothing was ever that easy.

Red walked over to Morgan's desk and pulled the coat off his chair. She buried her nose in the material and inhaled deeply. Morgan's scent filled her lungs. A new kind of pain took over as she closed her eyes. This ache hurt more than anything the people of Nuria could do to her. Because no matter what they did, it would never touch the pain of loss she felt with Morgan gone.

Red had been sitting at Morgan's desk for an hour when the vidcom chirped. She knew who it was even before she picked it up and pressed a button. Commander Robert Santiago, the head of the International Police Tactical Team. The screen brightened and her grandfather's sullen face came into view. Despite the circumstances, her heart lurched in happiness at the sight of him.

"Gina, you look like crap," he said, moving closer to the viewer.

"Feel like it, too," Red said, automatically moving back so her image blurred a little. She could just imagine what she looked like, and she didn't think her grandfather needed a closer inspection. If he got a good look at her, he might come down to Nuria, and that's the last place she wanted him to be. It was one thing to ruin your own reputation, she wasn't about to ruin his. He'd worked far too hard to get to his position. "It's good to see you," she said. "I've missed you so much."

"You, too, special one." He gave her a small smile. "Where's Morgan?" he asked without prelude.

She felt the color leach from her face. "He had to leave town for a short while. I expect him back soon," she lied.

His bushy brows lowered over his eyes in suspicion, but he didn't say anything further. "I just received a very interesting report about a noncommissioned sheriff station employee who's been accused of brutality. Would you know anything about that?"

Red sank back in Morgan's chair. "It doesn't make sense," she said.

"What doesn't?" he asked.

"He just hit the wall," she muttered.

"Gina, I need you to start from the beginning, since they're requesting the tactical team to intervene."

Intervene? The word rang in Red's head. How dare Maggie ask for outside help to handle this situation. She'd been so worried that Red would bring in IPTT because of her inability to control her wolf, and now she was calling in the troops.

Red blew out a frustrated breath. "I know what I'm about to tell you is going to sound crazy, but it's the absolute truth."

Concern marred his face, making him appear older than his years. "Just tell me what happened."

"I was heading to the food dispensing station to grab some lunch. John Green popped out of an alley on my way there and told me his friend was down and he needed help getting him to the emergency care center. When I went to call it in, he tried to stop me. I should've known something was up then, but I didn't listen to my gut. I was too preoccupied with—" *What was she going to say? She was thinking about Raphael's kiss and hadn't been paying attention to her surroundings?* She didn't think her grandfather would appreciate that news either. Red shook her head at how stupid she'd been. "It's not important." She waved the thought away. "I did end up calling it in, but the station said they never received my request for backup. Of course, I didn't know that at the time."

"Then what happened?" her grandfather prodded.

"I followed him into the alley. Figured my backup would be there any minute. There was a bunch of debris in the area so I didn't immediately spot his friend. The guy told me he was on the other side of some metal pipes that were lying against the wall."

He interrupted her to ask. "Is his friend okay?"

"Yes, no—I mean, I don't think he ever had a friend. I think the whole story was made up to get me into the alley." She scrubbed her hand over her face. "It doesn't make any sense."

"You're right," he said. "Why would someone go to that much trouble?"

"I don't know, but that's not the strangest part. When we reached the location he'd supposedly left his friend in, he apologized to me. At the time, I had no idea what he was apologizing for. The next thing I know, he took off full speed for the wall. He didn't even put a hand up to break the impact. The crunch of bones shattering sounded awful. I thought he was mentally unsound."

Robert Santiago sat back, his expression thoughtful as he digested her words. "That *is* odd. Did he say anything else?"

"No, not to me. I only received the apology. After that, he hit the wall again, then started shouting for help. Townspeople flooded the alley. The second they arrived he claimed brutality and asked them to protect him. It was so bizarre I didn't know what to do." She sighed. "I still don't. Why would someone do something like that?"

"Has anything else happened lately that stands out?"

Red thought about telling her grandfather about the murder, but how could she? If she said one word, he would send the IPTT in to investigate. It wouldn't matter that the man was an unknown or that a report had already been filed. She knew her grandfather well. He'd do anything he could to protect her and would continue to until his last breath.

By the time IPTT finished its investigation, the town of Nuria would come under scrutiny. That was something she just couldn't have. Red had promised Morgan she'd protect the town. She'd continue to do that, even if they didn't want her protection.

"No, it's been pretty quiet." Her gaze dropped. She couldn't meet his eyes and lie a second time.

Misunderstanding her evasiveness, Robert spoke. "It'll be okay. I'll hold the files for as long as I can. That should give you a week to get to the bottom of this mystery. Something is obviously going on in Nuria. I know you can handle it. I trained you myself. If you have any more problems— anything at all—call." He smiled as she looked up.

"Thank you, Commander," she said.

"I'm not your commander anymore, special one."

She looked at him, staring at the deep lines in his face and his white crop of hair. The mole on his cheek dipped and rose with every movement of his mouth. He was sitting behind his desk, surrounded by real books. She could almost smell the rich scent. It made her homesick.

"Thank you, Grandpa."

His eyes sparkled at her words. "Anytime, special one. Anytime."

Red slumped in the chair as the screen dimmed. She had

a week, tops, thanks to her grandfather, to uncover who was behind Green's sudden appearance. It was a given that she was being set up. If it was Roark, then he was going to elaborate means. Red just couldn't figure out what he would gain from her being sanctioned. It could create problems for her career, but it wouldn't stop the new tactical team from forming. Unless he thought she'd be arrested.

The question played in her mind until she feared she'd go mad. She stood up and dropped Morgan's jacket over the chair before heading out the door. The sheriff's station was quieter now. She figured Maggie and the townspeople must have personally escorted John Green to the emergency care center.

She debated whether to follow, but in the end decided against it. She wouldn't get anywhere questioning him further. He'd obviously come here to do a job. Now that he'd performed his duty, would he leave? Stick around? Maybe he hadn't yet finished.

The was a frightening thought. He'd already caused a lot of damage with the wall stunt. What if that was only part one of his plan? She paced back and forth, her mind working overtime.

"You're going to wear a hole in the concrete floor if you keep that up," Takeo said, stepping out of the back room. Juan followed.

"I didn't expect to see you guys here."

He laughed. "Where did you want us to go?"

"It's not a matter of want." Red shrugged. "I just figured you wouldn't stick around for long after the show. Where's Demery, by the way?" She swallowed hard and braced herself for the news that he'd quit. She really couldn't blame him. It seemed as if bad luck was following her.

"He's over at the emergency care center," Juan said, looking decidedly uneasy.

Red frowned. "What's he doing there?"

The two men looked at each other and her eyes widened in concern.

"Spill it, gentlemen. I can't handle any more surprises today."

Takeo ducked his head sheepishly. "I thought it might be a good idea to have him stay close to John Green. You never know what he might overhear with those vamp ears."

"You could've gone yourself," Red said.

Takeo shook his head. "Probably not a good idea. I'm more likely to beat the truth out of him. Demery is easygoing enough to stick with diplomacy."

Red wanted to be mad that they'd taken it upon themselves to investigate the case without her knowledge, but all she could muster was gratitude. "Thank you," she said quietly.

"For what?" Takeo asked.

"For believing in me."

Juan laughed and Takeo joined him.

Red's brow furrowed. "What's so funny?"

"You," Juan said.

Color flooded Red's face until her ears started to heat. She didn't appreciate being laughed at when her world was crumbling.

Juan held up his hands in defense. "We're not trying to piss you off."

"Could've fooled me."

"It's true," Takeo said. "I think you're missing the obvious."

"I'm missing something."

"Tell her, Takeo," Juan said.

"We saw John Green when he arrived. His face was pretty smashed, like he'd taken a beating. But the way we see it, if it had been you who did it, he'd be in far worse shape."

Red blinked as his words sunk in. "So you think I'm innocent because he wasn't hurt more."

"Exactly," they said in unison.

She shook her head. "Gentlemen, there is so much wrong with that line of thinking that I don't know where to begin."

"You have to admit it's true," Takeo said.

Red laughed. "Yes, it's true. If I'd set out to hurt him, there'd be more broken than just his face and shoulder."

Juan's expression grew serious. "Who do you think sent him?"

"Roark Montgomery."

Takeo gaped. "The politician?"

"That would be the one," Red said.

Juan stepped forward. "But why would he do that?"

Red's stomach twisted. "He has a plan for the world, and it doesn't include the Others. It also doesn't help that I shot off three of his fingers, when he was trying to kill Morgan Hunter."

Both men blinked as if they hadn't heard her correctly.

"You shot him?" Juan asked.

"It's a long and rather tedious story, but yes, I shot him. He didn't leave me much of a choice."

"Can you prove he's behind what's been happening in Nuria?" Takeo asked.

She shook her head. "Not yet. Not unless I can get John Green to confess, and that's not likely to happen, since I won't be allowed anywhere near him."

"Yeah, that could be a problem for you, but not for us," Juan said.

"No, I want you guys to stay out of it. Whatever Roark is up to, it only involves me as far as I can tell. I don't want you guys coming onto his radar. You don't know what he's capable of." Red thought about Morgan and his cousin, Kane. They'd been as close as brothers once. Then one day Kane tried to kill him and came damn close to succeeding. The pain on Morgan's face when he killed Kane was still etched firmly in her mind. It was better to keep Juan, Demery, and Takeo out of this for as long as possible.

"We're training to be part of the Nurian Tactical Team," Takeo said.

"Which is why I need you to stay out of this. You aren't done with your training yet. You still have a lot to learn. Roark is a killer and has many assassins at his disposal. They can be anywhere. They come in all guises, including members of your family."

Juan's brown eyes widened. "That's not possible."

"Believe me, it is." She ran a hand through her hair, dislodging her ponytail.

"There has to be something we can do," Takeo insisted.

Red looked at him, meeting his amber gaze. "There *is* something you can do."

"Name it," he said.

"Go get Demery before the townspeople spot him and something bad happens to him."

Takeo scowled, but before he could say anything more, Juan grabbed him and dragged him out of the sheriff's station. "You heard the commander," he said. "Let's go."

Red gave Juan a small smile and watched the men walk out into the fading sunlight. It would be dark soon. Raphael would be rising, if he hadn't already. She longed to contact him to vent her frustrations, but knew she couldn't. They were still friends as far as she was concerned, but the kiss they'd shared last night complicated matters. And the last thing Red needed in her life was more complications.

chapter fifteen

Bannon pushed the synth-papers around on his desk. He'd been doing reports for so long his eyes were crossed from staring at the pages. He'd had more and more administrative work since Gina Santiago left. Gone were the days of heading out regularly on patrol. He missed being in the thick of the action. Missed taking down unknowns. Hell, he missed riding around with a team of twelve men in the cramped space of a stinky maglev shuttle.

Never thought there'd be a day he'd admit that, but it was the truth. He grimaced, shoving the papers across his desk. A new recruit jumped when their gazes met. He hit a button on his compunit. There were still three reports left to go. Bannon glanced at the clock. If he made it out of here by five it would be a miracle. He looked over and saw the grunt, Catherine Meyers sitting at her desk. At least he wasn't the only one stuck working desk duty.

Maybe he'd give her the rest of the reports to finish and knock off early. Bannon was grinning when his vidcom chirped.

John Green signed the last of the documents needed to release him from the emergency care center. The nurse thanked him and left his room. He'd been patched, fed, watered, bathed, and changed. He looked out the window. The sun was just starting to set on the horizon. Despite the self-inflicted injuries, it was the best he'd felt in years.

He flicked up the collar of his shirt, admiring the brand-new tan fatigues the town had given him. He glanced down the length of him, turning from side to side. *Not bad,* he thought. They weren't the most flattering thing he'd ever put on, but at least they were clean and didn't carry the same holes and baggage as his previous wardrobe.

He stared in the mirror, his green eyes glittering from behind the black circles that had formed. They'd repaired his shoulder and broken nose. In a few days, he'd be able to breathe better than he ever had. His tawny hair had been styled neatly, thanks to the woman at the sheriff's station who'd taken his false statement. Maggie something. It wasn't important. She'd fulfilled her role rather quickly. Almost as if she'd been eager to harm the other woman. It wasn't any of his business. He shook his head and went back to inspecting his appearance.

All in all, not bad for a man who'd spent the last two years of his life drifting from place to place running cons.

He pictured his latest victim. John thought her name might be Gina. Beautifully exotic with her golden skin and black hair, she'd been willing to help him. She didn't even wait for backup. He was still surprised about that. Most people, particularly those living on the fringe near the boundary fence, rarely went out of their way to help a stranger. It was too dangerous. John had found out the hard way when he'd been trapped and imprisoned by that snake of a politician.

A twinge of guilt hit over what he'd done to her, but it didn't last long. He'd had no choice but to set up the woman. Knowing who she was, or anything else about her, hadn't been part of the deal. Freedom was. John would do anything for his freedom. If he'd had any doubts before, this proved it.

He'd tried to shut out the town's malicious rumors. They'd vilified the woman while the medics worked on him. If Gina knew what was good for her, she'd leave this place. Just like he was about to do.

John thanked the medical personnel and strolled out of the emergency care center. It wouldn't take long to reach the location for the meet. It was only a few blocks away. A shuttle would be waiting to take him north. Once it arrived, he could leave this whole nightmare behind him.

The vidcom rang as I was about to knock off for the day. I couldn't remember much about the conversation, only the suggestion to head to Nuria. I'd been driving for hours. My maglev shuttle cruised over the desert, hovering a foot off the ground. My eyes scanned the horizon, but there was nothing but miles and miles of sand. It sifted over the road, covering the only sign that mankind had ever been here. With it came the intense heat, licking at my senses.

My mind seemed fuzzy, as if something was clouding it. I tried to think, but it was too much effort. I pressed the lever down harder and the vehicle lurched, speeding toward the lights in the distance.

Nuria . . . The last remaining wart on the desert's smooth rump.

There was something I needed to do in Nuria. I thought hard and an image came into my mind. Tawny hair, green eyes, tall, medium build. A man was waiting for me. A man with a tracking device inside his watch. A man I planned to kill.

I knew he'd be behind the water trader. That had been predetermined. It took me awhile to find the place since I had to go through back alleys and side streets. The dark didn't help. I'd forgotten my night-vision goggles.

Buttoned up for the night, the town had just drifted off to sleep. There'd been several close calls as I worked my way to the back of the water trade building. I'd become adept at slipping into shadows, blending into walls. Stealth was the only way I'd make it out of here once the job was done.

Not long now, I thought, glancing at my navcom for the time. He should be waiting. Convenient. Blending with the shadows, I traveled through the belly of Nuria, scurrying past the heart before anyone could see me. The night had grown darker, more menacing, easily hiding other predators. Sweat clung to my forehead and pressed my clothes to my body.

A flash up ahead drew my attention and I stopped, dropping into a crouch to scan the area for movement. The light came again and I realized the man had lit up an illegal smoke stick.

My shoulders relaxed slightly. It felt good being back in action. I crept forward as the man drew deep on the stick, filling his lungs with smoke. He held his breath a few seconds before letting it out. Smoke spilled out of his nose and mouth in a steady stream.

He looked around nervously. Maybe it was because I was late or perhaps he was concerned about getting caught with the contraband. Either way I'd never know. He wouldn't live long enough to tell me.

The knife with its strange blade slid easily into my hand. The grip only took a second to conform to my palm, making the weapon instantly feel like part of my arm. The cool steel was smooth on one side and unusually jagged on the other. It looked like no other knife I'd ever seen and left behind unusual patterns that made identifying the weapon nearly impossible.

The man was still puffing away on his smoke stick as I inched closer. His tan fatigues did little to conceal him in the dark, but I had no doubt they'd be effective during the day. Too bad the sun wasn't around to help him now.

Despite my combat boots, my feet were silent upon the hard, cracked ground. Adrenaline pumped in my veins, but

I remained calm. I'd done this before and I'd do it again. I picked up a small rock and tossed it to the man's right. His head jerked as it pinged off something hard and metallic. His body remained tense as he listened, attention diverted. This was almost too easy.

I slipped up behind him and slashed quickly. Arterial spray hit the wall in a shower of crimson. He didn't even have time to gasp, much less scream. His eyes were wide as the realization of his impending death set in. His fingers slacked, dropping the smoke stick that had been wedged between them. It hit the ground a second before his knees did. He fell forward, face down on the dirt, his clean fatigues slowly turning red.

I watched the blood drip down the wall, while listening to the bubbles gurgle out of his throat. The rivulets were mesmerizing. It was only when the sound stopped that I decided it was safe to leave. My job here was done. I had to get back. After all, there were reports to make.

chapter sixteen

A loud banging brought Red bolt upright in the rest pad. It took her a second to realize the pounding was coming from outside her room. She threw the covers aside and shook her head. She'd skipped going out in the desert last night to work on the change after the day she'd had. Instead, she'd gone to bed early and had planned on sleeping in. A fist connected with the door. Someone obviously didn't care about her plans.

"Hold on. I'm coming," she said.

Red grabbed her pants off the chair and pulled them on. She didn't bother with a shirt, since her T-shirt covered anything important. She pressed her palm on the panel and the door slid open. The man in charge of supplying Nuria with water stood outside her door, scowling.

"You're going to make me late on my run," he said, glancing at his watch.

Red yawned. "Why didn't you go around back?"

"The gate's locked. I can't get in."

"Sorry," she said, turning away from him. "I thought I'd left it open. Give me a minute to throw on my shoes and I'll be right down."

He grunted and left.

She reached for her overshirt and pulled it on, then

grabbed her boots. It only took a minute to lace them up. She ran a hand over her sleep-covered face and trudged out of the door.

Red made her way across the empty bar area to the back room. She'd only managed to knock over a few stools on the way. The place was quiet—no one was up yet. She wished she could say the same. The rest pad had been feeling particularly good this morning. She pressed her hand to a panel, but the door refused to budge. Red kicked it once and it slid open. She took a step outside. Her boot hit something slick and she nearly tumbled down the stairs on her ass. She caught herself before she fell. Her hand came back wet with blood.

Red glanced down and froze. It took her a second to register what she was seeing. When she did, panic set in.

She backed into the water trader as the delivery man shouted. "Are you going to open the gate or what?"

Red couldn't answer. She couldn't seem to find her voice. All she wanted to do was run back upstairs, climb into the rest pad, and pull the covers over her head. She had to be dreaming. This had to be some kind of a nightmare. She looked at her blood-covered hand again, then out the back door. The man from the alley was still lying facedown in a dried crimson puddle.

"Listen, lady," the deliver guy shouted. "I don't have time for this sh—" His words strangled in his throat as he finally saw the body.

Red heard retching as he emptied his stomach contents on the parched ground. She forced her feet forward until she could see the body clearly once more. He appeared to have been killed in a similar manner to the last man, if the blood spatter was any indication. But this time there was no laser blast wound to exonerate her.

She had no idea how long she'd been standing there when she heard a commotion coming from behind her. Red turned in time to see Maggie and a couple of deputies approach. The delivery driver must have contacted the sheriff's station. They didn't look happy, but then again, they rarely had since Morgan left.

Maggie and the men pushed past her, shoving her out of the way. Red heard Maggie gasp. She looked up in time to see her glare. Red didn't return her stare. She was still in shock over the discovery.

A lot happened over the next few minutes. Officers came and went. Jim Thornton arrived to pick up the body. He gave a preliminary finding. The man had died last night sometime between eight and midnight. From the looks of the wound, the same weapon had been used. There was no evidence of a laser rifle blast. Whoever had killed him wanted it to be quiet.

Everyone in the room turned to look at her. The condemnation was easy to see. It was the growing fear that surprised her. Red swallowed hard. They looked away and began talking among themselves, but no one said a word to her. In fact, very few people dared to look in her direction again. It was as if she wasn't there. Wishful thinking on their part.

Red began to tremble. She fisted her hands, digging her nails into her palms to calm herself. She tried to recall anything unusual about last night, but nothing came to mind. It had been quiet. Even the new recruits had retired early for the night. Speaking of which, where were they?

Maggie said something to Jim, then stepped forward. Two deputies flanked her, looking decidedly uneasy. Did they think she was going to bolt? She gave them both a hard glare and they took a step back. She would've laughed, but the situation wasn't funny.

"We need you to come with us," Maggie said.

"Where?" Red's stomach knotted.

"To the station."

"Why?"

Maggie's lips pulled tight over her mouth, thinning until they disappeared. "I'd rather not discuss it here," she said, looking around.

Red followed her line of sight and realized that a small crowd had gathered in the bar area. She spotted the new recruits toward the back. They were staring at her, but she couldn't tell their thoughts from their blank expressions. She wondered how long it would be before they turned in their notice and left, too. She really wouldn't blame them for quitting. People were dropping faster than Jim could dissect and recycle them.

She had no doubt that the killer was long gone. Like a phantom, he'd slipped into town, murdered, and left. The thought that they were dealing with a professional made her ill because Red knew how hard they were to catch.

Professional killers didn't make mistakes. They rarely got caught. Trouble was, she only knew one professional killer and that was Raphael Vega's brother, Michael Travers. She doubted he could slip into town without Raphael knowing it. What if he *did* know and hadn't said anything? Morgan had done the same when she'd suspected his cousin Kane of killing several women. It had taken more murders and an attack on her to convince him to investigate. What if Raphael was protecting Michael?

The thought chilled her and she shuddered. Michael was far more dangerous than Kane could ever be. His powers were unlike anything she'd ever encountered. She'd read about telekinesis, but Red had never heard of anyone who actually had the ability. That was, until she met Michael Travers and he'd turned her own gun on her while she gripped it in her hand.

She'd thought they'd come to an understanding. Maybe she was wrong. Red decided to keep her theories to herself until she came up with proof. She wasn't about to go for a replay of what had happened with Morgan.

The town of Nuria was angry enough with her. She didn't need to give them more reasons to hate her.

"Okay, I'll lead the way." Red walked to the front of the

water trader with Maggie trailing in her wake. The crowd parted, their eyes wary. She met their gazes. She didn't want them to think she had anything to hide. She didn't realize the deputies hadn't followed until she and Maggie had stepped out the front door.

She glanced back and saw them working their way to the stairs. "What are they doing?" she asked, frowning.

"They have to check your room."

"Why?"

"It's procedure."

"Am I under arrest?" Red asked.

"Not yet," Maggie said.

"Then I don't understand why you're taking me to the station," Red said as they walked down the sidewalk.

"We need to take a statement. You're a witness. You can't exactly investigate yourself. And since Morgan left me second in command, the job falls to me," she said.

"You're not law enforcement," Red said, reminding her she had no real power.

"Neither are you—anymore," she snapped. "Don't worry I'll make sure a deputy is present so everything is official."

"It doesn't matter now, but shouldn't Green have been in the emergency care center? *You* made such a show of taking him there yesterday. I'm surprised they released him so soon."

Maggie blanched at the accusation in her voice. "He checked himself out."

"Didn't you have someone guarding him?" Red's voice rose before she could stop herself.

"Why should we? He wasn't a prisoner," Maggie snapped back.

"No one said he was, but you were obviously concerned for his welfare. Why stop there?"

"I'm not the one who's suspect here. And I don't appreciate your tone," Maggie ground out between clenched teeth. "I thought I'd give you a chance to explain things before I type up your official statement. Did you have any contact with him after he left the sheriff's station?"

Red's jaw clenched and her mind started to clear. "No! You told me to keep away and I did. I went straight back to the water trade depot after leaving Morgan's office. I was there all night until the water delivery driver woke me."

"You didn't go out into the desert?"

"No, I skipped last night. The day was long enough without that frustration heaped upon it." How could Maggie think she'd gone into the desert after everything that had occurred yesterday? She'd been accused of assault by means of an out-of-control inner wolf. The last thing Red wanted was to try to bring the wolf out.

"I don't suppose you have any witnesses to prove it?" Maggie asked.

"Not hardly. I didn't pass anyone on the way back." Raphael hadn't stopped by since she'd told him they couldn't have a relationship. Now she wished he had. At least that way she'd have someone to back her story. She glanced at Maggie, who continued to wait for her answer. "I went to sleep. Alone. If you haven't figured it out yet, someone is trying to set me up."

Red's mind scrambled in search of clues. This was the second time a killer had slipped into Nuria undetected. Either they were familiar with the area or they'd been given very specific directions. If Roark had another insider working for him, who could it be? Maggie was the obvious choice, but that answer was too easy. She wasn't capable of controlling her emotions. The murderer had been methodical. Nothing about the kills indicated a lack of control. It didn't completely rule her out, but it was a good bet someone else was behind these deaths.

Maggie looked at her in disbelief. "Who would frame you? It's not like you're important enough to garner that kind of attention."

Red let Maggie's personal comment slide, instead focusing on her question. "My first thought was Roark Montgomery. You know how he feels about the Others."

Maggie flinched and her bravado shrunk a little at the utterance of his name. "W-why would he do that?"

"You'd have to ask him," she said. "Or better yet, maybe I will."

"Nuria has had enough trouble, thanks to you. It doesn't need any more."

"You're the one who contacted IPTT," Red reminded her. "My guess is that's exactly what Roark wanted."

Maggie frowned, fear replacing her righteous stance. "It was for your own good. Morgan should've never left you in control."

Red's body began to heat. It felt like scorpions were scurrying beneath her skin. Pain racked her. She groaned as the wolf tried to break out. She sucked in a breath and held it. *Not now. Please not now.* Maggie took a step back, her eyes widening at the growing threat. It was her fear that allowed Red to pull herself back together.

"You forget I wasn't the one who convinced Kane to kill. I didn't even know him then, and I'd certainly never heard of Nuria. Sometimes I wish that were still the case. But it's not. So before you go accusing me of all the wrongs that have been perpetrated on this town, you need to take a long, hard look in the mirror. Everyone here does. You're all responsible for the things that have happened, because you could've done something about it and chose not to."

Maggie's face flushed and her nostrils flared. In the end though, she couldn't meet Red's gaze. "You'll still have to make a statement while the deputies search your room."

"Let them search. They aren't going to find anything other than a few days' worth of dirty clothes. I didn't bring much with me."

"You still have your weapons," Maggie reminded her.

"Yes, I do. The ones I don't wear are packed in a duffel bag under my rest pad. They haven't been fired in quite a while. Hopefully the deputies dust while they're searching under there."

"I'm surprised you can make jokes at a time like this."

"I don't find any of this funny. Particularly the part where you, a civilian, take me in for questioning." Red started walking, and Maggie had no choice but to follow. "You forgot one very important fact."

"What is that?" Maggie asked.

"If I was going to kill the guy, I wouldn't do it on my doorstep. And you damn well would never find the body."

Maggie and a deputy named Sams grilled Red for the next two hours. Sams did most of the questioning with Maggie interjecting often. They hadn't bothered to take her into Morgan's office or into the back room. Instead, they'd kept her front and center so the people who wandered by could hear what was being said. That included the three remaining recruits she'd hired. Red found that the most humiliating of all, which was probably Maggie's intention all along.

The deputies who'd been searching her room, returned empty-handed. She knew they would. They looked somewhat disappointed. Thanks to the new murder, the International Police Tactical Team was due to arrive tomorrow. She had to do whatever it took to keep them away from Nuria, at least until she could control the environment. That meant one thing—meeting them on their home turf.

Decision made, Red stood, cutting Maggie off midsentence. The chair she'd been sitting in fell back, hitting the floor with a loud clang. Everyone around her jumped. She didn't bother to pick it up.

"We're done here," Red said to no one in particular.

"I'll tell you when we're done." Maggie rose to stare her

down. It would've worked better if Red hadn't been five inches taller than the petite woman.

Red glared at her. "No, you won't. I've put up with your bullying and underhanded behavior long enough. I can't believe I fell for your nice act when I got here. In fact," she said, looking around, "I can't believe I thought I'd found a home in this town. Morgan's only been gone for a few weeks and look at you all. Making power grabs and throwing out baseless accusations. You're trying to undermine his authority. You're trying to undermine me. Well, enough is enough. I'm not putting up with it anymore." She strode toward the door.

"Where do you think you are going?" Maggie called out after her. "Deputy Sams is not finished with you yet."

Red looked back over her shoulder. "To IPTT to clean this mess up."

The three recruits were waiting for her outside the sheriff's station. They must have slipped out the back door during her interrogation with Maggie and Sams.

"That's telling her," Takeo said.

"What do you want?" she asked, eyeing them.

"Are you really leaving?" Juan asked.

Red nodded. "I don't have a choice." She hated to bring this mess to her grandfather's door. She could only imagine what was going through his mind. Would he believe her when she claimed innocence once more?

Demery looked at her. "There's always a choice, mon. You could stay."

"You don't get it," she said, shaking her head.

"Then explain it to us," Takeo said.

"If I don't go, then IPTT will send a team here. Despite what's been happening to me, I cannot afford to let them poke around. They might accidentally uncover something. It's not like they'd have to look too far." She gazed at Demery, who wore his protective suit.

"She has a point," he said, looking down at his special clothing. "It would be hard to explain this, if someone asked."

"Exactly," Red said.

"Takeo, you and Juan blend in a lot easier, but what happens if your chimera feels threatened and attacks? How would you explain that?"

"I . . ." he said, pausing to think of a logical explanation. "I suppose that would be a little difficult. I'd have to kill the person."

"Yeah, and I'm sure the tactical team wouldn't notice a missing member." She snorted. "I appreciate that you guys are sticking by me, but that might not be the smartest move. Right now, someone is out to get me. And if it's the someone I think it is, no one around me will be safe."

Juan approached. "You can't go it alone."

Red balked. "I've spent my whole life going it alone. It's a road I'm very familiar with." She didn't like it, but it was the truth. She'd let herself get comfortable having Morgan around. He'd been her strength. Looked out for her. Now that he wasn't here, she needed to stand on her own two feet again.

Juan nodded. "What would you like us to do while you're away?"

She wanted to tell them to run, get as far away from Nuria as possible, but she didn't think they'd listen. She knew she wouldn't if their roles were reversed. In the end, Red could only think of one thing for them to do. "I need you to keep your eyes open. Anyone starts acting strange, make a note of it, but do not approach. I repeat, do not approach the target. We need to prepare Nuria for IPTT's arrival."

"I thought you said they wouldn't be coming, if you went there first," Demery said.

"No." She shook her head. "My going to them will only delay the inevitable. They will eventually descend upon

Nuria, but hopefully it'll only be a few team members and not an entire unit."

"Do you think Roark has someone working from the inside?" Takeo asked.

Red sighed. "I don't know. It happened the last time, but I don't know if that is what's happening now. No one I've seen has been acting suspicious. I know that doesn't mean a lot, but there were signs the last time. This time there haven't been. It's like we're dealing with a ghost."

"We'll make sure to keep an eye on everyone." Juan looked at Takeo and Demery. They both nodded in agreement. "We'll report our findings when you get back."

"You *are* coming back. Right?" Takeo asked.

Red didn't answer. She wasn't sure what to say, since she'd seriously considered staying at IPTT. She was sure her grandfather, Commander Robert Santiago, would give her her old job back. The danger to her still remained, but with the change in the Nurians, she thought it might be safer with the team.

She looked at Takeo, Demery, and Juan. It was easy to see their concern. They knew without her saying a word that she was seriously thinking about abandoning them. They waited patiently, preparing to gauge her sincerity. If she lied now, they'd know it.

Red sighed. "I'm not sure," she said eventually. "If I decide to stay, I will contact you to let you know." It was the best she could do.

The drive to IPTT headquarters took hours. She'd borrowed Jim Thornton's maglev shuttle or it would've taken even longer. The gold dome glowed from within as she approached the 150-foot-high monolith. Concrete dormitories branched out from the central hub, which housed a thousand people.

She could see the rows of stainless steel beams marking the entrance to the main headquarters. The pyramid glistened under the artificial light in the biodome. There was nothing welcoming about the design. It was meant to intimidate and protect the sloped walls from hydrogen car bomb blasts.

Red watched the recruits being put through their paces. They trained in shifts, so while some slept, others worked. It made the International Police Tactical Team a hard place to attack. Her stomach fluttered as she circled around the back to the shuttle parking area. It had only been a little over a month and a half since she'd left, but it felt like a lifetime ago.

The agency, which was in its 150th year of existence, had been the only real home she'd known. Red didn't realize how much she'd missed it until now.

She parked the shuttle and stepped out. Two tactical team members approached. She didn't recognize either one, which wasn't a surprise. There were too many to remember everyone.

"State your business," the first man said.

"I'm here to see Commander Robert Santiago."

"Name," the other man said, hitting a button on the navcom hugging his wrist.

"Tell him Gina Santiago is here to see him."

The men's eyes widened and they looked at each other, suddenly unsure of protocol. "We-we'll let him know that you're here."

"Is he at headquarters or home?" she asked, showing the men more patience than she felt. Red wanted to see her grandfather. She needed to be around someone who'd let her cry on his shoulder. Someone who loved her and didn't look at her with fear in his eyes.

"He's at headquarters, ma'am," the second man said.

"Thanks," she said. "I'll find my own way there."

He stepped in front of her, blocking her exit. "Um, we can't let you do that, ma'am."

"Why not?"

They looked at each other again and shifted uncomfortably. "Because you're a civilian."

His words caused Red a fresh flood of pain. For a second, she'd allowed herself to forget she was no longer a tactical team member. No longer part of this great complex. His words brought home just how alone she was.

"Of course," she said, motioning for them to lead the way.

Red followed the two team members into the front doors of IPTT headquarters. The first thing she noticed was they'd changed the scent that pumped through the A.I. filtration system from the stinky sharp mint to a soft buttery vanilla. Red inhaled, letting it seep into her body and calm her tense muscles. It was a nice change.

She stepped up to the weapons detectors and stripped off her pistol. It was the only weapon she carried these days. As she stepped through the detectors, a green beam showered her from above, scanning the length of her body.

"Foreign material has been detected on the boots," a computerized disembodied voice said.

Without thought, Red unlaced her boots and dropped them into the nearby recycling bin. A pair of blue booties shot out of a slot. She slipped them on and walked through. A readout appeared on the other side of the scanner. Red went to pick it up, but one of her escorts beat her to it.

"She's clean," he said. "No biologicals or explosives detected."

Red waited for her gun to reappear. It didn't. After a moment, she turned to her other escort. "Where is my laser pistol?" she asked.

"No civilians are allowed to be armed inside headquarters. You'll get it back when you leave."

Her heart sank. Of course, she'd forgotten once again that she was considered a civilian here. Red nodded to the man and proceeded forward. Steel desks filled the area, along with compunits. A few officers looked up when she neared, but otherwise didn't acknowledge her presence.

She didn't see Bannon—thank goodness. Red wasn't in the mood for a confrontation. The last thing she needed was to be charged with assault *again*. She followed her two escorts toward the back of the room, where a long hallway led to her grandfather's office. Red slowed when she found herself hurrying. She couldn't wait to see him. It had been too long.

The men stopped outside the wooden door that marked the commander's office. Red stepped forward and ran her hand over the smooth surface, while a camera popped out of the door and scanned one of her escort's eyes. The door clicked a second later, indicating that the lock had been disengaged.

"Come in," Robert Santiago said, his voice strong and commanding.

One of the men opened the door, while the other held her back. "Sir, you have a visitor," he said.

Red could see the bookshelves that held rare volumes made of paper and bindings. From here, she could even smell the tomes. Holographic pictures of extinct animals hung on the walls in an explosion of color and life. A knot formed in her throat at the sight. She loved this room. Loved the way it made her feel. Loved that it represented her grandfather's Old World charm.

"Who is it?" the commander asked.

"It's me, Commander," Red said.

"Gina?"

She looked down at the hand that had held her back and raised an eyebrow. The man stepped aside and allowed her to enter. Her grandfather had risen from behind his desk.

His brown eyes sparkled as he smiled. Red waited for her two escorts to leave and the door to close before she rushed past the burgundy monstrosity of a chair and into her grand-father's open arms.

"I've missed you so much," she said, fighting back tears that flowed despite her valiant effort.

"Here now," Robert Santiago said, patting her on the back. "Everything will be all right."

Red sniffled, wiping at her face. "No it won't, Grandpa. I'm in big trouble and I don't know how I'm going to get out of it."

chapter seventeen

organ kept the list of employees who were supposed to be working in 47F. So far he'd been unable to locate a single scientist. He'd systematically
gone through the list, searching in the computers and in the facility for the individuals tied to the project. Every name he'd
investigated didn't appear to exist. He was down to the last
name on the list, a Dr. Finley. If Morgan couldn't locate this
researcher, then that would end his search. He'd know for
sure that none of the people were here at the lab. And never
had been. His wolf shifted restlessly, sensing danger.

But why create a fake project and assign false names to
front it? Morgan pinched the bridge of his nose and winced
as his second headache in as many days took up residence
behind his eyes. He'd risked so much coming here. The
thought of failing was unthinkable. But if the project didn't
exist and the workers weren't real, then why advertise the
two new clones? What was he missing?

Morgan felt like the truth was staring him in the face and
he just couldn't see past the images of Sarah and Joshua. He
could hear their laughter like it was yesterday. Unfortunately,
he could also hear their cries of terror. No, he hadn't been
there when the bomb hit his home, but he'd been in enough
similar circumstances to have witnessed the aftereffects.

He glanced down at his watch. His break was nearly over. Morgan had one more place he planned to check, then he'd turn in his resignation and head back to Nuria. Back to Gina. He'd seen metal crates being unloaded in bay 32. They were probably nothing, but it wouldn't hurt to check. Afterward, he'd head over to the Eye of God and ask about Dr. Finley. Someone had to know him.

Morgan picked up the pace, his booted feet slapping the concrete floor as a strange urgency gripped him. He was fifteen feet from the door that led into bay 32, when he smelled something. Something familiar. Before he could place the odor, a blast blew him into the air and down the hall. Morgan's head and back smacked the floor at the same time and he saw stars floating in front of his eyes.

A wave of scorching heat followed the blast. Morgan tried to put his hands up to protect his head, but he was having trouble moving. The cacophonous sound came next, thundering in his cranium, rattling his spinal column.

He looked up in time to see two people running out the door. They were on fire, their skin melting in waxy drips onto the floor. They were screaming. At least he thought they were screaming. The blood rushing through his veins was deafening, and the sound of the blast had taken care of the rest of his hearing. It would be an hour at least before he'd hear properly.

Morgan forced himself to sit up. It took a lot of effort. His arms didn't want to cooperate. He scooted, using one leg to get over to the wall, then used it for leverage to stand.

It hurt to breathe. Black smoke billowed out of the gaping hole where the door to bay 32 once stood. Morgan limped to the opening and tried to see inside. It was impossible. The thick angry cloud swallowed everything around it. If anyone was left inside, they were as good as dead.

A commotion started behind him. Sensing it, Morgan turned, expecting to see the sweepers. Instead, he saw Roark Montgomery pointing directly at him.

"Arrest that man," he shouted over the chaos.

Pete and another man he'd passed during rounds stepped forward and grabbed him.

"What's going on?" Morgan said, struggling to break out of their grip.

Pete refused to meet his eyes, and his young face remained downcast and flushed. "Don't make this any harder than it already is," he whispered.

They slipped restraints on Morgan's wrists and brought him forward to face Roark. The man was smiling. Morgan had the sudden urge to kick his teeth down his throat.

"What am I being arrested for?"

Roark smirked. "Why, sabotage, of course."

"Sabotage?" Morgan snorted. "You're out of your mind. I didn't sabotage anything. I was walking toward the room when a bomb went off."

"That's for the Republic of New Mexico to decide. Put him in the transport."

Morgan was half dragged and half carried outside before being shoved into Roark's awaiting transport. He grunted as he hit the floor. "This isn't right, Pete, and you know it. I didn't blow anything up."

Pete looked around to make sure Roark wasn't near enough to hear. "Then what were you doing over there?"

"Looking for Dr. Finley."

"Who's that?" Pete asked.

"Someone who's supposed to be part of the cloning operation, but as far as I can tell, he doesn't exist. And now I know why." Morgan let his head fall back against the hard transport floor. He'd been so stupid. The whole thing had been staged. Sarah and Joshua had never been up for cloning. It was a ruse. A ruse to get him to leave Nuria. To leave Gina. And it had worked. Pain blossomed in his chest as he realized how vulnerable she was all alone. If anything happened to her, he'd never forgive himself.

Roark came walking up with the man who'd interviewed Morgan upon his arrival. From the familiar way they were talking, leaving no doubt they'd known each other for a while. Pete glanced at both men, then focused on the gates of the complex and frowned. "Shouldn't we call the authorities?" he asked, looking like the wide-eyed innocent he was.

"Leave that to me," Roark said.

"But it's procedure when anything happens here at the lab." He pulled out a small screen and pressed a button. "See." Pete held the screen up to their faces. "It's under section fifteen."

Morgan saw the look exchanged between Roark and the man he'd been talking to when he walked up. Fear shook him. If Pete didn't stop this line of questioning his life would be in danger. Maybe it was already too late.

"Roark's planning to take me straight to the detention center in Taos. Isn't that right, Montgomery?" Morgan glared at the politician.

"Of course. Where else would I be taking you?" he said, eyeing the young guard contemptuously.

Pete looked back at Morgan as if he wasn't sure whom to believe. Morgan gave him a brisk nod. "Thanks for everything, Pete. It was nice working with you. Please tell the Eye of God it was fun while it lasted."

"You sure?" Pete asked, clearly torn.

"Yeah, you better get back inside where Coleman can *see* you."

Pete's eyes widened as the warning Morgan sent him finally sank in. "Right." He nodded. "Good luck," he said, then sprinted back to the building before the man with Roark could stop him.

"You were so easy," Roark said. "I'm really surprised you came running when you saw those old vid-clips of your dead wife and child. Did you really think they were going to be cloned?"

"Obviously, or I wouldn't be here." Morgan rolled until he could sit up. "I do have one question for you."

"What's that?"

"What did you hope to gain?"

"Isn't that obvious?" Roark asked.

Morgan shook his head. "No, it's not." He'd thought of many possible outcomes, but none seemed worth the trouble Roark had gone to this time.

Roark smiled and the act chilled Morgan to the bone. It was the first time he nearly broke eye contact with another man. "The destruction of the two people who've caused me more trouble than either of you is worth."

"What have you done to Gina?"

Roark laughed. "Nothing. *Yet.*"

"What in the hell does that mean?" Morgan nearly choked on his anger.

"Let's just say I've been keeping her busy while I chip away at her impending career. I daresay she probably won't be accepted by the Nurian sheriff's department or the new tactical team. Unless of course, you make a habit of hiring murderers."

Morgan flinched. What had Roark been doing to Gina while he'd been here chasing the past? He could only imagine what she'd had to endure. Yet she'd said nothing. And he'd only made it harder by leaving her.

"Where are you taking me?" he asked, wondering if Roark would give him a straight answer.

"Someplace that will have you begging for death before I'm through." Roark turned to the man who'd escorted him out. "Give me," he glanced at his watch, "a two-hour head start, then make the announcement."

The man nodded and smirked at Morgan. "I'll be here if you need any help," he said with unbridled glee.

Roark turned back to Morgan. "Settle in. We have a long ride ahead of us," he said, then shut the door in Morgan's face.

* * *

Red sat in the burgundy velvet chair that was so big she could swing her legs beneath her. It had taken an hour, but she'd finally stopped crying. Her grandfather's shirt was wrinkled where she'd been gripping it, but he didn't seem to mind. He'd ordered a new pair of boots to be brought to her and now sat back behind his desk, worry clearly written on his weathered face.

"Now tell me what has you so upset?" he asked.

"You haven't heard?" Red looked up in surprise.

"Heard what?" he said, then leaned forward.

This was worse than she thought. Red hated to be the one to break the bad news to her grandfather. "I don't know where to begin."

He smiled. "I've always found the beginning to be a nice place to start." Robert Santiago winked at her.

She shook her head. "I'm so sorry about everything. I tried. I tried so hard to fit into Nuria. But my best was never good enough."

"I'm sure it's not as bad as you think," he said softly.

Red's gaze met his. "No, it's worse. You already know about the complaint filed against me for brutality."

Her grandfather sobered. "Yes, that's a very serious charge." His vidcom beeped. He pressed a button. "Hold all my calls," he said.

She waited for him to disconnect, then continued. "I didn't do it. I know I'm being set up."

"Roark?" The name came out like a curse.

"Yes, who else? He's had it out for me ever since I shot him."

He grimaced. "Have you found any proof since we last spoke?" He pushed synth-papers around, straightening already neat piles.

Red knew he needed something to do with his hands. She gripped the arms of the chair and pushed herself up, tucking a leg beneath her. "None. It's just a gut feeling. The whole situation smells like a professional job."

"You know what I think of gut feelings," he said.

She did. Robert Santiago was a man of science and a follower of the law. He wanted solid proof, not suppositions. He didn't believe in chasing feelings. He'd told her time and again they were misleading, especially when it came to the job. "I know, Grandpa, but too many strange things have been happening to be mere coincidence." She sat back and the cushions cradled her.

"Such as?"

Red hadn't wanted to tell him about the unknown and the wild accusation that he made against her, but she didn't have a choice. Maybe her grandpa would be able to give her advice, but he couldn't do that without all the facts.

"A few days ago, a man came into town. I'd never seen him before. He found me when I was eating a late lunch. He started screaming about me leaving him. He accused me of forgetting him. As if we'd had a relationship."

He frowned. "Did you know this man?"

"No, Grandpa. That's just it. He was a stranger. To make matters worse, the man turned up dead the next day. Jim Thornton discovered he was an unknown during dissection. I've encountered a lot of unknowns over the years, but I'd never seen that man before in my life."

"There's something definitely going on."

"Then yesterday on my way to lunch, I was called into an alley. You know what happened next."

"I still can't believe that you went," he said admonishingly. "I trained you better than that."

"I know it was stupid. I knew it at the time, but I wasn't expecting to be ambushed and I really did think my backup would show at any moment." She mentally kicked herself again for the rookie mistake.

He nodded. "I still don't understand why he did that. It

was risky. He could've been easily caught in his own trap, which tells me he was desperate."

"I agree," Red said. "But there's more."

"I'm not sure my heart can take much more." He pressed a hand to his chest and rubbed. She started to rise from her seat, but he waved her back. "I'm fine. Please continue."

Red reluctantly sat back down. "The same guy ended up dead on my back doorstep this morning. There was blood everywhere. I slipped and nearly fell in it."

Robert Santiago's brown eyes widened. "This isn't good, special one. How was he killed?"

"His throat was slit just like the first guy. Although the first guy was also shot."

"I take it you think it's the work of the same killer or killers?"

"Absolutely." She nodded. "That's why I believe I'm being set up. The bodies have been placed in areas I frequent. Most people in town think I'm a murderer."

He propped his elbows onto his desk. "What does Morgan have to say about all this?" Robert asked with a wave of his hand.

Red felt her face heat and her gaze dropped to her hands.

"What's wrong?" he asked.

"Morgan needed to take care of some personal business. He left several weeks ago. He left me in charge until he gets back." And she'd done a damn fine job of running Nuria into the ground.

"Where has he gone? Surely the business can't be as important as what's been happening in Nuria."

Red couldn't tell him. She wanted to, but how could Red explain that Morgan had gone after his wife and child, when it was hard for her to accept. "Take my word for it, it's important."

"Why don't you let me decide what is and is not important."

She shifted in her seat under his regard. "I'd rather not talk about it."

"I thought you two were getting along."

"We were. We are. It's just that a lot has been happening lately. He has stuff he needs to take care of. I have to let him handle things on his own. I thought while he was away things would be the same in town. But I don't fit in at Nuria any better than I did here. I'm starting to think I made a mistake."

"Do you love him?" he asked.

"Of course I love him," she said. Of that Red had no doubt.

The viewer activated in her grandfather's office. They both turned to face the screen as it glowed to life.

"What now?" he muttered at the interruption.

"We interrupt your workday for this important announcement," the broadcaster said. "A bomb has been detonated at the Santa Fe Cloning Lab Corporation. Five people have been killed and several others injured. The prototype for Project Scarlet is among the many items destroyed. The on-site investigators are calling the act sabotage."

Red's heart began to pound in her chest, threatening to bruise her. *Please let him be all right and not involved.* A picture of Morgan flashed on the screen and she gasped.

"Morgan Hunter has been detained in connection with the bombing. Sources confirm that he was a security guard for the company. His previous employment lists him as the former sheriff of Nuria in the Republic of Arizona. He's been taken in for questioning."

"No! They're wrong!" she shouted. Morgan wasn't a murderer. That thought was quickly followed by a second realization. He was alive. Morgan was alive. Her relief was short-lived as the severity of the situation sank in. "They can't just take him away. Grandpa, shouldn't IPTT be the ones questioning him?"

"I thought you said Morgan left on personal business.

What was he doing at the Santa Fe Cloning Lab? You have some explaining to do, young lady. What aren't you telling me?" He demanded as his sharp brown eyes latched onto her face.

"I've told you everything."

"Gina? Time is of the essence. I need to know the truth if I'm to help Morgan."

She looked at him, silently pleading with him to believe her. He was frowning and shaking his head as he stared at the screen.

"Morgan would never hurt anyone in order to destroy the lab. I know he wouldn't. He's a good man." But even as Red said the words, she remembered what Morgan had told her before he left. He would do whatever it took to prevent the Santa Fe Cloning Lab from destroying the memory of his dead wife and child. And from the looks of it, he'd made good on his promise.

chapter eighteen

Red stared in horror as Morgan's picture rotated on the screen. The image was from his I.D. at the Santa Fe Cloning Lab. Dark circles marred his tired amber eyes. A day's growth of hair covered his chin. He looked so different, so lost.

The announcer spoke again. "We repeat. The former sheriff of Nuria, Morgan Hunter, is suspected of blowing up a portion of the Santa Fe Cloning Lab today, destroying what could've been a revolutionary vaccine for mankind. No reason for the sabotage has been given. He is currently being held in an interim facility in Taos for questioning, but will be moved soon. Standard admission tests have detected genetic anomalies in his blood. Stay tuned for more information."

The room spun as Red fought to get air into her lungs. Her grandfather came around his desk and shoved her head between her knees. "Breathe, special one."

"This can't be happening. It can't be real. What am I going to do?" she gasped. "I have to see Morgan. I have to find out what happened. There's no way it went down like they said."

Robert Santiago crouched next to the chair until they were nearly at eye level. "I don't think that's going to be possible. We don't even know who's holding him. Besides, I think it's best you stay far away from him, Gina. They've already started testing his blood. Soon they'll discover how different it really is, and then he'll be beyond our help."

Her head jerked up as pain infused her. She couldn't let that happen. Red didn't know what she was going to do, but she couldn't let them use Morgan like a lab experiment. "I know who's holding him. Roark." Her grandfather pushed her shoulders back down, encouraging her to slow her breathing some more. "It has to be him. He's behind everything."

"You don't know that for sure," he said patiently.

"But you could find out for me, Grandpa. You could use your contacts. It's important. I really need to see him. Make sure that he's okay. Then I'll figure out a way to get him out of there."

Robert sobered. "If he's guilty of the crimes they say, there will be nothing you can do."

"I realize that, but he's not guilty. I know he's not." Red's heart squeezed as she prayed that was the case. What was she going to do if it turned out that Morgan was behind the sabotage? They'd put him in detention for the rest of his life, if they didn't decide to execute him instead. If he'd killed those people and destroyed that vaccine, then execution was a good possibility, since its destruction would cost the lives of hundreds of thousands.

He frowned, causing the thick lines on his face to nearly swallow up his brown eyes. "I'll see what I can do. I hope that he's worth it."

"He is," she said, rubbing her tired eyes.

Robert Santiago rose and walked behind his desk. He pressed a button on his vidcom and called Samuel Duncan, the leader of the Republic of Missouri.

"Hello, Sam, how's it going?" he asked.

"It was quiet and calm until that announcement."

Robert nodded in agreement.

"Listen, Bob, you've never been good at dancing around a subject," Sam said. "What can I do for you?"

Her grandfather laughed. "You know me too well." His smile faded as he looked at the man. "I have a favor to ask of you."

"Shoot," Sam said.

"My granddaughter needs to get in to see the man who was arrested today for that bombing."

Sam sucked air sharply through his lips. "Not sure that's going to be possible. He's due to be questioned."

"So he's been delivered to your republic?" Robert asked.

"I didn't say that," Sam said.

"Yes, you did." Robert grinned.

"Okay, maybe I sent orders for him to be brought here, but he isn't here yet. He's being processed at the Taos detention center."

"The arrest happened pretty fast, don't you think? Not really time for a proper investigation."

Sam rubbed his chin. "Yes, we really lucked out. An investigation could've taken months or even years, if he hadn't been spotted on scene."

"That is lucky, but still circumstantial. Don't you think? He is a security guard there after all." Robert sat forward. "Who was the brave soul who caught him?"

"Wouldn't you know, it was Roark Montgomery. The damn glory hound. Has to have his face splashed on all the viewers." Sam shook his head in disgust.

Red gasped. Her grandfather gave her a sharp look and shook his head in warning.

"You may want to watch your back, Sam," he said.

It was the Republic of Missouri leader's turn to frown. "Why's that?"

"Because I think Roark might be angling for your job and then some."

"Oh, that." His shoulders relaxed and he shook his head. "He's been after that for years. Hasn't managed to get it yet."

"He's gaining in popularity," Robert said. "His followers are turning into zealots. You know what happens when that occurs."

"Yes, I know." He sobered. "We'll have a war on our hands. Luckily, he has such wacky agendas that he drives the honest voters away. He'd be a lot better off if he'd stop spouting off about the Others or uniting the republics," Sam said.

"There are some people who'd like to see the republics united," Robert reminded him, without touching on the subject of the Others.

He balked. "Yes, and there are even more people who would fight to keep that from happening. Either way, no one wins."

"You're right. Well, I'd consider it a personal favor if you can get my granddaughter in to see Morgan Hunter. I doubt Roark would accommodate me."

Sam's dark brow rose. "He won't have a choice if I tell him to let her in. I still run this republic. Until I step down or the people decide they don't want me to lead any longer, that will remain the case."

Robert smiled. "I appreciate it, Sam. If I can ever do anything for you, just give me a shout. Next time you're out this way stop by. We can grab a synth-drink and talk about old times."

Sam chortled. "Sounds good to me," he said, disconnecting the call.

Red sat up. "Thank you, Grandpa."

"I hope you know what you're doing, Gina." The concern was evident in his voice. "I don't like you going into that republic without backup."

"I'm not on the team anymore."

"I know, but old habits die hard. Speaking of which . . ." He reached into his desk drawer and pulled out her old navcom. "I want you to take Rita with you. If you don't have backup, she's the next best thing. She'll make sure to notify me if anything goes wrong."

"I can't, Grandpa." She shook her head and looked at the communication device that had served as a surrogate friend for so many years.

"Yes, you can," he said, rising to come around the desk and put the navcom on her wrist.

Rita came to life the second he clasped the band. "Gina, where have you been? My systems have been unable to detect you for almost two months."

Red laughed. "Sorry, Rita. I had to go away for a while."

"Well don't do that again," the navcom scolded in a nasal voice.

Robert laughed. "Just like old times," he said, smiling.

"You really should keep her." Red started to remove Rita. She'd just gotten to the point where she no longer missed the navcom. She didn't want to get reattached and have to give her up again.

He shook his head. "I'd feel better if she was with you. At least that way you'll have a second set of senses helping you scan your environment. Roark isn't going to be happy when he's forced to allow you in to see Morgan. Be careful."

"I always am," she said, standing to hug him. Red held on a long time, not wanting to release him. In the end, she knew she had to go. "I'll call after I've seen him."

"Use Rita. I've had her modified to contact me directly."

Red grinned. "So that's why you wanted me to take her with me. You want to keep tabs on me."

"That's only one of the reasons." He grinned. "Here are the coordinates for the facility Morgan will be kept in."

She logged them into Rita. "I better go," she said, looking around his office one more time. She inhaled, trying to hold the memory in her mind.

"Take care, special one. And remember, if he's guilty, then you'll have to let him go."

"I'm aware of that," she said, knowing that she'd never be able to do so.

The trip to the Republic of New Mexico took four excruciatingly long hours. Red drove straight through without stopping. By the time she reached the facility, the sun was slowly sinking below the horizon and she was exhausted. Anxiety beat inside of her. She didn't know what to expect when she finally got to see Morgan. Would he look the same as the photo, or had he been injured? She hadn't actually considered that he might have been hurt in the blast. Red had been too grateful that he was alive.

She parked the shuttle, staring at the electromagnetic fence that surrounded the detention processing center. Smaller than prisons in the twentieth-first century, the detention center acted as a filtering system. Prisoners were held there before the tribunal met to decide their fate. Depending on the findings, they would be released, executed, sentenced to labor, or sent in for reprogramming.

Red shuddered at the thought of having Morgan reprogrammed. She'd once met a man who'd been reprogrammed. He had no knowledge of his history. They'd changed his face, fingerprints, and erased much of his memory. The scientist who'd performed the procedure had called it a clean slate. Red called it legal mind rape.

She hurried, her booted heels slamming the pavement. She approached the guarded gate and stopped. "Gina Santiago to see detainee Morgan Hunter."

The guard nearest her raised his navcom and hit a button. He scanned what she presumed was a list of names. Red held her breath. Had her grandfather's friend Sam been successful? She'd hate to think she'd come all this way and wouldn't be allowed entry.

"Santiago," he said. "Here it is. A last-minute addition." He pressed a button and the gate opened. "Weapons will be collected at the next checkpoint."

Red nodded.

"Walk straight ahead. Guard number 11174 will process you."

She followed the walkway toward an imposing gray building that looked like a grounded storm cloud. There were no bars on the windows because there were no windows. She stepped through a set of doors and nodded to the two guards waiting.

Inside, the building seemed even more immense than it had from the outside. Gray halls led off in four different directions. There were black stairs at the end of each hall that led to goodness only knew where. Electromagnetic fields crackled, causing the hair on the back of her neck to stand on end. The lights had been converted to natural light to make up for the lack of windows. It also kept the prisoners calm.

Red looked from hall to hall. Guards patrolled every inch of the facility. She had no idea how many people were being held here. Hadn't bothered to ask. She only cared about one man.

"Place your weapon in here, please," the guard said, indicating her pistol.

Red pulled the weapon out of the holster and set the gun down in the container he held. The second her hand was clear of the box, it folded in on itself, securing the gun.

"You can get the pistol back when you leave," he said. "Now step through the scanner."

She proceeded forward as a bright yellow light engulfed her. After a few seconds, it was too bright to keep her eyes open. She closed them against the glare. The light was warm as it spread over her body in search of hidden weapons and explosives.

"All done," the guard said after a minute. "Follow guard 77737 to cell twenty-two alpha."

Red followed the dark-haired bull of a guard down the middle hall on the left. The cell doors were open by design, only giving off the occasional spark to let the prisoners know they were still locked up. Most of the cells were empty, as she'd suspected, but a few were occupied. The prisoners stared at her. Whether it was curiosity over her presence or simply wondering whether she was a new resident, she didn't know. Red avoided eye contact.

The guard continued to the end of the hall until they reached a flight of stairs. He looked back at her. "We have to go up another level."

Red motioned for him to continue and climbed after him. They were now on the second level, and from the looks of it, the detention center went up at least another two. She was relieved that they stayed on the second floor.

"This way," the guard said, stopping three doors down.

Red looked past him. Seated on a small rest pad that had been hastily tossed into a corner sat a man whose back was to them. Despite not being able to see his face, Red recognized Morgan. He had bandages around his ribs and his hands were covered in a dozen or so cuts. He didn't turn when the guard lowered the power on the door. She stepped inside. The room didn't hold much: a chair, a waste dispensing unit, and the rest pad. Just enough to exist.

"What are you doing here?" he asked, his voice rough. He hadn't turned to look at her, which meant he'd identified her by scent. "You shouldn't be here."

"I came to see how you were holding up," she said, walking to the only chair in the room. Red sat before her trembling knees gave out.

"I'm great. Can't you tell?" he said, swinging around. His face was bruised. Blue, black, and purple covered one cheek and eye. Without being able to shift, Morgan hadn't been able to heal himself.

Red gasped before she could stop herself. "Is that from the blast?"

Morgan shook his head. "Roark made sure I got here relatively unharmed." He shrugged and looked over her shoulder toward the guard waiting in the hall. "I was given a warm welcome when I arrived. Apparently, a lot of people are pissed off about the lab."

Red glared at the guard. "Can you give us a little privacy? It's not like we can go anywhere."

He scowled, but stepped back a few more feet.

"What happened?" Red asked, lowering her voice.

"I was set up," he said without inflection.

Unable to stand the distance between them, Red walked over to the rest pad and dropped down beside him. Underneath the blood, sweat, and pain, she could smell the man she loved and her heart melted in response.

"Gina, your blood pressure is rising," Rita piped up. "Please do something to stabilize it."

Morgan looked down at her wrist and gave her a small smile. "Well that explains why they let you in. How is your grandfather?"

"He's fine. Worried, but fine."

Morgan's smile faded. "He has reason to worry," he said, all warmth gone from his tone. "You shouldn't be here. Roark might return any minute."

Red ignored his plea. She wasn't concerned about Roark right now. She needed to find out the truth. "What happened at the lab? We heard that it was blown up. It's been all over the viewers."

Morgan scowled. "It wasn't the whole facility, only a section of it. I was there when it happened, but I didn't set the charge. Don't know who did for sure, but I suspect it was the man who hired me."

"What were you doing there?"

"I was checking out an incoming shipment and looking for a scientist by the name of Finley. From what I could uncover, he doesn't exist. Neither do any of the other scientists on my list, who were assigned to make the Scarlet vaccine and the clones."

Red frowned. "You mentioned that before, but that doesn't make sense."

"No, it doesn't, but Roark stated that the clones of my

wife and child were never there when he had me arrested. With all the other information I've managed to piece together, I believe him." He let out a heavy breath. "I've been such a fool."

"What about the vaccine? They say you destroyed Scarlet." Red looked over her shoulder to check on the guard.

Morgan's head dropped and he snorted. "I'm sure Roark made sure the news said a lot of things. But as far as I can tell, the vaccine never existed. It was a ghost, a sham, like the clones of my dead family. He just wanted to get me away from Nuria, away from you." Pain filled his eyes as he met her gaze for the first time. "And he succeeded. Can you ever forgive me?"

Red leaned forward and embraced him, careful not to squeeze too hard. Her lips touched his in a tender kiss. "There's nothing to forgive. When I heard about the explosion, I didn't think I'd ever see you again." She buried her face in the crook of his neck.

He gently stroked her hair. "Shh . . . It's okay."

A lump formed in her throat. "No, it's not okay. You're being framed and I intend to prove it."

Morgan's eyes chilled. "You will do no such thing. I need you to go back to Nuria. The town is vulnerable without you."

Red laughed before she could stop herself, the sound quaked with bitterness. "Nuria doesn't want me."

Morgan frowned. "What are you talking about?"

"They all but ran me out of town," she said.

He brushed a tear from her face. "Why would they do that?"

"I told you why. It's because I'm a stranger. The second you left everyone closed ranks, keeping me out. Maggie, Jim, just about the whole damn town turned on me. While you've been chasing your tail at the lab, I've been getting framed for murder."

He searched her face. "Roark said something about that,

when he put me in the shuttle. That doesn't explain what's happening in Nuria. I know these people. They protect their own."

"I felt the same way, until the two men came into town. Both hassled me and later ended up dead. The last one had time to file a formal complaint against me. Maggie personally called in IPTT to investigate. Claimed it was in my best interest to cooperate. Do you have any idea how humiliating it is to have your grandfather, your former commander, receive a brutality complaint?" She growled in frustration. "I know Roark is behind their arrival, but I can't fight him and the town at the same time."

"So the killer is still on the loose?" he asked.

"Yes. Like you, I've been led on a merry chase that's ended up coming full circle. Recruits are quitting. Maggie's on a power trip. The town doesn't trust me. Most of them are afraid of me because of my—" She stopped short and looked at the guard. He was staring down at his boots, but she had no doubt he was listening intently to their conversation. "My lack of control."

"I can't believe Maggie would do such a thing."

Red gave him a sad smile. "I knew you were going to say that."

"It just doesn't sound like her. She cares about you."

Red snorted. "Maggie and the others cared about me as long as you were around. The second you left, they accused me of running you off. As if that wasn't bad enough, they insinuated that I was sleeping with Raphael and the new tactical team members. The final blow came when they added murder to the already full stack of accusations leveled against me."

Morgan sat in silence, digesting her words. He couldn't believe Nuria would abandon Gina the moment his back was turned. He'd done everything for that town. Protected them. Lied for them. Killed his own cousin for them. And this was the gratitude he got?

"I'll talk to them," he said, before cutting himself off. He'd been about to say, when he got back, but Morgan knew there was a very good chance he'd never see Nuria again.

Gina must have realized it, too, because she looked away. Before she did, he saw tears glistening in her eyes.

"I need you to be strong. We both knew going in this might be a one-way trip for me, but I had to try anyway. I couldn't allow them to hurt my family." He choked on the last word. Why hadn't he just let the past remain buried? Why had he run off, when the present needed him so much?

"I know, but it doesn't make it any easier."

He squeezed her hand. "I've missed you so much," he whispered, brushing her lips reverently with his fingertips.

Tears slipped down her cheeks and she quickly wiped them away. "It's not fair," she said. "We just found each other and now this."

"I'll figure something out. I always do." The lies slipped easily from his mouth because Morgan knew how much she needed to hear them.

"Maybe my grandfather can help. He's friends with the republic leader in charge of corrections. He can put in a good word for you."

Morgan's head jerked vehemently. "I don't want him involved. What if that's what Roark was after all along?"

"I don't follow." She frowned.

"Roark told me he was after us, but what if that was another lie? What if he really wants your grandfather? If the commander steps in, Roark could question his loyalties and claim he's unfit to lead the tactical team."

"Could he do that?" Fear colored her features, making her seem more fragile than a synth-egg. Her hands started to shake.

"Look what he's accomplished thus far. I'm in detention and you're about to lose the only thing you ever loved—your job."

"That's not the *only* thing I ever loved," she murmured.

His grip on her tightened. "Promise me when you leave here that you'll go into hiding until this mess blows over."

Their gazes met and locked. "You know I can't make that promise," Gina said softly.

Morgan pulled her close as fear threatened to rip his heart from his chest. He had no idea how he'd get out of this mess. No idea how he'd prove his innocence. He couldn't protect Gina from in here and Morgan had no doubt she was in danger. He'd been a fool to chase the past. A fool to leave the one thing that meant more to him than anything else in this crazy world. And he was about to lose it all.

chapter nineteen

Roark fumed as he sat behind his desk. How dare the leader of the Republic of Missouri force him to drop off his detainee at the Taos detention center? How had Sam even known Morgan Hunter was in his custody? Roark grimaced as he recalled the news report he'd arranged.

Of course Sam knew that he had Morgan—the whole world knew. Thanks to his associate's premature announcement, it had cost Roark a fortune in credits to ensure he'd regain custody. He slammed his fist down on his desk, causing the nearby items to jump and tumble onto their sides.

His vidcom buzzed, interrupting his tirade.

"Roark here," he said, his tone clipped.

"The woman has arrived," the voice said, before cutting off.

Roark smiled. The fact that Gina Santiago was visiting Morgan meant she'd gone to IPTT headquarters for help. Technically, they hadn't done anything wrong by getting her in to see the detainee. But if they inserted their power any farther over the line, Roark would have cause to ask for Robert Santiago's resignation. And he knew just how he'd make sure that happened.

He glanced out his office window as workers inside the biodome hustled to their jobs as dawn broke. He had one more thing to take care of before he could put his plan into action. Roark pressed a button on his desk.

"Michael, I need you to come in here," he said. Just the thought of being in the same room as his assistant set his heart racing. His disgust over what he was, and the fact that Roark had allowed the man to work so closely with him, still left him shaken. Well he wasn't about to have an Other running around the office unless he could control him. And there was only one way he could do that.

Roark pressed another button. "Stand by," he said.

Michael entered his office a moment later. "Yes, sir. You called?"

"I did," Roark said smoothly, feeling anything but calm. Under his desk were two weapons, one meant to stun, the other meant to kill. If Michael made one wrong move, Roark would kill him. "Some disturbing news has reached me."

Michael frowned, his pale skin rippling with the effort. "Are you talking about the lab bombing, sir?"

"No, it's something more immediate. Right here under our noses, so to speak."

"I don't know what you mean," he said.

"You will in a moment," Roark said, firing the stunner.

Michael's eyes widened in shock as he looked down at the wound blossoming on his chest. "Why did you shoot me?"

Roark's heart thundered. The shot should have downed him instantly. Maybe his physiology was messing with the stunner's effectiveness. "You know why, you freak bastard," he said, firing again. What would he do if the man didn't go down? He moved his fingers to the other gun. The next shot would be fatal.

Michael dropped into a nearby chair and crumpled forward, but not before he sent out a silent cry for help to his brother.

* * *

Raphael awoke instantly and bolted upright. He looked around the room, trying to figure out what had disturbed him. The echo of Michael's cry remained in his mind. Pain-filled and distant, the sound bounced a few more times before fading away.

Michael, are you okay? He sent the message using the old form of communication the military developed back in the war. Silence met him. *Michael, I heard your call. Answer me.* Something was wrong. He could feel it. Raphael glanced down at the naked woman lying beside him. She'd been a poor substitute for Gina, but he'd needed a warm body to get lost in.

He stroked a finger down the side of her face and she snuffled in her sleep. He smiled and felt a flush of pride that came from loving her well. Raphael threw back the covers and stood. The air felt good against his bare skin. He glanced out the window. With dawn's arrival, it was too light to travel to the Republic of Missouri. He could do it, but not without a lot of pain and sunscreen. He'd have to wait until dark and hope he heard from his brother again.

Raphael walked into the cleansing unit and flipped on the viewer. An image of Morgan glowed to life and his mind froze. What in the world was going on? He turned up the volume, keeping it low enough to not disturb his lovely hostess from her beauty rest. He'd had better things to do last night than watch the news.

The words "sabotage," "bombing," and "detention center" were dropped like verbal land mines. They were followed by the word "escape" and then a picture of Red. He turned the volume up a little louder.

"We repeat. The man wanted for questioning in the Santa Fe Cloning Lab Corporation bombing has escaped. It is believed he might have been assisted by this woman. Her name is Gina Santiago. She is a former International Police Tactical Team officer and should be considered armed and dangerous. If you see her, do not approach and call the authorities immediately."

Raphael was moving before the last word faded from the screen. He had to find Red.

Red arrived in Nuria at dawn. She'd driven through the night. She was tired both mentally and physically, and wanted nothing more than to head to the water trader to go to sleep. She pulled the shuttle around to the rear of the dissecting lab and climbed out. Her back ached from sitting. She wasn't used to spending long hours riding around anymore. She looked up and saw a few people walking down the street. Red waved. When they saw her, their eyes widened and they rushed off.

Terrific. Nothing had changed since she'd been gone.

Red grimaced. She still didn't know how she was going to get Morgan out of the detention center. There had to be proof of his innocence somewhere at the Santa Fe Cloning Lab, but the question was, how could she get to it? She placed her hands on the small of her back and stretched, trying to work out the kinks.

Rita came alive on her wrist. "Gina, you have an urgent message from the commander."

Red frowned. What was her grandfather doing calling her so early? Maybe he wanted to see how her visit with Morgan went. "Go ahead and put him through."

Her grandfather's face appeared on the tiny navcom screen. "Hi, Grandpa. I just got back. Haven't even walked in the door yet."

His face was pinched with pain and his eyes darted as he looked around him. "Gina, what happened?"

"What do you mean?" She shut the door of the shuttle and walked toward the water trader depot.

"Where are you right now?" he asked.

"I told you I'm in Nuria. Where else would I be?" she asked, suddenly feeling tense. "Why do you ask?"

He looked around again. "Is Morgan with you?"

She blinked. "No, why would he be?" Dread seeped into her bones, anchoring her in place.

"He's escaped," he whispered.

"That's not possible. That place was locked down tight. There's no way he could've escaped. There aren't any windows, and besides, he would've told me if those were his plans." *Wouldn't he?*

"It's all over the news. *You're* all over the news," he added quietly.

"What do you mean *I'm* on the news?"

"Please be quiet and listen." Her grandfather glanced around again to ensure that he was alone. "They're saying you might have had something to do with his escape."

"What? That's insane." Her voice rose before she could stop it. Red stepped around the backside of the building to remain out of sight.

"You're wanted for questioning for possibly aiding and abetting the escape."

She looked around, feeling the sudden need to hide. "That's impossible. I didn't even have my gun. There's no way I could break him out, even if I wanted to. Morgan was still in his cell when I left him."

"I'm sorry, Gina, but IPTT has received orders to come to Nuria and take you in by force if necessary. While there we are to search the town for Morgan. And by 'we,' I don't mean me. I've been asked to step aside."

"But Morgan's not here," she cried. Red had no idea where Morgan was. Why would he escape without telling her? He knew her grandfather had pulled strings to get her in to see him. There was no way he'd jeopardize Robert Santiago's position. Not when he already suspected Roark might be trying to take over IPTT. Morgan was many things, but selfish wasn't one of them. It didn't make any sense. Red pulled herself together. She needed to think like an officer. "How much time do I have?"

He glanced down. "The team will be there in a matter of hours."

"Thanks, Grandpa. Thanks for everything. I'm sorry things have gotten so out of control."

"I should've never allowed you to go to that detention center," he said. "I should've never let you leave IPTT that first time."

"I couldn't stay your little girl forever." Red gave him a half-smile. "Besides, you didn't do anything wrong. Roark would've figured out some other way to get to us, to get me, eventually. Shooting him only sped the process up."

"What are you going to do?" he asked, fear leaching the strength out of his voice.

"There's not much I can do."

"You could run to no-man's-land," he said softly.

Red knew what it cost him to even suggest such a thing. "And then what? I'd be there all alone. I have no idea where Morgan is right now. I don't even know if he's alive." She choked back a sob. "I do know there's no way he escaped on his own without telling me. He would've at least said good-bye."

"I fear I have failed to protect you." Robert Santiago's broad shoulders slumped.

"No, Grandpa, you haven't. You've done a good job taking care of me. Now it's time for me to take care of myself. I was naive to believe leaving the tactical team and coming to Nuria would keep me safe. I should've gone after Roark and ended this when I had the chance."

"I will do my best to slow the team down, but I don't know how much good it'll do since they're already on their way."

"Was it Roark's suggestion that you step down?"

He smiled, but it came out more as a sneer. "Who else?"

"It's okay. I'll be all right. Who's leading the team?" she asked.

"Your old friend Bannon Richards. Of course Roark will be there to make sure he does his job."

"Terrific." She shook her head and sighed. "You'd better go before they realize you've contacted me. I have to prepare things before they get here."

He nodded.

"I love you, Grandpa." Her heart clenched and she swallowed hard. She couldn't fall apart now.

"I love you, too, Gina. Take care of yourself. And don't give them a reason to shoot."

Bannon didn't need a reason to shoot her. They'd butted heads on the job so much he'd probably be looking for an excuse.

"You know me," she said, then laughed. It sounded strained, but her grandfather played along.

Robert arched a brow. "Yes, that's why I said it."

She smiled and pressed the button to disconnect their call. Red slipped down the alleys to the back of the water trader. She pressed her palm on the screen, but the door refused to open. *Crap.* Red took out her laser pistol and fired, shattering the scanner, leaving it smoldering. The door slid open. She stepped inside and froze, listening for any signs that she'd disturbed the residents. She glanced at the time on Rita's screen. The place would be opening its doors in thirty minutes.

Red took a deep breath, then stepped around the corner and walked right into Takeo. She jumped back, clutching her pistol. "You scared the crap out of me," Red hissed under her breath.

"I wasn't the one sneaking around," he said, his amber eyes glittering in the early morning light.

"I wasn't sneaking. I was trying to be quiet. I didn't want to wake anyone."

"Would that have anything to do with the latest news announcement?" he asked.

"I've been driving all night. I haven't seen any viewer reports."

He cocked a hip in the doorway. "Well, you're real popular right now. Word is you had a hand in busting your man out of the detention center in the Republic of Missouri." He was watching her closely, taking in her slightest movement, waiting to see if her scent changed.

You didn't have to be an Other to know he was trying to detect if she was lying.

"I went to the detention center and saw Morgan. When I left, he was still there."

Takeo frowned.

Juan stepped out from behind a nearby pillar. Red made a mental note to put bells on them. "She's telling the truth," he said, giving her a sad smile.

"I know she is," Takeo said. "I'd smell it on her if she were lying. So what happened?"

Red laughed mirthlessly. "I have no idea. I just found out about the escape moments ago as I was parking the shuttle."

"Morgan didn't tell you that he was going to try to break out?"

She brushed past him. "No. In fact, when I left Morgan said he didn't think there was a chance he'd be leaving anytime soon."

"That's strange," Demery said, walking down the stairs. "I would've thought if he'd planned an escape he'd at least tell you so you could meet up later."

"Funny," she said. "I was thinking the same thing."

"Do you think it was staged?" Takeo asked.

Red shrugged. "Everything else has been. Why not this?"

"But how did you get dragged into it?" Juan asked.

Red realized once again she'd played right into Roark's hands. She sighed. "I went there to see him. I needed to know he was okay. My mere presence made it easy for Roark to tie me to the escape."

Demery motioned with his hand. "But that doesn't explain the timing. He would've had to escape right after you left."

Red ran her fingers through her hair, pulling out her ponytail. "Roark has people everywhere. When I first met him, he had a man in Nuria. An Other no less."

The three recruits stilled. "You mentioned the man on the inside before, but you said you didn't think that was the case now," Juan said.

Red threw her arms up in the air. "I don't know where he's put people, but nothing would surprise me. It's obvious he had someone working for him at the Santa Fe Cloning Lab and the detention center. If you can get to people in secure facilities, a town isn't going to pose a problem."

"What about the dead bodies?" Demery asked, moving to sit on the bar.

"They were just his way of distracting us from the bigger picture. If he could ruin my career while he was doing it, all the better."

"Is that what he's trying to do?" Juan asked.

Red turned to him and leveled her gaze. "No, he's trying to destroy all the Others. I guess he figures if he can take out me and Morgan, it'll be a lot easier, since we're trying to organize the Nurian Tactical Team."

Takeo stepped forward. "What do you want us to do?"

"Nothing. The International Police Tactical Team is on their way. I need you to stay as far away from me as possible. Roark won't think twice about taking you out if you stand against him."

Takeo grinned, flashing fangs. "We aren't that easy to kill."

Demery nodded. "Yeah, mon. I've had a lot of people try to kill me throughout the years and I'm still here."

Red looked at him, surrounded by his protective suit.

"Yes, and right now, you're extremely vulnerable. One tear in that suit and you'd go off like a bomb. I, for one, do not want to see that happen."

He cringed.

"I'm going to jump in the shower before the tactical team arrives to search Nuria. I want all three of you gone by the time I get out. Understood?"

The three men looked at her. Red could tell they were debating whether to defy her.

"We don't run from fights," Juan said.

"There isn't going to be a fight. They have us outgunned, outmanned, and outmaneuvered. It wouldn't be a fight, it would be a massacre. And despite how everyone in town has been treating me, I'm not about to let the tactical team annihilate the Nurians if I can prevent it."

chapter twenty

Morgan awoke with his head pounding. He tried to move and felt metal bite into his wrists. He winced and forced his eyes open. A bright light glared in his face, causing him to shut them once again. Morgan licked his dry lips and tried again, but the light hurt too much.

The last thing he remembered was sitting in his cell at the detention center. Gina had just left and the pain of separation had been excruciating. He'd heard the electromagnetic door defenses drop right before something hit him. Well, hit wasn't the right word. Hitting would've been far less painful than whatever they shot him with. Searing heat had sliced his skin, pulling his flesh apart until the world around him faded to black.

Morgan had no idea how long he'd been out. Was it hours? Days? Weeks? He forced his eyes open and looked to the side, away from the light. Shackles secured his wrists. He tried to stand and his right foot clanked. He looked down at the chain binding one of his ankles. He couldn't risk shifting until he determined where he was.

He glanced around. The walls were dark and slick with human misery. He could smell it, along with blood, urine, sweat, and feces. There didn't appear to be any windows, but there were bars. He was in some sort of cage.

He shook his head to clear it. The room spun and Morgan gulped air to keep from vomiting. He shouldn't have breathed so deeply. The sour air did little to soothe his stomach.

"I see you're finally awake," a voice called out from the other side of the light.

Morgan's head shot up, but the brightness blinded him. He tried to raise his hand to block the light, forgetting about the chains. They pulled taut and he groaned. "Where am I?" he croaked.

The light was pushed aside. Morgan's eyes slowly adjusted until he could finally see his captor. Roark Montgomery stood against the far wall, grinning smugly.

He quickly looked around. Morgan didn't know how long he'd have before Roark changed his mind and shined the light back in his face. The rest of the room was suffocatingly small. Other than the one door, there didn't appear to be any way out. The rusty cage that held him was barely big enough to accommodate three people. It reminded him of the circus cages used in the twenty-first century to house the lions. "I should've known," Morgan said.

Roark nodded. "Yes, you should have, but you didn't. Neither did your lady, although I believe she suspected, since she went above my head to get in to see you at the detention center."

"Am I in another part of the building?" Morgan asked, wondering if this was solitary confinement.

Roark's grin widened. "No, haven't you heard? You've escaped with the help of your accomplice, Gina Santiago."

Morgan frowned. "Escaped?"

"Well, that's what everyone believes, thanks to a few well-placed guards and some friends with access to the viewer broadcasts."

Morgan felt his stomach drop as understanding dawned. "You're going after her." It wasn't a question.

"I told you I would." Roark canted his head. "It's taken you a while to catch on."

"Sorry," he said, to keep him talking.

Roark scowled. "Are all the Others as thick as you are?"

Morgan tried to shrug, but the movement was hindered by the chains. "You brought me here and put us through all this just to get to Gina." He'd thought for sure Roark had been angling for Commander Robert Santiago's position.

"No one shoots *me* and gets away with it. It's a pity, really. She had a promising future with the IPTT before she started lying with beasts." He pulled a face that showed his disgust.

"Is that what this is all about?" Morgan spat dried blood out of his mouth. So Roark was still under the impression Gina was normal. At least that was some consolation.

Roark shook his head. "Do you really think I'd go to this much trouble for revenge?"

Morgan looked at him, meeting his flat gaze. "Yes, I do."

Roark laughed. "Then you're a fool. Revenge is only a side benefit. As long as you're both around, I'll never be able to quietly eliminate the Others and unite the republics for the purebloods."

"I didn't think that 'quiet' was on your agenda. You seem to have gone out of your way to draw attention to your actions."

"I've always considered myself and my actions rather subdued," Roark said.

"I'm sure, but you should probably read your history vids. Elimination of an entire race of people has been attempted again and again throughout time and it has *always* failed."

Roark's eyes narrowed. "It won't fail this time because you're going to give me the proof I need. You're going to show the world that you're a monster."

"Why would I do that?"

"Because it's the only way you'll ever escape this place, especially now that I've captured the spy you planted in my office. The chains on your wrists and ankle are too small for your hands and feet to slip through, but a paw might have a chance."

He glanced at the bindings. "I don't know what you're talking about," Morgan said.

"Oh please, don't play stupid. I saw you fight Kane. He was your cousin, right? That's how I was able to trace your personal history so far back. He gave me all the information I needed. Must have been hard to kill him. I bet you still mourn his death."

"Shut up," Morgan spat. So Kane had done more than kill women and try to take Gina away from him; he'd also broken the trust they'd shared. He'd betrayed Morgan and the Others. His cousin's treachery stung, but Morgan refused to give Roark the satisfaction of knowing how deeply he'd hurt him.

Roark watched him closely, amusement lighting his eyes. "I didn't realize my assistant, Michael Travers, was sending you information. I admit the man had me fooled, but not anymore."

Morgan kept his expression neutral. Michael had helped them a little and had planned on sending them more information if it was needed, but otherwise, they hadn't heard from him. "I don't know what you're talking about."

"I really wish you'd stop lying to me," Roark shouted. "I don't accept it from purebloods, and I certainly won't accept it from a filthy animal." He pressed a button on the side of the wall and Morgan's chains electrified.

He screamed, his body bowing under the current as pain shot through him, blackening the skin touching the metal.

Roark released the button and the electricity shut off. "Lie to me again and I'll leave it on until you're nothing but char on the floor."

Morgan gasped, his heart racing. His ears were ringing and his limbs wouldn't stop shaking as the last of the deadly current swept through his body. Sweat broke out across his forehead. It had been a long time since he'd been tortured. Not since the war had he experienced this much agony. The thought of Roark getting his hands on Gina and subjecting her to similar treatment left him cold. He couldn't allow that, even if he died trying to stop him.

"What have you done to Michael?" he asked, wondering if he could somehow get word to Raphael.

Roark's smile returned. "He's been chipped. It's amazing what happens when you place an artificial intelligence chip in the frontal lobe of the brain. Did you know that you can induce schizophrenia? Make the person see malicious shadows? Science can accomplish so much these days with a single touch of one tiny button." He pulled out a device that wasn't much smaller than his palm. It had a green button in the center that stuck up like a pimple on its black face. He thumbed the button, stroking it lovingly.

Morgan swallowed hard. He had no doubt Roark had done what he'd professed. The man didn't make idle threats. The question was, had he implanted him as well?

Roark pressed the button. Morgan braced himself, expecting pain and delirium to start at any second, but nothing happened. Morgan cocked his head. It was then he heard screams and thrashing. They were far away, but still close enough for his wolf to detect.

"I can't hear his agonizing cries," Roark said with a malicious grin. "But I know you can."

"I thought Michael worked for you for years. I only met him recently, so he couldn't have been spying all this time."

Roark frowned. It was obvious that hadn't crossed his mind. He quickly recovered. "It doesn't matter when his betrayal started. All that matters is that it did. I can't believe I allowed an Other so near me." He shuddered. "I should've been able to detect him."

"Why?" Morgan asked. "We aren't so different than you. We have the same wants and needs."

Roark slammed his palm down on the button on the wall. Electricity shot through the chains and straight into Morgan's body. He bit his tongue and tasted blood as all his muscles stiffened and convulsed. Roark kept it going for a few seconds. Morgan felt the skin at his wrists and ankle split. He couldn't prevent the cry that ripped from his throat.

Roark released the button. "Don't you *ever* compare yourself to me or any other pureblood. You're an abomination. They should never have made you."

Morgan gasped. "People do strange and desperate things in times of war," he murmured. "I'm curious, though. Was there ever a finished clone of my wife and child at any of the labs?"

Roark laughed. "No. I stumbled upon them quite by accident—thanks to the information Kane shared about your kind. I had no idea that creatures like you could live so long."

"Funny, there was a time when we were called heroes."

Roark scowled. "That was a mistake, but the scientists paid for their arrogance by losing the war."

"Was there ever a Scarlet vaccine for blood mutations?" Morgan still had mixed feelings about that. What if he'd been wrong about its existence? What if he had destroyed the only thing that would give Gina a chance at a normal life?

Roark shook his head. "Nope, but I needed someone to blame for its destruction before my investors realized it didn't exist. When you showed up to 'save' your family, I knew it was the perfect opportunity to 'kill two coyotes with one laser blast.'"

"You know I'll never help you no matter how many times you shock me," Morgan said.

"You will eventually. Once the people see the truth on the vids about your kind, see that monsters truly exist; they'll come running to me for help. Uniting the republics will take no effort at all."

"If you really do have Michael under your control, why don't you just use *him* to show the world?"

Roark's expression soured.

"Oh," Morgan laughed. "I see. You don't want anyone to know you've had an Other working for you all these years. I suppose that would cause quite a bit of embarrassment."

"You must really love pain," Roark said as he hit the button on the wall, sending another jolt of electricity through Morgan's system.

Morgan's head fell forward and he allowed his body to sag. He clenched his jaw to fight the pain and worked to regulate his breathing so he could feign unconsciousness. He'd been so blind. Not being able to find the clones had been his first warning. Morgan had ignored it in order to get to the bottom of the cover-up. Well, he'd found out the truth as the trap sprang closed. Now his mistake might very well cost Gina her life.

The sad part was, he couldn't even warn her. If he did, Roark would have the proof he'd been looking for. So he was stuck. Bound to the wall like a rabid dog until all hell broke loose and madness overtook him. God help anyone who was around, when that happened.

Roark shut off the current and stood for a few minutes, staring at him. Morgan could taste his anger and disgust on the foul air that he sucked into his lungs. Now that Michael had been captured, the Others were in danger. More danger than they'd ever been in before.

Finally Roark snorted in displeasure. "How disappointing," he said. "Hopefully the girl will put up more of a fight."

Morgan waited for him to leave, then raised his head once more. His muscles continued to twitch. He pictured his lovely Gina and tried to imagine her hanging limply beside him. Pain crushed him, squeezing the breath out of his chest. He couldn't let that happen. Morgan focused everything he had on mentally reaching her.

"Run, Gina. Run," he murmured, hoping somehow she'd hear his pleas.

* * *

Raphael froze as Morgan's voice filled his mind. He'd heard his whispered cry. It had sounded so very far away. He had slathered his body in sun barrier and thrown on sunshades before rushing outside. The sun scorched his skin despite the covering. He inhaled, smelling Red's scent on the air. She was here. Somewhere close. Raphael poured on the speed, following Red's sweet aroma from the dissecting lab to the water trader. He should've known.

People were outside, waiting to be let in. He brushed past them and then turned to hiss, flashing his fangs in warning. People scattered, running in all directions. He had no doubt some would end up at the sheriff's station, but he didn't care. He had to get to her.

He forced the door open and rushed inside. Three men came out from behind the pillars, surrounding him. Red stood at the bar, her hand resting on her laser pistol.

"Where have you been? I've been looking all over town for you," Raphael said, eyeing the men. "Call off your dogs before I send them packing."

Red smiled and nodded to the men, letting them know everything was all right. The men relaxed, but didn't leave their positions. "I doubt that would be as easy as you think," she said.

Raphael smiled. "I like a challenge," he said, giving her a slow perusal.

Red stiffened. "If you've come here to ask about Morgan, I haven't seen him since I left him at the detention center."

His smile dropped. "I know he's nowhere near here. I just received a message from him."

"How? He's alive? Where is he? Is he okay?" she asked.

"How is unimportant. As to where he is and how he's doing, I don't know." Raphael shook his head. "What is important is the message itself. He wants you to run. Get far away from here."

Red gave him a sad smile and slowly shook her head. "I'm not leaving Nuria unprotected," she said. "IPTT will tear this place apart looking for me."

"Don't be daft, woman. Nuria can take care of itself," Raphael growled.

"So can I," she said, arching a brow.

"Apparently not, if you're being accused of breaking a detainee out of detention," Raphael reproached.

Red's lower lip trembled. "Roark is behind this whole thing," she said. "I just can't prove it."

Raphael reached out and touched her cheek before quickly dropping his hand. "You can't fight him if you're dead."

"I won't let him destroy the town. I promised Morgan I'd look after Nuria. And I plan to keep my word."

"How are you going to do that?" Raphael asked.

Red bit her lip. "I don't know yet, but I'll think of something. I have to, for everyone's sake."

The door to the water trader burst open and Maggie came rushing in with several deputies in tow. "I knew I'd find you here," she said, watching Raphael and the others warily. "A friend just called from the Republic of Colorutah and said that the tactical team is on its way. What were you thinking bringing Morgan here? You're going to get us all killed."

Red stepped past Raphael. "Morgan isn't here."

Maggie scowled. "Don't lie to me."

"Use your wolf to discern the truth. I'm not lying. I don't know where he is," Red said. "I wish I did."

She ignored her. "The report said you helped him escape."

"She didn't," Juan said.

Maggie swung on him. "How would you know? You're probably just sticking up for her because she's sleeping with you. She's probably sleeping with you all."

"We wish," Takeo muttered and Demery laughed.

Maggie glared at him until he stopped, then faced Red once more. "Wherever you're hiding him, you need to leave now. Or I'll be forced to have the deputies arrest you and hold you until tactical team arrives."

Red let out a frustrated breath. "I told you, I don't know where he is. The last time I saw Morgan he was locked up."

"So you admit you were there," Maggie said.

"I never denied it, but I didn't break him out."

"This town has had nothing but bad luck since you arrived."

If Red hadn't been watching closely, she would've missed the fear in the woman's eyes. She'd never understood why Maggie had changed after Morgan left, but now she did. Maggie needed someone to blame for all the pain that had been heaped upon the Nurians. She couldn't blame Morgan or anyone from here. Her only option had been to target an outsider, and Red was the only outsider around. At least she knew now what motivated the woman.

"I'm sorry you feel that way," Red said. "I came to Nuria to do a job. I stayed because I fell in love and thought I'd found a place where I finally belonged. I realize now that place doesn't really exist. Despite all the pain you and the other people in town have caused me, I won't let the tactical team level Nuria."

Maggie's gaze searched hers. After a few seconds, she nodded and left. Clearly torn between duty and loyalty, the deputies lingered behind until Red dismissed them.

"What are we going to do?" Takeo asked.

"*We* aren't going to do anything. You guys are going to get out of town before the team gets here." Red turned to Raphael. "I know I don't have the right to ask this of you, but I need you to get in touch with your brother. I have to find out what Roark has planned. The only person who might know is Michael."

Raphael reached for her hand and pressed his lips to her knuckles. "I will try to do this if you grant me one favor."

"Which is?" she asked.

"Please allow me to bite you."

Her eyes widened. "Why do you want to do that?" she asked, looking around at the recruits, who were staring at her with a mixture of surprise and amusement.

"Other than the pleasure . . ." Her eyes narrowed and Raphael held up his hands. "It will allow me to speak with you when words are not possible."

"Like you talk to your brother?"

Raphael's expression dimmed at the reminder of his brother.

"What?" she asked. "Is there something you're not telling me?"

"I fear it may be too late," he said.

"Why do you say that?" Red paused, an unwelcome feeling gathering in her gut.

"Because his last message to me was cut short and I haven't been able to reach him since. It came shortly before Morgan's plea."

Red recalled her first encounter with Michael Travers. On top of being a genetically engineered vampire, he'd also displayed frightening psychic abilities. If those powers fell into Roark's hands, heaven help the people of this world. Not even an army of Others could stop Michael Travers if he was bent on destroying them. Her fear must have shown on her face because Raphael gave her hand a quick squeeze.

"I know," he said, as if she'd voiced her concerns. "I will find him."

And kill him if necessary was left unspoken.

Raphael stepped forward and gathered Red into his arms for what he was sure would be the last time. She felt good there. Her soft curves met the hard planes of his chest. It took effort not to crush her to him.

"I didn't agree," she said breathlessly.

"No, but you didn't protest either." Raphael looked around at the recruits. "Gentlemen, can you give us a little privacy?"

They looked at Red. She nodded. "It's okay. Just go upstairs for a moment."

They didn't seem happy about it, but they did listen. Raphael waited until the last man had left, then brushed his thumb over her lower lip.

Awareness flared in her hazel eyes. "What do I have to do?" she asked.

He smiled. "Just relax. This shouldn't hurt. I've been told my bite brings pleasure."

She arched a skeptical brow. "I'm sure." Her tongue darted out wetting her mouth. Whether from nerves or anticipation Raphael didn't know. But she now had his undivided attention.

He stroked the side of her face, trailing his fingers down her slender throat.

"This doesn't have any meaning, does it?" Red asked. "I mean when Morgan bit me, it meant something. Does your bite have any meaning attached to it?"

Raphael debated how to answer. On the one hand, he bit people for sustenance. On the other, his bite could bind him to the person he was biting. He hadn't allowed himself to be bound to any woman. The thought of her having so much control over him was frightening . . . *and incredibly alluring*. He debated whether to deliver that blessedly cursed bite. It was selfish, he knew. But he longed to have Red in his life in a deeper way than she currently existed.

Morgan's plea replayed in his mind. Raphael couldn't do it. It wasn't her that prevented it. Or even himself. It was the thought of what Morgan was going through to save her. Despite everything that had happened, he still considered the man his friend.

"No," he said finally. "The bite will only allow me to speak with you."

"Okay," Red said. "I think I'm ready." She braced herself.

Raphael smiled again, then kissed her lips tenderly. He didn't try to deepen the kiss, instead, he allowed his lips to slide over her jaw until he could nuzzle her ear. He sucked the lobe between his fangs and worked it with his tongue. Her skin was so soft and succulent, he longed to taste every inch of it. If only they were on a rest pad and not standing in the middle of the water trader.

Red trembled beneath the onslaught of his attention. Raphael groaned, releasing her lobe to lower his mouth to the pulse pounding in her throat. His tongue laved the area, the toxin in his saliva numbing the skin. His fangs wept as his hunger rose with each swipe.

"Relax," he said, breathing the word against her heated skin. Gooseflesh rose on her arms and he felt her nipples harden against his chest. He swallowed a groan. She had no idea what this was costing him.

Raphael closed his eyes and opened his mouth, then bit down. Pleasure erupted inside him as her warm, salty blood rushed past his lips. He growled, making happy noises in his throat as he sucked the delicious sweetness into his mouth. The taste exploded on his tongue, sending his senses soaring. He felt the room spin as intoxication set in. He took two more greedy swallows before he forced his mouth away. Raphael swiped his tongue across the wounds to help seal them.

"Is that it?" she asked. "I thought it would take longer." Red was pliant in his arms. Openly seductive. She licked her bottom lip.

His ragged breathing filled the silence. "Almost done," he said on a gasp. His gaze followed the movement. It would be so easy to take what she unconsciously offered. He watched the rise and fall of her small breasts. Desire scorched him, frying his senses until all that was left was raw need. He prayed she couldn't see it burning in his eyes.

Red was breathing as hard as Raphael. Not since Morgan had bit her during their lovemaking had she felt something so sensual. She was painfully aroused, shaking with pent-up desire, and there wasn't a chance of it being assuaged. She took a trembling breath and let it out slowly. Her body raged at her, but she ignored it.

"What else needs to happen?" she asked, when her mind could finally string words together.

Raphael looked up, his eyes swirling with untapped passion. "Now, you must drink from me." His voice was hoarse as he whipped out a knife and carefully sliced the skin at his throat.

Red hesitated. She wasn't sure if she could do that when she wasn't in her wolf form, no matter how wonderful it had felt a moment ago.

"Please," he begged, his voice guttural. "It's the only way." Raphael reached up and cupped the back of her neck with his large hand and coaxed her closer. Red resisted for a second, then acquiesced.

Her mouth closed over his wound and the tangy spice of his blood brushed her tongue. She started to pull away, but he held firm.

"Swallow," he said, his body trembling beneath her. "You must swallow."

Red took a deep breath, closed her eyes, and swallowed. The initial taste burned her throat, nearly choking her, then it began to change. His blood wasn't so much sweet as it was addictive. She sucked, drawing more of it into her mouth. The taste broadened, going straight to her head. Red groaned.

"That's it," Raphael encouraged. "Drink from me." He sounded like a man on the verge of orgasm. And maybe he was. Red was too far gone to tell.

She sucked harder, drawing him into her body. Her senses came alive, sharpening to the point of pain. She wanted to pull away, but she couldn't. It was like the first time she'd had real chocolate. The full-bodied sweetness had swirled around her tongue, teasing her with its sinfully rich goodness. The synth stuff now paled in comparison.

That's enough, the voice in her mind said.

Red continued to drink.

Gina, can you hear me? The voice came again, stronger this time.

She stilled, realizing the words hadn't been spoken aloud.

That's better, the voice said.

It took Red a moment to recognize Raphael's voice in her head. The tone was different. She started, even though that had been the point of this exchange.

"It will take some getting used to," he said aloud.

Red slowly pulled away from his throat. "Yes, it will."

"I need you to try to speak to me," he said.

She frowned. "How?"

"Just think the words and I'll hear them."

"All the time?" she asked, horrified.

Raphael laughed. "No, not all the time. You have to think of me in order for me to pick them up."

Red bit her lip. "Was Morgan thinking about you when you heard him?"

His expression changed, becoming unreadable. "No, but there *are* exceptions."

"Such as?" Her unease grew.

"When someone is in great pain or experiencing fear, they can project their thoughts loud enough for me to hear them."

She gulped, nodding in understanding. "So Morgan was still alive, but he was scared and in pain, when you heard him." Red's heart cracked a little. She'd been enjoying Raphael's bite while Morgan had been suffering. What was wrong with her? She didn't deserve the man.

Raphael shook her. "We are doing this for a reason. Don't

ever forget that. You deserve all the happiness that Morgan can offer you."

She nodded.

"Now try it again."

"Okay," she said, thinking about the tactical team. *I don't know if I can stop them on my own,* she thought.

No matter what happens, know that you will never be alone. He met her gaze and she saw the truth in his statement. And despite everything that had happened and was about to occur, she found a modicum of peace.

chapter twenty-one

The tactical team arrived in late afternoon, a steady stream of maglev shuttles and weaponry. The sun glistened off their thick armored plating. The roar of the engines deafened even the most secretive of thoughts. A plume of dust followed in their wake, as the shuttles lowered one by one to the ground. Tactical team members poured out of the vehicles in angry swarms of black and took up position, weapons aimed at all parts of the town.

Despite what her grandfather told her, Roark led the team with Bannon Richards by his side. Red noted the irony as she stepped into the doorway of the sheriff's station. He'd come here to start his war. The streets were empty. Most of the people had been evacuated to nearby farms. A few had remained, carefully concealed behind the reflective windows in their homes and businesses. Maggie, Jim, and several of the deputies were hunkered behind their desks.

Roark stepped out of the nearest shuttle. He'd foregone his regular suit and donned what Red could only describe as desert fatigue chic. The sunshades on his eyes reflected the town as he scanned the streets. He was here to see and be seen. Red looked around, half expecting to see viewer reporters lurking in the alleys.

"She's here somewhere," he said. "Search every building. She has to be keeping him nearby."

"Stay here," she said to Maggie and the others positioned inside the sheriff's station. Maggie nodded, then ducked down. Red took a deep breath and stepped out of the shadows of the doorway. "I'm right here," she said.

Everyone tensed as she walked into the center of the street. The tactical team swung their weapons around until they were all trained on her. Red swallowed, but otherwise didn't move.

"Roark, I'm flattered you'd go to this much trouble for me."

His jaw clenched. "I don't like it when people try to flout the law."

She leveled him with a stare. "That's funny, neither do I."

"Where is he?" Roark asked.

"If you're talking about Morgan, I don't know. The last time I saw him he was at the detention center. I believe under your orders."

Roark laughed. "They weren't my orders. I'm a humble civil servant. I don't wield the kind of power your grandfather has at his disposal." He glanced around at the teams and nodded. Several broke formation and fanned out.

"I can see that." She snorted in disgust. "Believe what you want. It's the truth."

He smirked. "We'll see. I have the team searching the town."

"They won't find anything, but you already know that." Red looked at her nails and gave him her best bored expression. "You're wasting precious tactical team time."

"You'll forgive me if I don't take an accomplice's word for it."

"I had no idea I'd already been convicted," she said, noticing the uneasy looks on the faces of a few tactical team members. "Have the tribunal laws changed?"

Roark's face reddened. "You know very well they haven't. We've come here to find Morgan and take you in for questioning."

"Good thing I've come out to turn myself in then," she said, ignoring his statement. "This town and these people have nothing to do with our fight."

He looked around. "That remains to be seen." Roark looked back over his shoulder and Bannon jumped down along with a redheaded woman that Red had seen before at headquarters. Catherine Meyers. The name popped into her head. She recalled what else she knew about the woman, which wasn't much, other than there was more to her than what she projected.

"You two join in the search," he said, then leaned down and whispered something in Catherine's ear.

Red watched as the woman's expression changed. At first her face slackened, then her eyes grew distant, almost unfocused. Suddenly Catherine appeared to snap out of it because she glared at her. For a second Red thought for sure the woman would shoot her. She shivered under her chilling regard.

Suddenly Catherine turned away and took off in the opposite direction that Bannon headed in. Red tensed as Bannon looked back and sneered. She would like nothing more than to knock that smirk off his face, but he wasn't worth starting a war over. Red felt someone watching her and she cautiously looked to her left. She saw Raphael and a few others lurking in the shadows, waiting to come to her aid. Red shook her head in warning. Roark was looking for an excuse to open fire. If they came out, he could claim they'd put up resistance.

She couldn't give him any reason to shoot. Red slowly raised her hands in surrender, even though it pained her to do so.

Keep an eye on the woman, she said to Raphael. *Her name is Catherine Meyers, and there's something not quite right about her.*

He nodded and quietly slipped away.

Red knew what it was costing Raphael to be out in the

sun. The sunscreen didn't help much at this time of day. He'd tried to keep his thoughts hidden from her, but she still managed to sense his agony. Looking at him, no one would know he was in pain.

Roark watched her with something akin to disappointment on his face. "Drop to your knees in preparation for detainment."

Red did as he asked. She saw her new recruits move forward to stand where Raphael had been moments ago and her body tensed. What were they doing here? They should've left as she'd asked. Maggie poked her head out the door. Red couldn't tell what she was doing until a viewer appeared on the sidewalk.

The screen glowed to life and an announcer's face appeared. "The woman wanted for questioning in the detention escape scandal has surrendered without incident." Suddenly a picture popped up with Red kneeling in the middle of the street and the tactical team surrounding her. Red glanced at the sky and saw the image do the same. She realized then that a satellite was tracking her movements.

Roark watched the screen, his face growing redder by the second. He swung around and looked at the team behind him. "Who ordered this to be broadcasted?"

Murmurs rumbled throughout the group, but came to no consensus. The team members looked at each other and shrugged.

Red's lips twitched.

"Gina, the message to the broadcasters has been sent," Rita's voice piped in.

"You," Roark spat, whirling to face her.

Red shrugged, not bothering to correct him. She hadn't sent the message. It had been her grandfather. She hadn't known it until Rita spoke, but since Red didn't want him involved, she decided to take the credit. "I'm sure the leaders of the republics are keen to see how you handle the apprehension of a person of interest. Since you're always out to impress them, I thought this moment would be no exception."

You'll pay for this, Roark mouthed.

"I have no doubt." They were ballsy words from a woman in her position, but she had little choice. She'd done what she had to in order to save her grandfather, to save Nuria. Public opinion meant everything to people like Roark. She'd gambled her life and the lives in this town on the fact that he wouldn't commit political suicide under the watchful gaze of the world.

Bannon returned from his quick check of the buildings. Some of the recruits that Roark had sent out were with him, but she noted the short redheaded woman was not.

"Hunter's not here," Bannon said to Roark. "His heat signature didn't appear when I scanned the buildings and his chip isn't registering in the area."

Roark didn't seem particularly fazed or surprised by his statement. "Shackle her," he said, pointing to Red.

Bannon grinned. "With pleasure," he said, stepping forward to slip the restraints onto Red's wrists. "I've waited a long time to do this," he whispered in her ear, tightening them until they cut off her circulation. "I'm going to make sure I enjoy every second."

"Don't get too used to it. There will come a time when I won't be wearing these and then you'll get your comeuppance."

"Are you threatening an officer?" he asked, yanking her to her feet. "I'd hate to think I'd have to use force on you because you're resisting arrest." He made a show of patting her down for weapons, taking longer than was necessary. He squeezed her thighs, kicking them wide until she nearly toppled forward. He cupped her sex, lifting while he searched her. When he reached her breasts, he kneaded them under heavy hands. "I want to make sure you aren't concealing any contraband," he said, giving them a final rough pinch.

Red bit the inside of her mouth to keep from crying out. She had left her pistol in the sheriff's station. She hadn't wanted them to accuse her of reaching for a gun. "Was it good for you, too?" She laughed, ignoring the revulsion she felt from his touch. "I think we can safely say I'm not concealing anything. Oh, and for the record, I don't need to threaten you." She smiled and the temperature seemed to drop around them. "You will pay for this. That's a promise."

He jerked her forward, nearly dislocating Red's shoulder in the process. She winced. "We'll see who's laughing in the end," he said, tightening his grip on her arm until she knew bruises would appear.

"What has he promised you?" Red asked. "I mean, you have to be getting something out of this. As I recall, you're not one to do something for nothing."

Bannon glared at her. "Other than the pleasure of locking your ass up, it's none of your business."

"It mustn't be much, if you're that tight-lipped. I've never known you not to brag, unless there wasn't anything to brag about. You do know you're being used, right?" she asked.

"Shut up," Bannon hissed, manhandling her some more. "Can't you just come quietly?"

"Truth hurts, doesn't it?"

"I said," he jerked her around to face him, his nose inches from hers, "shut your mouth." Spittle sprayed Red as he shouted. She used her shoulder to wipe it off her face.

"I believe I hit a nerve," she said.

"Roark's going to knock that smart mouth right off you," he said.

Red met Bannon's blue gaze. "You better pray you remain useful to him."

"Why?" Bannon quipped.

"Because the people who outlive their usefulness don't tend to continue to breathe for long."

Fear flashed in his eyes, then they hardened to ice. "I know what you're doing, and it's not going to work."

Red shook her head. "You always were thick as a boulder."

Raphael found Catherine Meyers sneaking behind the buildings. "Need some help looking?" he asked, staying to the shadows to avoid the direct sunlight.

She glanced up, startled, and Raphael's head swam a second before clearing.

His eyes narrowed. "Now that's an interesting trick, how did you do it?"

Her gaze widened and Catherine took a step back. She drew her laser pistol and pointed it at his chest, then fired. Raphael barely had a chance to get out of the way.

"Don't come any closer," she warned. "Or I'll fire again."

"Did your trainer teach you to shoot before you send out a warning?" he asked, taking a step forward.

"Yes," she said, aiming and pulling the trigger. "My orders are to take out the Others and anyone considered a sympathizer." She glared at him and the dizzying sensation came again, stronger this time. "You're here, so you must be an Other or an Other sympathizer."

Raphael let the wave of power wash over him. His thoughts swirled in his head. He tried to catch them and put them back into logical order. "Never let it be said I don't like a challenge." Raphael rushed her before she could take aim.

They struggled with the gun. It took nearly breaking her hand to get her to release it. What was wrong with this woman? He held on, feeling his body spring to life. It had been a long time since he'd fought hand to hand. And it had never been with a woman. But this one seemed determined to kill him. How intriguing.

"No!" she shouted, grabbing for the weapon. The pistol went off again, hitting the back of a nearby building, scorching the wall. The sound echoed in the narrow space. It was followed by a thick thud as the weapon hit the dirt.

"Now that wasn't nice," Raphael murmured against her ear. His heart was racing and so was hers. He hadn't been this worked up in years. "I'm only here to help."

"Let me go," Catherine said, managing to scratch him. Blood welled up on the back of his hand. The scent caused his fangs to extend.

Her eyes bugged as her gaze latched onto his teeth. "You're an Other." Her power flowed through him and he struggled to remain upright.

"Don't do that," Raphael warned, on the verge of losing control. She had no idea what she was messing with, and yet she fought on. He beat back the blood lust that threatened to rage. If he didn't get himself under control, he'd throw her down on the ground and take her right here in the alley. He forced himself to focus on the source of her energy. "Have you always had the ability to create confusion?"

Her pixie face paled and fear filled her green eyes as she continued to struggle. Her knee shot up and caught him in the solar plexus. Raphael grunted, but didn't let go. Instead, he pulled her closer, squeezing her like a python in order to control her.

He didn't realize his mistake until he had her against his body. Despite her small size, she had *very* womanly curves. Full and lush, like goddesses of long ago. Her chopped hair hid her beauty, but it was there, lurking just below the surface, waiting to be coaxed out. The sudden awareness almost caused him to release her.

She twisted in his grasp. "I didn't do anything. I don't know what you're talking about. If you don't let me go, I'm going to scream." Her gaze darted around in search of escape. There would be none for her today. She managed to work a hand free to punch him.

Raphael's head snapped back and he smiled, licking the blood oozing from his lip. He got a hold of her arm once more. In some cultures, this would be considered foreplay. Goodness knows he was getting harder the longer they fought. "Catherine, did you know that when you lie the tips of your ears turn pink?"

Her fingers moved of their own volition to her ears before she realized what she was doing. "How did you know my name?" she asked.

"I'm curious, does Roark know what you are? Does the team? Or have you kept yourself hidden?" he asked, slowly walking her backward toward the dissecting lab's rear entrance.

"I don't know what you mean." Fear flashed in her eyes, before quickly being doused with anger. "Let me go or you're going to be sorry."

"That's an empty threat. You and I both know that." He inhaled, taking her strangely alluring scent into his lungs. Raphael still couldn't readily identify her Otherness. She was a puzzle. And he *loved* puzzles. "I only asked a simple question. I'm genuinely curious. Can't you do me the courtesy of answering, since I've yet to hit you back?"

She glanced at his hands, no doubt taking in their large size for the first time. Raphael had no intention of striking her, but she didn't know that.

"Roark doesn't care who or what I am," she said with a little too much bravado.

"Now that's where you're wrong, little one. He cares very much." Raphael tilted his head. "My guess is he doesn't know or you'd be locked up, buried in some hole, praying for a glimpse of sunlight."

She trembled. "Are you going to tell him?" she asked hesitantly, looking oddly vulnerable.

Raphael's heart stuttered in his chest. "That depends," he said, surprised by his reaction to the fiery urchin.

"On what?" In a flash, Catherine was back to fighting and being indignant.

"On what happens next," he said, pressing forward. The door opened behind her and she fell inside.

Raphael landed on top of her before she could get up. "Now, you and I are going to have a talk."

"I don't know anything. I'm here under orders just like everyone else."

"Your orders were to shoot first and ask questions later? I find that odd given that no one else has fired a shot."

The fear was back in her green eyes, along with genuine confusion. "My orders are . . . they are . . ." She blinked. "I always follow orders."

Raphael noted her hesitance, her confusion. She wasn't lying. He would have scented it on her had she been. She genuinely couldn't remember. He'd known soldiers who'd had their thoughts altered, but that had been a lifetime ago. He stared at her, memorizing her lightly freckled face. For a moment, he saw another's face superimposed upon hers. Just as quickly it faded from memory, replaced once again by Catherine's. Raphael inhaled, taking in her musky scent. "Despite your protests, you aren't like everyone else."

"I am, too," she squeaked. "Now let me up. You're squishing me."

He shifted, allowing her to breathe easier, and then carefully probed her mind. Raphael was met with a wall that had no beginning and no end. *Very interesting.* He pressed harder and her hand tried to fly to her head, but he held her down.

"Ouch!" she said, glaring at him. "What are you doing to me? Whatever it is knock it off."

"Apparently nothing." Raphael had never met anyone he couldn't access mentally, at least to some degree. Others were harder to gain entry to, but it was possible. The trick was getting past their defenses. She had defenses like he'd never seen before.

Raphael nuzzled her neck and felt her shudder beneath him. Her breathing deepened and she stopped struggling. Her scent changed subtly and he smiled. So she was enjoying their tussle, too. Maybe it wouldn't be impossible after all. Raphael hadn't intended to seduce her. That had been the furthest thing from his mind. He just wanted answers. Or at least he had until she intrigued him.

Catherine moved restlessly beneath him and his shaft hardened instantly. The response was both unexpected and unwelcome. He took a breath and closed his eyes. Raphael's fangs ached with the need to bite her.

"Meyers, report," Roark's voice blasted over her navcom, shaking them both.

"Tell him you're okay," Raphael said, squeezing her wrists in warning.

"No way," she said.

"Do it or I'll take you away from here so fast they won't ever find you."

Catherine stared into his eyes, gauging his words, then finally did as she was told. Raphael released a breath he didn't know he'd been holding. "Meyers reporting all clear."

"We heard shots. Is everything okay?" Roark asked.

"I'm fine. I want to stay here and look around some more. I'll catch up with the team tomorrow."

"You sure?" he asked.

"Yes, sir."

"What about the shots?" he asked.

"Thought I spotted something." She glared at Raphael. "Turned out to be nothing."

As she responded to Roark, Raphael let his teeth graze over her soft neck. She flinched when he *accidentally* sliced her.

"Sorry," he whispered, then quickly lapped at the cut so

there would be no evidence of his intrusion. Her blood was sweet, despite her prickly personality. Raphael sucked lightly, swirling his tongue along her rapidly beating pulse. He had to taste her blood in order to break through the defenses in her mind. It wasn't as effective as a blood exchange, but it would still work. He pushed his will inside her once more. The walls shook and a crack appeared, splintering down the center. Raphael locked eyes with her and shoved harder.

He got a flash of the field where the new recruits trained from her memories. He frowned and nuzzled her neck once more. Laser blasts exploded in his mind, nearly blinding him. Raphael jumped up off Catherine.

"It was you," he snarled, drawing away.

"What?" she asked, her expression dazed from his invasion.

"You were the one who destroyed the training equipment outside of town. I saw everything."

She shook her head and scrambled to her feet. "You're mad. I did no such thing. I'm a member of the tactical team. I uphold the law. I don't break it."

"Don't lie to me." But even as Raphael said the words, he realized the woman's scent hadn't changed. She wasn't lying. Or at least she didn't think she was lying.

She brushed off her hands and looked around for her weapon, obviously forgetting she'd left it outside. Or maybe she was just looking for something else to use in order to attack him again. "You just stay away from me." Catherine was shaking now and it had nothing to do with the desire he'd elicited moments ago. She hugged herself and began to pace.

Raphael followed her thoughts. They were jumping all around like a maze that had been scrambled, which didn't make sense. Unless . . .

"Come here," he commanded.

She swung on him. "I'll do no such thing."

"I said come here," his voice lowered and he pressed his will upon her. He hadn't wanted to do it, but he needed the truth.

Her feet dragged as Catherine crossed the floor, moving ever so slowly toward him. Her lungs were heaving by the time she stood in front of him. She'd fought him every step of the way and he couldn't help but admire her for it.

"How did you do that?" she asked.

"Why should I answer you, when you feel disinclined to answer me?" He grabbed her arms and pulled her close, pressing her chest against his.

"What are you doing?" Catherine asked suddenly breathless.

"Seeking the truth. The whole truth. Even the things that are hidden within your mind," he said, a second before he bit into her neck. This time Raphael didn't treat her gently. He needed answers. And he wanted her to feel fear and pain. If she was the one behind the sabotage, she wouldn't be leaving Nuria. He'd make sure of it.

Her blood flooded his mouth. Raphael closed his eyes and groaned at the savory flavor. His hands loosened and slowly dropped, inching their way down her arms and over her waist. Information was coming at him so fast he could barely process it. He saw the training facility. Saw her shooting it up. He even saw her escape.

Raphael was about to release her, when the cross-hairs of a rifle flashed in his mind, quickly followed by a single blade. He saw a man fall, then another. He wouldn't have thought anything of this, given her job, had it not been for the location of the second kill. He recognized it as the back of the water trader depot.

Outraged, Raphael shoved her away, blood dripping down his chin and onto his shirt. "You! It was you who killed them."

She was pale, whether from the blood loss or discovery, he couldn't tell. She trembled and retreated a step. "I—I did no such thing. I don't know what you're talking about." Catherine clutched her head and cried out.

"I should do Nuria a favor and execute you right this second. If there wasn't an entire tactical team on the other side of this building, I would."

Catherine's head throbbed like she'd been punched in the face repeatedly. Memories she didn't understand or recognize flashed in her mind, ending in blood and bodies. "I couldn't have. There's no reason for me to have come here before."

"Then how did you know where you were going when Roark ordered you to search the area?" he asked.

"I did—" The words cut off in her throat. She *had* known where she was going. Or at least something about the place had seemed vaguely familiar. Like a remembered dream or a chance memory, she'd wandered the back alleys as if they were second nature. But that was impossible. She'd never been to Nuria before today. "I don't understand what's happening."

"There's nothing to understand. You're a killer and a saboteur. Both of which can get you executed."

"I didn't do the things you say I did." Catherine frowned and rubbed her temple. "At least I don't think so. I can't remember."

"How convenient." Raphael knew he had to kill her. She'd given him no choice. He considered various methods, and decided on snapping her neck. She didn't deserve a quick death, but he couldn't bring himself to draw it out. He swallowed, taking in the remnants of her blood, relishing the flavor while it lasted. It scalded his throat. He licked his lips and froze as a strange aftertaste hit him. He hadn't noticed it before. He'd been enjoying her too much. "What have you taken? Did you swallow poison in an attempt to thwart me?"

"What are you talking about now?" Catherine's fingers knotted in her short hair.

"You've imbibed something."

"I haven't taken anything other than a few sips of water on the way down here." She picked at her empty holster, probably wishing it still held her gun.

"Your blood doesn't lie. Now tell me what you've taken." Raphael swirled his tongue around his mouth. He'd tasted this before. It had been a long time ago, but the essence was familiar.

She inched toward the door. "I'm going to leave now. This conversation is over."

"You've killed two people and sabotaged a training area. Don't you even want to know why?" he asked.

"No." She shook her head. "If I've done the things you think I have, then I must have had a very good reason."

He snorted. "Like starting a war?"

"I knew you were crazy when I first laid eyes on you," Catherine said. "You had that kind of look about you."

"That is what Roark is trying to do," he said softly, ignoring her verbal jab. "Start a war."

She shook her head and winced. "You're wrong. All he's got are grandiose ideas about uniting the republics. He's not the first of his ilk to have that dream and I doubt he'll be the last."

"Is that what he told you when he recruited you to kill for him?" Raphael watched her, searching for any sign of deception, but as of yet, could detect none.

"He did no such thing. He just wanted my help on the campaign trail. So you're wrong. Dead wrong," she said, backing away from him.

"Am I?" he asked. "I remember now where I've tasted

that essence in your blood. It was in a spy who'd been sent to kill me years ago. They'd doused him with influ-gas. I didn't recognize it at the time. It was only later after I'd killed him that I found out why he'd acted the way he had."

"Influ-gas? That's not possible." Her lower lip trembled. "I couldn't have been drugged without knowing it." Fear shadowed the green in her eyes.

"Sure you could. The spy I killed had no idea he was operating under a drug's influence. That's what makes it so dangerous. I'm sorry, but whoever gassed you has turned you into an assassin."

"**W**hat's taking so long?" Roark asked just before shots rang out. A smile ghosted his face before he carefully hid it.

Red's heart dropped.

Everyone froze and looked around, tense, weapons at the ready.

"Should I send Private Meyers's backup?" Bannon asked, pulling his weapon.

Roark shook his head. "Not yet. Meyers report," he said into his navcom.

Silence met Roark's command.

"Meyers report," he repeated.

"Meyers reporting all clear."

"We heard shots. Is everything okay?" Roark asked, making a show of being concerned.

Red wasn't fooled for a minute. He didn't care if the woman was killed. It would be the excuse he was looking for to level the town. And if she happened to kill an Other, well that meant one less creature for him to have to deal with.

"I'm fine. I want to stay here and look around some more. I'll catch up with the team tomorrow," she said, her voice a harsh gasp as if she was out of breath.

"You sure?" Roark asked.

"Yes, sir," she said.

"What about the shots?"

"Thought I spotted something. Turned out to be nothing."

Roark looked around. "You heard her. She's fine. If she needs help, she'll call."

Bannon hesitated, his gaze going in the direction Catherine had headed in. "Do you want me to check it out? Make sure she's not being held against her will?"

Roark glared at him. "I gave you an order."

"Yes, sir." Bannon looked back at Red. "Get a move on," he said, dragging her.

"Don't say I didn't warn you," she said, before turning her thoughts to Raphael. She pictured him in the moments before he bit her, then sent out her thoughts. *Are you okay? I heard the shots.*

Tinkling laughter filled her mind.

I am fine. Just a minor altercation, nothing I can't handle. What about you?

I'll be all right. Red said what he needed to hear. It was the only way to get out of Nuria without declaring war.

If you aren't back soon, we are coming to get you. She knew exactly who he meant by we. Red thought about her new recruits and doubted they were ready for this kind of mission. *That's a promise.* The thought plunged into her mind, brooking no room for argument.

Despite Red's resolve to remain strong, Raphael's statement came as a relief, even if it turned out to be wishful thinking.

chapter twenty-two

R ed was loaded into a transport shuttle without incident. Roark hadn't been able to level the town, thanks to the viewer broadcast her grandfather had organized. And she'd done her part by fulfilling her promise to Morgan to protect Nuria. Red had done it the only way she knew how. She'd sacrificed herself.

She knew she'd be taken to the detention center at IPTT headquarters first before being moved to the larger facility in the Republic of New Mexico for processing. Maybe once she was there, she'd find out what happened to Morgan. There was always someone who liked to brag. She settled back for the long ride. It wasn't until the tactical team broke off from Roark's vehicle that she'd realized there'd been a change in plans.

"Where are they going?" she asked him.

Roark didn't look back. "To IPTT headquarters."

"And why aren't we going with them?" Her stomach fluttered as nerves set in. "Shouldn't they escort me to their detention center for processing?" Red shifted, trying to get comfortable in the hand restraints.

"You aren't going to any detention center. Did I forget to mention that?" He laughed.

And just like that the flutters in her stomach turned to fear.

"That's against regulations," she said. "I'm only wanted for questioning. You can't hold me longer than forty-eight hours."

His eyes narrowed in the mirror, which allowed him to see the entire back end of the shuttle. "I'm afraid you'll be with me longer than that."

"Which republic are you taking me to?"

"Missouri."

"So we're skipping IPTT and going straight to the detention center in Missouri? I want to see Samuel Duncan when we arrive," she said, trying to squelch the panic. The republic leader would be able to get word to her grandfather.

"I'm not sure if you've noticed, but you are in no position to make demands."

She'd noticed. Bannon had taken great pleasure in placing the restraints on her as tight as they could go. Red had already lost some circulation in her hands. If it hadn't been for her navcom Rita sending pulses to keep the nerve endings stimulated she would've lost all feeling.

"I'm not hiding Morgan," she said, changing the subject.

"I know."

Red blinked. That hadn't been what she'd expected him to say. In fact, he'd made a grand show of having Nuria searched by his two lap dogs and the rest of the team.

"What do you mean, you *know*?" Her eyes narrowed on him. Was he about to make a confession? Red wished she could see his face.

"Isn't it obvious?" He shrugged. "I have him. I guess fucking animals has dulled your instincts."

Red didn't respond to the insult, concentrating instead on getting as much information out of him as she could. She hit the record button on Rita. He'd accused her of losing some of her tactical team instincts, but Red would show him just how much she remembered. "Then why do you need me?" she asked.

"For pure enjoyment." Roark grinned in the mirror. "You'd

have been dead by now if Kane hadn't fallen for you and fucked things up. He had orders to kill you."

"What you're doing is highly illegal. If the tactical team found out, you would be arrested and your career would be ruined."

He stopped the shuttle and scrambled back to where she sat on the floor. He grabbed her by the front of the shirt and lifted her off the ground. "But they aren't going to find out," he hissed. "I'll report your escape just like I reported Morgan Hunter's. Everyone will assume you two are together."

"They won't believe you." She tried to shift so Rita could pick up the whole conversation.

"Don't think I've forgotten how you used that navcom to keep me from leveling Nuria." Roark released her and reached down, ripping Rita off her arm.

"What are you doing?" Her eyes widened.

Roark dropped Rita onto the floor and raised his booted heel.

"No!" Red shouted a second before it came down hard.

"Gina?" Rita's garbled voice came out. "What's happening?"

Roark raised his foot again and stomped until wires bulged out of every crevice.

"Stop it! Can't you see she's broken?" Tears sprang into Red's eyes as he ground the navcom under his boot.

"G-Gina . . . can't . . . find you. Contacting comm . . ." The light on Rita's screen dimmed and her voice died.

Roark looked at Red's teary face and laughed so hard he doubled over. "Your expression is priceless. It's just a *navcom*," he said, returning to the driver's seat. "You'd think I'd killed your grandfather."

Red stared down at what remained of Rita and shifted around until she could touch the pieces. The components were still warm. Fresh tears welled in her eyes. She didn't think the lab guys at IPTT headquarters would be able to repair her this time. Red ran her fingers gently over the shattered device. She sniffled as her heart broke. She'd had Rita for as long as she could remember. And now she was gone, just like her family. Red should've never taken her back from her grandfather. Rita would've been safe had she refused.

"I'm sorry," she murmured, knowing in her last functioning moments Rita had tried to save her.

Tears dropped onto the shuttle's metal floor in soft pings. Red stared at the pile of rubble until her eyes stung. After a while, the shuttle's rocking cadence lulled her to sleep.

Red came awake with a start as Roark's boot connected with the bottom of her shoe. He drew back and kicked her again.

"Get up," he said. "We're here."

"Where's here?" she asked, looking out the window. She could see a biodomed city off in the distance, but they were still several miles away.

He jerked her out and she nearly fell onto the desert floor. If he hadn't caught her, she would have. "Don't bother trying to escape, it won't do you any good," he said, taking her to a nearby hydrogen car. A man she didn't recognize stood outside of it, waiting patiently.

"What's going on? Who is he?" Red asked.

Roark didn't answer her, and instead turned to the man. "Take it a little farther out and blast a hole in the side. We need to make it look good if they find the wreckage. I'll park your car around back for you to pick up later."

"Yes, sir," the man said, and climbed into the transport shuttle.

Roark shoved Red into the passenger side of the car and then took a seat behind the wheel.

"Why are you doing this?" she asked, watching the man drive off in the shuttle with what remained of Rita. There was no way she could stop him.

"We have to make your escape look good," he said. "By

the time I'm done, everyone will believe Morgan Hunter helped you. There will of course be a massive man-hunt. It'll be a public relations nightmare for your grandfather. I wouldn't be surprised if he's asked to step down."

"You're going to pay for this." The ride to the city didn't take long. It seemed that Roark had thought of everything. Of course, her grandfather would never believe the reports, but there wouldn't be much he could do, given his tenuous position.

Red glanced at the location with her peripheral vision. She recognized Roark's building from the files she'd seen at headquarters. He tossed a cloak over her head, hiding her face. Roark walked with his hand at her back, making it look like they were out for a casual stroll. No one would guess he was escorting a prisoner.

She wondered where Michael was. She'd never seen Roark without his assistant. Raphael had said he'd sensed something was wrong. "Where's your assistant, Travers?" she asked, as a couple of people passed them. They were dressed in suits and didn't pay attention to her or Roark. "I thought he always did your dirty work for you."

He leaned close to her ear. "If you're expecting help from him, you can forget about it. I know what he is. I've made sure he won't cause me any more problems."

Red stumbled and he jerked her upright. She debated whether or not to lie, but decided against it. She needed to find out what had happened to Michael for Raphael's sake.

"What have you done to him?" she asked.

"Nothing the filthy animal didn't deserve."

Red flinched. She had seen Michael's power. He'd frightened her more than any creature she'd encountered thus far. What could Roark have done to him—short of killing him—that could keep him down?

"He's been with you for a long time," she said. "Always doing your bidding and cleaning up your messes."

"You mean he's been spying on me for years," Roark ground out between clenched teeth.

"He's been loyal to you. More loyal than you deserve."

Roark snorted, then picked up his pace. Red trotted to keep up. "You don't know a thing about loyalty. Your mind is muddled from spending so much time around the creatures." So he didn't know about her yet. He thought she was a pureblood. Red tucked the information away. "You want to know the truth about Michael Travers? Well I'll tell you," he said, not waiting for her to answer. "He drinks people's blood. I saw it with my own eyes. It was disgusting. Inhuman. Vile. The man's a monster and I would've had him killed long ago had I known."

"He's not the monster," Red said. "You are."

Roark's elbow shot out, catching her just below the ribs. Red's breath rushed out in a whoosh as she doubled over. He jerked her upright as she gasped for air.

"Come on, my dear. You don't want to keep Morgan waiting." Roark pulled her through a side door that didn't seem to be in use. He walked her down a hall, then made an abrupt right-hand turn into a stairwell she hadn't seen. The stairs were dark and the air stank from disuse. He led her down at least four flights. Red kept count. The sound of their breathing muted suddenly.

Red wished she could knock on the walls to test their solidity. The stairs stopped abruptly. It was darker here, but Red had little trouble seeing. The hall was filled with discarded office items, some dating from the twenty-first century.

"Where are we?" she asked, looking around. Few doors dotted the area and the ones that did appeared rusted shut.

"Your new home," he said cheerfully, yanking the cloak off her.

Red tried to break free, struggling in his grasp. He was stronger than he appeared. Roark tightened his grip until pain shot through her arm.

"Don't make this any harder than it needs to be."

"Harder for whom? I'm surprised you're willing to get your hands dirty," she said, trying to get him angry so he'd slip up.

"I made a mistake. I trusted an animal to do a man's job. If you want something done right, as the saying goes."

They reached the end of the hall and Roark raised his palm to the door. The panel didn't look like any Red had seen before, which meant it had probably been custom made for him. That would make using it later impossible. She'd have to break it when she made her escape.

The door opened, revealing a tiny room with a single cell against the far wall. Shadows crept in from all sides swallowing the contents. Red squinted. Then she saw the outline of a man. He groaned and her eyes widened. "Morgan?"

His head rose with effort and he stared at her, his amber eyes glowing in the dim light from the hallway. "Gina? Is it really you?"

"Yes, I'm here." Red tried to rush forward, but Roark held her back. The second she stepped over the threshold, the smell hit her and she gagged.

"Not so fast," he said. "You'll be joining him soon enough."

She spun to face Roark. "I can't believe you've had him all along. What have you done to him?"

"You'll see. While the world searches for the elusive fugitives, I'll know they're safe and sound in my prison." Roark walked her over to the cell and opened the door. It creaked on its hinges. He leaned down and grabbed an ankle shackle, clamping it on her. He undid her wrist bindings and quickly backed away before she could strike. "Enjoy your reunion. It shall be short-lived." Roark locked the cell and left the room without a backward glance.

Red turned to Morgan. His face was bruised and swollen, gaunt from lack of food and water. How long had it been since Roark had fed him? His clothes were soiled. She could see sores on his wrists. She tried to reach for him, but her fingers could only brush the tips of his.

"You shouldn't have come here," he said, through chapped, split lips.

Red glanced at the closed door. "I wasn't given much of a choice. He came after me in Nuria and brought the tactical team with him."

"Your grandfather?"

"No, my grandfather wasn't allowed to come because of the conflict of interest. They'd posted my picture all over the viewers, claiming I was an accomplice and wanted for questioning in your escape."

Morgan shook his head. "As you can see, I didn't get very far," he said, giving a painful laugh. "Not that I tried."

"Why didn't you shift? You could've at least healed your wounds so you could escape."

"He has the place under electronic surveillance. He vowed to broadcast the vid-clip if I shifted. It would play right into his plans to expose the Others. I couldn't do that. The whole is worth more than a single individual."

Red swallowed hard as the full import of their situation hit her. "Not to me," she whispered.

"Is Nuria okay?" he asked, tilting his head to look at her.

"It's safe for now. My grandfather had Rita broadcast my apprehension, so Roark couldn't massacre the town like he'd planned." Red choked on the name of her navcom.

Morgan's gaze sharpened, despite the pain he was in. "What happened?"

Red shook her head. "It's nothing. I'm just being silly."

"Gina, tell me."

"Roark destroyed Rita. Stomped the life right out of her. I couldn't do anything but watch." She laughed to hide her sob.

His features softened. "I'm sorry," he said. "I know how much she meant to you. I'm sorry for everything."

"It's not your fault," she said quietly.

"Yes, it is. If I hadn't gone off after my family, we wouldn't be in this mess."

"Roark was determined to get us one way or another. If this ploy hadn't worked, then he would've used another. I should've killed him when I had the chance." Something squished under her toes and she grimaced.

"We both should have," he said.

"Where's Michael?" she asked, hoping that he might still be around, despite Roark's claims.

Morgan shook his head and groaned. "I don't know exactly what's been done to him. I heard screams. It sounded like he was being tortured. Roark is carrying around some kind of device in his pocket that messes with an A.I. chip he's implanted in Michael's head."

"Oh, God, that must have been what Raphael sensed."

"What do you mean?" he asked, trying to face her.

"Raphael came to me and said something was wrong with his brother. He was concerned, but there were more pressing things to take care of. He must have felt Michael's pain when Roark implanted the chip. I should've told him to go find out."

"It wouldn't have done any good. If anything, it would've gotten Raphael killed." He shifted and the chains holding him squeaked.

"Why?" she asked. "I don't think Michael would kill his own brother. Not after so many years apart."

"Roark claims he can control Michael's actions. If that's true, he wouldn't have a choice."

Red's eyes widened. "Pray that he's wrong." She tried to imagine Michael's power turned into a weapon. Red trembled at the thought.

"It could all be a lie. Like everything else," Morgan said.

"Or it could be the truth. In which case, Roark now controls the ultimate weapon."

chapter twenty-three

Raphael left the dissecting lab with the Catherine in tow. He wasn't sure exactly what he was going to do with her. It wasn't as if he could keep her here for long. Part of him knew he should kill her and be done with it, but he couldn't ignore the pull he felt toward her. He also couldn't ignore the fact that the woman had been drugged.

She might continue to be drugged if she returned to IPTT headquarters. Roark had gotten to her once, he could get to her again. He had no doubt Roark was behind the drugging. He was the only one ballsy enough to use a drug that had been outlawed. Raphael looked at Catherine. She was small, but far from defenseless. Yet even she wouldn't be able to resist the effects of influ-gas for long.

She'd been lucky that he'd been able to detect it in her bloodstream. Had he not, he would have killed her instantly for what she'd done to Red. Even now, Raphael didn't know how deep she was into this conspiracy. But he would find out, no matter how many days it took to get her to remember.

Raphael led her to the share space after collecting her weapon. He kept a firm grip on her because he didn't trust her to go quietly.

"Who are you? Where are you taking me?" she asked.

"Back to the scene of the crime," he said, daring her to deny his claims. "You may call me Raphael."

He pushed against the back door and waited for it to open. Raphael stepped inside and listened. Other than the drone of the water pump, he couldn't hear anything.

"Come," he said, pulling her inside. He walked her up the stairs past Red's room to a door at the end of the hall. He hadn't stayed here in over a month. Hadn't wanted to once Red moved in. He pressed his palm to the scanner. A second later the door slid open, revealing a heavily shaded burgundy-colored room with a cleansing unit attached.

It felt good to get out of the sun. The salve he'd put on earlier was starting to wear off. He could already feel the blisters rising on his skin.

Raphael shoved Catherine onto the rest pad. "Stay," he said, shutting the door behind him. He blocked her view and quickly keyed in a code that would lock the door and prevent her from opening it. He turned back and crossed the room to the lone chair that sat against a small desk. Raphael pulled it out and slammed it onto the floor in the middle of the room. "Sit," he said.

"I'm not your synth-pet," she growled.

"I said sit!"

Catherine rose slowly from the rest pad, her eyes wary as she made her way to the chair. "What are you going to do?"

"Torture you." Raphael purposely let her think of the worst possible scenario. But there were many types of torture. Not all required pain. What he had in mind might hurt her pride but it wouldn't bruise her body. He reached into a drawer and pulled out several scarves he used when the mood struck him and the bed sport turned kinky. "I'm going to get answers. It would help if you cooperated, but it's not entirely necessary."

"What are those for?" She pointed at the scarves obviously expecting to see something else.

He hid his smile. "They will ensure I have your undivided attention."

Catherine shook her head. "I'm not going to just let you tie me up." She took a fighting stance.

"Have it your way," he said, moving so fast she couldn't track his movements. Raphael was upon her before she had a chance to blink.

She squealed and began to struggle. Raphael managed to slip one scarf over her wrist and tighten it, then he lifted her off her feet. Catherine kicked out and connected with his knee. He grunted, letting her know she'd hurt him, but kept walking until he reached the chair. Raphael dropped her onto the seat and then quickly looped the other end of the scarf around the chair, effectively shackling her.

"Let me go, damn it." Catherine yanked at the scarf, but only succeeded in tightening the knots.

He reached for her feet and she kicked at him. This time he was ready for her. Raphael caught both of her feet and quickly unlaced her boots. He yanked them off, along with her socks, then moved to the belt at her waist.

"W-what are you doing?" she gasped, trying to hold onto her pants with one hand and get free with the other.

"Making it so it will be easier to question you. I find that nudity stops most physical fights." He continued to strip her. Within a couple of minutes she was naked, with her arms and legs bound to the chair.

Catherine's breath was coming out in billowy gasps. Her legs were spread, exposing her sex—thanks to her ankles being tied to the chair. She'd never been so humiliated and regrettably turned-on in all her life.

"I demand you release me this instant. You've violated at least three laws that I can think of off the top of my head."

Raphael looked at her askance. "More like four, but who's

counting? Now, let's get down to business. How long have you been working for Roark Montgomery?"

"I don't work for Roark. I'm a tactical team member." Catherine spouted off her identification chip numbers just like she'd been taught to do in training.

He shook his head, his disappointment clear. "Please don't lie. It's unbecoming in one as lovely as you."

"I'm telling the truth," she said. It hit her a second later that he'd called her lovely. She'd been called many things over the years, but lovely wasn't one of them.

"No." He shook his head. "You're not."

Raphael undid the buttons at his wrists and rolled up his sleeves, exposing pale, muscled forearms, dusted with a sprinkling of dark hair. His movements were exact and prac- ticed, almost sensual in the ease with which his fingers folded the fabric. She wondered if those hands would be as demand- ing on a woman's body. A hot flush covered her cheeks and Catherine forced her gaze back to his face.

Raphael appeared focused on what he was doing, but she didn't miss the quick glances he made at her breasts. He might be fierce and relentless, but he wasn't entirely unaf- fected by her nudity. Catherine hoped that would be enough to keep her alive. She forced herself to relax.

"Now, I'm going to ask you once more, how long have you been working for Roark? If you lie again, I'll have to come up with a suitable punishment." His gaze raked her and despite her fear, Catherine felt her nipples harden.

Raphael's eyes locked onto the jutting peaks and hunger flared in his dark depths. Catherine's breast grew heavy and heat swept her body. She swallowed hard.

"I don't work for Roark. I only met him a few weeks ago."

Raphael looked at her. "I should tell you now I'm able to sense when you're lying. The statement you just made is both the truth and a lie," he said matter-of-factly. "The question is which is which?"

She scowled. "I am not lying. Roark called me and Lieutenant Bannon in to work security for some upcoming appearances. Nothing was ever finalized. I haven't spoken to him since."

He stepped forward and her breath caught.

"You have to believe me." She shrunk back in the chair and braced for a blow that never came.

Raphael did believe her. He could smell the truth oozing out of her pores. He could also smell the lush wetness emanating from her spread legs. If the light was brighter in this room, he had no doubt he'd see her glistening. He turned away, trying to gain control of his needs, his hungers. Raphael licked his lips and rolled his shoulders. He took a deep breath, then turned back to face her.

The visual impact of her naked body hit him in the gut, nearly knocking the breath out of him. She was all rounded curves and hidden valleys. The fact that she was bound and defenseless made her even more appealing. He felt himself harden under her perusal.

"W-Why . . ." his voice rasped. He cleared his throat and tried again. "Why would Roark want you to work security? As a private in IPTT, you hardly have the experience to take on such a job."

She shifted and tried to close her legs. The scarves wouldn't allow it, so she stopped and straightened. "He said it was for show. Something about letting people know he could relate to the commoners, too." Catherine shrugged.

"Don't you think that seems odd?" he asked, stepping closer, despite the warning going off in his head. Her powerful gift hit him with gale force and he swayed. Raphael shook his head to clear it.

"Roark's request might be a little strange, but as you can tell I'm certainly capable of doing the job," she said, jutting her chin out. "Besides, I'm not in the position to question orders. I'm still on probation."

"I thought you said you didn't answer to Roark." Raphael dropped to his knees in front of her and her eyes widened.

"I don't. What are you doing?" she asked, scooting her bottom back. She didn't get far, a scant half inch at most.

"I need to make sure you aren't lying. Your story seems to change every time I ask you a question."

She squeaked in alarm. "You said you could tell whether I was lying by sensing it or something."

Raphael grinned. "That's correct, but it's not the only way to uncover the truth." He licked his lips. "Your powers might be so great they can mask the truth. I have to be sure." He reached out and skimmed a finger over her collarbone, following the graceful slope to the soft mounds of her breasts.

Catherine shuddered, but it wasn't out of fear. She was painfully aroused. Gooseflesh rose on her arms and over her body. She watched a smile ghost his sensual lips before he suppressed it. His cool fingers glided down between the peaks of her breasts and her breath caught in anticipation. Would he touch her? Did she want him to? Her body certainly did, if her hard nipples and the moisture pooling between her legs were any indication.

She knew she should be fighting him. At least putting up a pretense of a struggle. So what if he kissed like a bandit. This man was the enemy. At the very least, Raphael had kidnapped her and kept her here against her will. She didn't want to even think about the fact he'd bit her or that she'd found it pleasurable after the initial pain. And it had been pleasurable. She'd nearly come apart in his arms.

Catherine watched him kneel before her and her breath stuttered. There was something darkly menacing about him, in stark contrast to his pale skin and gentle caresses. His black eyes shimmered like mercury, always moving, missing nothing.

"They say truth has a distinctive taste. Only one way to find out." He moved closer, his hot breath fanning over her flushed skin.

She quivered in anticipation. Heaven help her. She wanted him. Wanted what he offered, even if it was in the guise of seeking information. His head dipped and his mouth latched onto her aching breast, while his hand closed over the other.

Catherine arched as his tongue swirled over her pebbled flesh, teasing it with consummate skill. She felt the brush of his fangs. One wrong move and he'd slice her open, but he was careful and oh-so thorough as he sucked and worried her engorged nipple. Catherine closed her eyes and groaned. "W-what are you doing?"

He released her with a slight pop. "I would think that would be obvious," Raphael said, stroking a nail over her other nipple. It immediately sprang to life. "You have magnificent breasts," he said. "So lush and full. A man could happily feast upon them for days."

"This is wrong," she gasped as he pinched her.

"It doesn't feel that way to me." His mouth moved soothingly, easing the sting. Raphael was doing things she'd only read about in e-books. He clamped down and Catherine moaned, struggling to get closer.

She had to stop him. This had gone too far. She was losing her ability to reason. "Please," Catherine begged, not sure what she was asking for.

"Please what?" he asked, making his way down to her stomach with gentle kisses. His soft hair brushed her flesh, heightening her awareness.

Catherine's thighs quivered as he neared her navel. His tongue made lazy circles around it, teasing the edges, but not quite dipping inside. By the time he entered the shallow indent, her hips were moving restlessly of their own volition.

The ache coming from deep inside her was gathering force. Soon it would be too late.

"I can't," she said, trying to clear her mind, but it was impossible. Catherine didn't want to climax. Not this way. Not for him. He had enough power over her. Yet, her thoughts refused to leave his talented mouth as he tongued her navel. She gripped the arms of the chair until her knuckles turned white.

"No one is forcing you to do anything," he said, nibbling on her ribs. "We're just having a conversation."

They were talking? Talking about what? For the life of her, Catherine couldn't remember. His hands latched onto her calves and he began to knead his way up her legs. His thumbs neared the apex of her pleasure, but didn't go any further.

Catherine braced herself, the nerves in her body hypersensitive. He was so close. She wanted him to stop—and she desperately needed him to keep going. Her clit throbbed, keeping time with his kisses. He was back to lavishing her breasts with attention. Was it possible to orgasm from that alone? Catherine hadn't thought so before, but now she wasn't sure. If this was his idea of torture, she couldn't imagine what it would be like if he loved a woman.

Her head dropped back and her jaw clenched as she reached for completion. It remained elusive, balancing on an edge she couldn't tip. Catherine growled in frustration when she realized she wouldn't get there without him. And she knew by the lazy way he was teasing her breasts that he wasn't about to go any further unless she asked.

She looked at the top of his dark head. He was watching her through his long lashes, a smile playing on his sensual lips. He flicked his tongue over her flesh and Catherine felt fire shoot through her veins. She mewed as her body demanded release.

"You bastard," she ground out.

His lips twitched in amusement. "I've been called far worse."

"Why can't you—" She couldn't do it. Catherine couldn't bring herself to ask for what she wanted—no, *needed*. It would mean that he'd won. And she couldn't stand the thought of that. He continued his sensual assault. Her body's demands grew louder. "Raphael, please," she grit between clenched teeth.

He arched an insolent brow, refusing to make it easy on her. "What do you want, little storm?"

"You know damn well what I want," she said, as a second wave of power rushed out of her. "And don't call me little storm." It sounded too much like an endearment. "My name is Catherine. If you can't remember that, then call me Chaos."

Raphael held onto her, his mouth teasing her already aroused flesh. He was so hard he'd passed the point of pain. He wanted to fuck her so badly he could taste it, but he wasn't about to do that without her permission. He may be many things, but he wasn't a rapist.

"I'm afraid you'll have to spell it out," he said, hoping she gave in soon for both their sakes. He could walk away if she said no, but it would cost him.

"I need you to . . ." she said, her words trailing off. "I need you."

"For what?"

She growled in frustration and slammed her fists onto the chair. "Do I really have to say it?"

"Afraid so," he said, nipping the inside of her firm thigh.

"This sucks! I know I'm going to regret this," Catherine said.

Raphael stopped what he was doing and looked at her. Her freckled skin was flushed a lovely shade of pink to match her upturned nipples. Her feminine musk filled the air as her body wept for his. "I have no doubt we both will," he said, in complete honesty.

"Let's fuck and get it over with," she growled. The command had come out like sex was some kind of brisk chore to be ticked off a list.

Raphael frowned, then he leveled her with a sharp gaze. "I do many things in a hurry, but *fucking* is not one of them. If that's what you want, then I'll just untie you now."

"That's—"

He held up a hand to cut her off. "Think carefully about your next words because if you agree to my terms, you'll be here for the night. I plan to take my time with you."

Raphael could see reason warring with her need. She wanted to tell him to go to hell. Part of him hoped she did. Sleeping with her was the last thing he should be doing, considering he might have to kill her later. But that didn't stop his body from pressing its own demands. He wanted her. Wanted to feel the soft wetness of her surrounding his cock, milking him. Wanted to feel her body's firm grip as he pulled out of her seconds before plunging back in. Wanted to taste her sweet blood as she climaxed again and again.

Aroused, she smelled so deliciously fragrant that his head spun. It affected him more than her power ever could. He inhaled and closed his eyes to heighten his senses. Need hit so savagely he nearly quaked.

"I want to stay," Catherine said quietly.

"It's about time," he said.

She glared at him. "Shut up before I change my mind."

Raphael hid his victorious smile behind a groan and dipped his head between her lush thighs.

chapter twenty-four

Catherine writhed in the chair, her hard nipples stabbing the air as he feasted upon her. His lips locked onto her clit and began to suck, worrying the sensitive nub with his teeth and tongue, continuing to build pressure. She'd tried watching him for a while, but her eyelids drooped, heavy with desire. He continued to stroke and suckle until the pressure inside her became too much. She screamed as the dam broke, sending ripples of pleasure rolling through her.

Raphael continued to feast upon her fevered flesh as Catherine attempted to catch her breath. He was having none of it. He quickly stood and stripped off his shirt and shoes. At the last moment, he dropped his pants, and her mouth fell open. She'd read stories about well-endowed men, but she'd never seen one in the flesh until now. She'd obviously been missing out.

Catherine was far from a virgin, but even so, she found Raphael's cock intimidating.

"What's the matter, little storm? You act as if you've never seen a naked man before," he said, a teasing glint in his eyes.

She gulped and forced her gaze away. "Not like that," she said.

Raphael threw his head back and laughed. "It's nice to know I finally made an impression on you."

He made quick work of her ties, then picked her up and carried her to the rest pad. Despite his obvious need, he laid her down gently. Raphael slid in beside her. "Now where was I?" he asked before going back to arousing her.

Catherine didn't think she had another orgasm in her after the last one, but she was wrong. Raphael was patient and thorough, demanding a response from her sated flesh. He brought her back to life in a matter of minutes and left her teetering on the brink of insanity.

"This time I want to be inside of you when you come," he said, kneeing her legs apart until she opened before him in offering.

The weight of his body felt good upon her, cooling her fevered flesh. His skin held a spicy scent, but was surprisingly soft beneath her fingertips. Catherine didn't know what she'd been expecting. It's not like she'd ever slept with a vampire before. And she had no doubt he was a vampire, after the fanging she'd received a few hours ago. She knew the Others were real, but she hadn't believed that vampires existed before today.

She did now.

Catherine felt his cock kiss her opening and tensed.

"Relax," he said, stroking the side of her face.

"That's easy for you to say. I'm not trying to put that thing inside of you."

He chuckled. "I promise I'll go slow," he said, nudging her.

She was wet from his ministrations and the head of his cock slid into her easily, despite her earlier reservations.

Raphael's smile faded and sweat trickled down the side of his face. His jaw clenched as he slowly worked his way deeper. She was small. Smaller than anyone he'd ever been with. He knew he would fit, but it wouldn't happen without some pain. He kissed her cheek, working his way to her ear. There he nuzzled and licked, teasing her lobe until she squirmed beneath him. Her movements caused him to slip in a few inches more.

She gasped.

"I'm sorry. I am going as slow as I can. If it's any consolation, it pains me, too." He rocked his hips gently, waiting for her body to adjust. She was so tight Raphael thought he'd scream from the sensation or go mad before he could bury himself to the hilt.

She canted her pelvis and he slid in further. Nearly there. Just a few more inches. Raphael bit the inside of his mouth and tasted blood. Sweat dripped from his face and landed on her voluptuous breasts. He watched the pulse jump in her throat, daring him to taste her once more. He closed his eyes for a second to resist the temptation.

Her fingers stroked down his sides until they reached his lower back. There, she sank her short fingernails in deep. "Yes," he hissed and pulled back a second before plunging all the way inside of her. Catherine gasped, then whimpered as he pierced her tender flesh. "I'm afraid I lost control for a moment. Pain and pleasure go hand in hand in my world." Raphael held himself perfectly still, his body throbbing with the need to thrust.

"It's all right. It doesn't hurt anymore."

When he finally felt her relax, he began to move. The heat of her was pure torture as his hips rocked, setting a rhythm as old as the ages. She stayed still for a few moments, but eventually rose to meet him. Her fingers bit deep again and Raphael relished the pain. It spurred him on. Urged him to take all she had to offer and then some.

Her soft murmurs grew to loud moans as she neared orgasm. He reached between their bodies and found her hidden flesh, then stroked it repeatedly with his thumbnail. Catherine cried out, her body engulfing him in a viselike grip, which in turn sent him over the edge.

Raphael's vision dimmed and he instinctively bit down.

Her coppery blood filled his mouth as he emptied himself into her willing body. Two things became readily apparent in that moment. One, once with this woman would never be enough. And two, he'd been a fool to think he could ever harm her.

Somewhere between their fight and his search for the truth, Raphael had found something he'd dared not believe exist. He'd found home in the guise of an enemy he could not afford to trust. What in the hell had he done?

They spent the rest of the night making love. Raphael would like to believe it was just sex, but he wasn't the type to delude himself. He recognized it for what it was, even if he didn't like it. Now that the pleasure was drawing to an end, it was time to get back to work. He ran his fingertips over her bare flesh, noting every freckle as he relished her softness. Raphael forced himself to release her. He rose and dressed quickly after showering, then urged her to do the same.

"Come on, we need to go to the sheriff's station."

"Why? I thought after last night you'd let me go." She stared at the rug, toeing it with her boot. "Are you going to turn me in?"

"I haven't decided yet. Now come," he said, moving to the door. "We have to uncover the rest of Roark's plans."

Raphael heard Maggie before they reached the entrance to the station.

"I don't know where she is, Commander. Roark sent out a broadcast claiming she escaped en route. The shuttle he took is ruined. I've seen the images Roark supplied. There's a hole in the side of it. Looks like it was hit by a cannon blast." She paused, listening.

Raphael couldn't hear what the commander was saying, but he could imagine. Maggie continued talking, but he didn't bother to listen further. He'd heard what he needed to hear. Roark hadn't made it to the IPTT detention center, which meant he'd had other plans all along.

There was no way that Red had escaped as he claimed or she would've come back here. She would have contacted him, if she were able. The fact that she hadn't meant she was far away. Too far to reach him, or she was dead. Raphael dismissed the latter option, refusing to accept the possibility. He'd know if she'd died, which meant he needed to find her.

He tried mentally contacting his brother once more, since distance didn't seem to affect their bond. *Michael, I need your help.*

Silence met him.

Raphael tried again. *Michael, can you hear me?*

Stay away, Michael slammed the thought into Raphael's mind, causing pain to reverberate through his skull. He brought a hand to his head. *Or they'll get you, too.*

Who are they? Raphael frowned.

The shadow people, Michael hissed the words. *They're everywhere. I can't keep them away.*

Raphael shuddered at the madness he heard in his brother's tortured voice. What had Roark done to him? Newfound fear blossomed inside of him, spreading like a weed over his soul. If Roark could do that to his brother, what would he do to Red now that he had his hands on her?

"There's been a change of plans," he said to Catherine, leading her away from the sheriff's station. He needed to find the new recruits.

"We can't just leave her," Takeo said to Demery and Juan in frustration. His hands balled into fists. He needed to hit something or someone. He turned and punched the column closest to him. It bowed under the impact. He shook out his fist, preparing to strike it again.

"We aren't leaving anyone, so calm down," Juan said. "But we can't rush in without a plan. We're outmanned. And we don't even know where they've taken her. Hell, they're claiming she's escaped."

"That's bullshit! She hasn't escaped. She's not the type to cut and run. Yesterday she faced down the tactical team. Someone who'd do that isn't likely to run away."

Demery grinned. "Leave finding her to me. She isn't blocking herself like the killer did when I tried to find them. It should be a piece of cake." He rubbed his gloved hands together.

"What if Roark has a way of blocking her location?" Takeo asked, pacing back and forth.

"He can't, mon. I would still be able to find her. Artificial blocking aids don't work against my abilities."

"But you said the killer blocked you," Juan said. "Maybe you're not as strong as you think."

"That was different. The killer wasn't using artificial means to block me. It was natural talent," Demery said.

"So he's an Other?" Takeo asked. "Wait until I get my hands on him."

"Don't know what he is, mon. Couldn't tell, which is odd, but he's definitely powerful if he can easily block me."

Raphael strolled into the room with Catherine by his side. All three recruits stiffened at seeing her.

"Isn't she the one we saw taking orders from Roark yesterday?" Takeo asked, his contempt evident.

"Yes," Raphael said.

"What is she doing here?" Takeo asked, staring daggers into the woman.

"Catherine's going to help us rescue Red."

"Call me Chaos," she said. "Everyone does."

"Don't you think she's a little on the small side?" Takeo asked, ignoring what she'd said. "Not to mention the wrong side of this equation. Seems to me the tactical team is part of the problem, or hadn't you noticed?"

"We can't trust her, mon," Demery said, shaking his head. "She's the enemy."

Raphael smiled, flashing his fangs. "We can now," he said.

The three men realized instantly what Raphael meant.

"Are you sure?" Juan asked. "I'd hate for you to be wrong and get us all killed."

Demery and Takeo turned to Juan. "There's no ignoring the bite, although I'd feel better if Demery and I bit her, too," Takeo said.

"Yeah, mon. At least we'd know what she was thinking then. Can't be too careful."

Raphael hissed in warning. "That's not going to happen," he said, pulling Catherine behind him. He'd never been territorial when it came to women, but she brought out the beast in him. His actions were met with three sets of raised brows. But Raphael was in no mood to explain himself. "I will take responsibility for her," he said, hoping that wasn't the wrong thing to do. What was he thinking? *Of course* it was the wrong thing to do, but he couldn't stop himself. He wasn't about to let the two men bite Catherine. She was his.

"You picked a fine time to become blood whipped," Takeo said, shaking his head in disgust. "I'm telling you now she makes one wrong move and we're fanging her."

The men would die trying, Raphael mused before reining in his wayward thoughts.

"How can she help?" Juan asked.

"I believe a demonstration is in order," Raphael said, pulling her out from behind him. "My dear, if you don't mind. Gentleman, feel free to threaten her."

Catherine took a hesitant step forward, her limbs trembling beneath her uniform. As soon as she reached the center of the room, the three men stepped forward, forming a tight circle around her. She closed her eyes. Raphael felt her power flow, washing over the recruits. Now that he'd taken her blood, it had little effect on him. Too bad he couldn't say the same about her.

The three men swayed on their feet. Juan dropped to one knee. She slipped away easily to rejoin Raphael. The recruits blinked several times and looked around in confusion.

"What the hell?" Takeo said, shaking his head to clear it. "What were we doing?" he asked.

"I don't remember," Juan said. He stood and reached for a nearby column to steady himself.

"Neither do I," Demery added.

Raphael waited for the men to notice them standing near the doorway. His arms were crossed and he didn't bother to hide his amused smile. "Gentlemen," he said, drawing their attention to him.

"What are you doing here?" Takeo asked, stepping forward. Aggression marked his flawless features.

Demery hissed at him from behind his protective mask.

"Enough with the theatrics. I've been here the whole time. Don't you remember?" he asked.

The men shook their heads again and frowned.

"My thoughts don't make sense," Juan said. "They're jumbled along with my psychic gift."

"Neither do mine," Demery added. "The last thing I remember is—" He clutched his temple and a vein popped out on his forehead.

"What did you do to us?" Takeo glared at Raphael.

"It wasn't me," he said. "I'd like you to meet Catherine Meyers. She has an interesting ability that will come in handy, when we find Red."

"She did this to us?" Juan gasped. "How?" His dark eyes narrowed in suspicion. "And why aren't you affected?"

"I'm not letting anyone fuck with my head." Takeo rushed forward to grab her.

Raphael pulled her out of the way, shoving her behind him. The move was revealing. "I wouldn't if I were you," he said in warning. "It does affect me just not in the same way."

"What kind of game are you playing, vamp?" Takeo asked.

"No game," Raphael said, shaking his head. "I'm quite serious. You touch her. You die."

"We can't trust her, especially if she has the ability to

leave us confused. What if she does that when we're looking for Red?" Demery asked.

"Yeah," Takeo added. "She could lead us right to slaugh-
ter and there wouldn't be a damn thing we could do about it."

"She won't do that," Raphael said.

"You can't know that for sure," Juan countered.

"Yes, I can," Raphael said softly. His gaze slid over her.

Takeo crossed his arms over his chest mirroring Raphael's
stance. "How can you be certain?"

"Because if she does, I'll kill her."

Catherine blanched. His cold stark words were in direct
contrast to his heated glances. How had she gotten herself
into this mess? She was still having a hard time processing
all that had happened. How could she have killed two people without knowing it?

Raphael had said she'd been drugged. Had Roark done
that when she and Bannon went to visit him? If so, had Bannon been drugged, too, or was she the "lucky" one? Catherine hadn't noticed any changes in his behavior, but she hadn't
noticed any changes in hers either. Roark was good. She'd
give him that. She'd always been so careful about showing
her power. Using it only when she needed it. Catherine had
thought she had hid it well. Yet this vampire had swept in and
uncovered the truth with an ease that left her head spinning.

She might have fucked Raphael, but she didn't trust him.
Catherine still couldn't believe she'd done that. Even now
she could feel the impression of his hands on her body, the
tiny brands his fingertips had burned into her flesh.

She looked around at the four men. Each was so different
from the other. Yet they all had an element of danger to
them. It was not only in their eyes, but in their stances as well.
They didn't trust her. The feeling was mutual. They were
monsters, even though they didn't look it from the outside.

Monsters that until yesterday she'd believed were more myth than anything.

Even now, she could see the hate in the exotic man's amber gaze. He would like nothing more than to tear her apart. Not that she could really blame him, if she'd done everything her seducer had claimed. As much as she didn't want to believe Raphael, something told her he was telling the truth. Catherine swallowed the bile threatening to choke her.

Why had she told the tactical team to leave her? Because Raphael asked? Ridiculous. She'd simply been in fear for her life. And the danger wasn't over yet. Catherine thought about calling the commander to throw herself on his mercy, but she didn't think Raphael would allow it. At least not yet. No, he had plans for her. Plans that sounded quite illegal.

She looked around and quivered. There'd be no escaping these men. Not now. Maybe never.

chapter twenty-five

Red glanced at Morgan. He'd passed out thirty minutes ago and she hadn't been able to revive him. His stomach was concave, but soon it would bloat from lack of food and water.

"Roark!" she shouted. "Roark, I know you can hear me. Morgan needs food and water or he'll die." She choked on the last word, fear beating at her. "Roark! Damn you!"

Red pulled at the chain around her ankle. It wouldn't budge. She examined the wall, pressing in various places to test its strength. It was slick, but solid, like the shackle imprisoning her.

The door opened. She stilled, expecting to see Roark. Hope blossomed as she recognized the man in the doorway. "Michael? Thank God you're here."

He scurried forward, carrying a tray of food and water. He opened the cage and set the tray down between them, then unlocked one of Morgan's wrists so he could reach the food.

"Michael, you have to get us out of here. Roark is going to kill us," Red said.

He didn't respond.

"Michael please."

His head slowly turned, his black eyes staring at her. The wild look in them caused Red to take a step back.

"What has he done to you?" She kept her voice low and soothing.

Michael opened his mouth to answer. A scream scorched the air where words should've been. He clutched his head, then started batting at the air.

"Keep them away," he gasped. "Don't let them get me."

Red looked beside her, trying to see what disturbed him so, but there was nothing there.

"Stay away," he said.

Michael's power slammed her into the cell wall, knocking the air out of her lungs as it lifted her off the ground. He continued swatting at invisible enemies, while his power held her long enough for him to back out of the cage and lock it behind him. He scrambled out the door, clawing at the walls like a trapped beast who'd tasted freedom but had it taken away. The second he was out of sight, Red dropped to the ground with a thud.

She struggled to her feet. "What have you done to him, you bastard?"

Roark's disembodied voice came out of a hidden speaker in the wall. "Watch your tongue or you'll end up just like him."

Red shuddered. She had to find a way out of here. She wouldn't end up like Michael. She'd die before she'd let that happen. She turned back to Morgan, who was starting to rouse now that his wrist was free.

"You have to eat," she said. "There's water on the tray, too. Can you hold it?"

He moaned when he tried to reach the water. His hand dropped as if the effort were too great.

"Morgan, I need you to eat so that you can get your strength back. We are going to get out of here."

His amber eyes flickered open and he looked at her.

"That's better," Red said. "Now drink the water slowly. You can't afford to throw it up. This may be all we get."

Morgan nodded and reached for the canteen again. This time he grasped it. He put it to his mouth and removed the cap with his teeth, then poured some of the liquid into his mouth. Morgan swallowed, choking.

"Have a little more," Red said. She didn't need much. It was more important that he hydrate. He'd gone without far longer than she.

"You need some," Morgan croaked.

"I will once you've drunk your fill. Make sure you get some of the food on the tray."

"I know what you're doing," he said.

Red smiled. "Yeah, I'm saving your life."

He flashed a half-grin back at her, then winced as his lip split. "I can't believe I was stupid enough to fall for his ploy."

"You weren't being stupid. You thought you were protecting your family. No one can fault you for that."

"You can. And you *should*," he said, placing the canteen on the tray so that she could reach it.

Red picked it up and shook it. There wasn't much left, but that was okay. She didn't need much. She'd done survival training with the tactical team. She could go for a long time without food or water. She placed her lips on the cap and tipped it up. The liquid was warm, but she didn't care. Red swallowed it, then put the canteen back on the tray.

"He only gave us these supplies so he could play with us longer," Morgan said. "You do know that, right?"

Red had suspected Roark hadn't given them the food and water to be humane. It didn't matter what his reasons were. All she was concerned about was their survival. And they couldn't survive without the basics.

"Yes, I know," she said. "And I don't care."

"You seem awfully calm about the situation." He slowly looked around the room.

"I'm not, but panicking won't help. It's better to focus, to think."

Morgan shook his head and reached for some food. "There's no way out of this place. I've examined every inch."

"You might have missed something," Red said. "Lack of food and water can leave you sluggish."

"I didn't. Believe me. I've had more time to study it," he said, scowling.

"We're belowground. Four floors if I counted right," she said. "Only two of the floors had doors opening onto them. My guess is that two are aboveground and two are below."

"That makes getting out of here even harder," he said.

"Maybe," she said. "Maybe not."

"What do you mean?"

"People know that I'm missing. Someone will come looking for me." Red thought about Raphael's promise.

"They think you escaped," he reminded her.

"Some will believe that. My grandfather won't. And neither will a few people in Nuria. All we have to do is survive long enough for them to find us."

"Roark isn't going to let them find us. He can't afford to have any witnesses. I told you about Michael."

Red sobered as she thought about Michael Travers. "I've seen him. You're right. I don't know what Roark's done to him, but he's not the same man that we met." She pictured Raphael and sadness welled inside of her. Michael was his only family.

Red twisted the chain that secured her to the wall.

"What are you doing?" Morgan asked.

"Testing it for weaknesses. Sometimes all you need to break one of these things is a little leverage."

The chain clanked as she wound it around and around.

"Be careful," Morgan said. His hands weren't shaking as bad now that he'd had some food. And he seemed more alert than he had been an hour ago.

"You should eat more," she said, her attention going back to the task at hand.

"I'm full," he said. "It's your turn to have a bite."

"I'm not hungry." Her stomach growled, making a liar out of her.

"Please have a couple of bites and a sip of water."

Red grabbed a small piece of what she assumed was synth-meat and took the canteen that Morgan offered. After a couple of sips of water, she placed it back on the tray. "I'm done. You need to have the rest. I plan to get out of here and I need you at full strength."

"We can't get out of here or he'll have the proof he needs."

"Screw his proof. Surviving is all that matters now," she said. "Hear that Roark? Fuck you!"

"I'm sorry for leaving you," Morgan said quietly.

Red stopped working the chain and looked at him. "What's done is done. Regrets are a waste of time. Right now we need to focus on the future. And that means breaking out."

"I knew that you were the right woman for me. You're strong enough to be an alpha, even without the . . ." He let the words trail off, but Red knew what he'd been about to say. The fact that she couldn't change was coming back to haunt her now more than ever.

"Is that the only reason you pursued me, because I was strong?"

He shook his head. "No, at least not after the beginning."

"Then why did you find it so easy to leave?" Red watched him carefully, since she wouldn't be able to smell any changes in him due to the eye-watering stench.

Morgan took a deep breath. "I've asked myself that same question multiple times. There are no easy answers."

She shifted until she was facing him. "I'm not looking for easy, I want the truth."

"When you came along, everything happened so fast. At first I was trying to persuade you to return to IPTT, then I didn't want you to leave. I was confused. When it turned out that Kane was involved with Roark, I was angry. Angry at Kane, but also angry at you for destroying what we had."

Red flinched, but didn't say anything.

"I thought I'd moved past my anger, but when Sarah and Joshua appeared, I realized I hadn't. I knew I needed to reconcile the past or we'd never have a future together. I'm just sorry it's taken me this long to realize how much you mean to me. I love you, Gina. And I hope it's not too late to make it up to you."

Red's head dropped and she twisted her fingers. "I've made mistakes, too," she said quietly.

"What mistakes could you have possibly made?" he asked, incredulous.

She closed her eyes unable to face his condemnation. "While you were away, Raphael and I became close."

Morgan stilled, his heart slamming against his ribs. Raphael, his friend, his nemesis, had always been competitive. Throughout the years they'd competed for jobs and women. He'd stolen Karen Martin from him. Had the vamp managed to take the one that meant more than life itself?

He growled in frustration. That was the old Morgan talking. The new Morgan would forgive her of any transgressions as long as she said she loved him. And only him.

"What do you mean by close?" Morgan asked, needing to know the truth while dreading it at the same time.

"He's one of the only ones who showed me kindness after you left. I was lonely. I needed a friend."

Morgan listened, trying to read between the lines of what she was saying. His imagination tortured him with naked images of Gina and Raphael. "How close?" he repeated, bracing for whatever she had to say and praying his heart could take it.

"I didn't sleep with him, if that's what you're asking," she said.

His body sagged in relief. It shouldn't have mattered, but it did. He needed to know he could trust her completely. That she wouldn't run off, if someone more appealing came along.

"What did happen?" he asked.

"I let him kiss me."

Morgan could live with a kiss, if it hadn't gone past that point. It hurt, but he could accept it. "It's okay," he said. "Anything else happen?"

"He bit me," she whispered.

A growl rumbled out of his chest before he could stop it. He could handle a kiss, since it was relatively innocent. A bite was another matter completely.

"Why did you allow him to bite you, Gina?" His body trembled as his mind tried to reconcile her words with the intimacy he knew occurred when an alpha male placed a bite on a female.

"He said it was necessary for my protection. You of all people should recall the benefits." she added hastily, glancing at the vid recorder tucked in the corner.

Morgan followed her gaze. "Don't worry Roark's after visual proof, not audio. Aren't you, Montgomery?" he shouted. "You know that old saying about a picture's worth." Morgan didn't want to ask, but he had to know. "Did you enjoy Raphael's bite?" He choked on the words. "I mean, did you enjoy it more than mine?"

"Why do you ask?"

Morgan hesitated, debating whether to tell her the truth, but in the end he knew he had no choice. If they were to make a go of it once they got out of this hell, they had to be honest with each other from here on out. "Because Raphael is an alpha, too."

"I thought you were the alpha," she said, her confusion clear.

"I am. That's why I've been running Nuria for so long. But there are other alphas out there. Alphas like Raphael, who have no wish to run a town or anything else. He chooses to live under me and serve when it suits him. It's an unspoken agreement that allows him to stay in Nuria when he pleases."

"I'm not sure I follow."

Morgan decided to be blunt. "You could choose to go with him, even though I put my mark on you first."

"Oh." Gina bit her lip. She remained silent in deep thought. "That's not going to happen," she said finally.

"You need to be sure," Morgan said.

"I am sure," she said.

"Why?" Morgan kept what little hope he had left tamped down.

"Because I'm not in love with Raphael," Gina said, shifting as close as she could to him. "And I told him as much."

Morgan started at her confession. "What did he say?"

"He said he understood, then let me go."

He couldn't believe Raphael had given up so easily. Morgan wouldn't have if he wanted Gina enough to try to steal her out from under him. Maybe his friend was softening in his old age. Morgan smiled at the thought.

"Thank you for telling me," he said.

"I figured since we were getting everything out in the open, full disclosure was needed."

"I love you, Gina."

"I love you, too."

"How touching," Roark said, as he walked into the room. "I'm surprised my teeth haven't rotted from listening to all this sickeningly sweet crap."

Gina and Morgan stiffened.

"I hate to break up this sappy reunion, but I thought you'd like to know I will be moving Morgan out tomorrow. I think it's best the authorities find your body quickly. We wouldn't want the animals getting to you first."

"Body?" Gina murmured.

"Yes, it's quite tragic," Roark said. "Two star-crossed lovers who in the end betray each other. Kind of like she did with Michael's brother Raphael. By the way, how does it feel to know some other guy has been sticking it to your woman, while you're off chasing your tail?"

"You bastard," Morgan snapped, yanking at his restraints.

"Are you angry enough to shift for me?" Roark taunted.

Morgan stopped at his words. "You'd like that, wouldn't you?"

Roark smiled. "I'd love it. Just the proof I'd need to present to the republics. Can you help him along, my dear?" he asked, turning to Gina. "Surely you must have learned a few tricks along the way."

Red stared at him, her body trembling in rage.

"Hmm, guess not," he said. "Looks like you only know how to spread your legs for the beast. I bet that makes you feel like a freak around them. I'm surprised they let a pureblood like you stay." He stepped closer, taunting her, but keeping just out of range. "What's the matter, bitch got your tongue?" Roark waved his hand in front of her.

Red swiped at him and missed.

"Close, but not close enough. Care to try again?" He leaned forward.

"Go to hell," she spat.

"Now why would I want to do that, when I'm so close to achieving my goals?" Roark asked, grinning like an idiot.

"This isn't over, Roark," Morgan said.

"It will be for you. Very soon." He spun on his heel and strode out of the room.

"What are we going to do?" Red asked in a whisper. Desperation clawed at her insides as she searched the same four walls for a way out.

"I don't know," he said. His head dropped back against the wall with a thump.

Red met Morgan's gaze. "I won't let him take you."

"You may not have a choice."

chapter twenty-six

Red and Morgan spent a restless night in the cell. Red couldn't stop thinking about Roark's threat. She had to do something. Even if Raphael and the new recruits were searching for her by now, they'd never get here in time. Roark would have Morgan taken out and shot somewhere in the desert. Hell, he may dump him in Nuria, so that he could go back and finish what he'd tried to start.

She knew that if their roles were reversed that's what she'd do. It bothered her that she was beginning to think like him. She'd learned to over the past couple of months. At first it had been to try to figure out what he was up to; now she needed to think ahead. Determine his next move before he made it.

Red faced the corner. Roark had set up the vid recorder close to the wall. It was trained on Morgan. She looked over her shoulder and spotted another mini-vid recorder in the wall. *Clever,* she thought. *But not clever enough.* If she angled herself right, the lens would only see her back. Roark still had no idea that she was an Other. That gave them the advantage. She hoped.

Red turned away from the vid and stilled her mind, concentrating on the wolf. It yipped excitedly. She chased it, willing it to come to her. It stayed just out of reach, shaking its black fur in her face as she pursued it. She opened her eyes and once again, a lone claw stuck out from her hand. This time it was shorter than usual. Terrific. Instead of getting better, her one ability was getting worse. She sighed, letting her forehead fall into the wall.

"Gina, are you all right?" Morgan whispered.

"I'm fine," she said, keeping her back turned until the claw receded into her hand. "I was just . . . It's not important."

Morgan twisted toward her. The chains binding him groaned. "I need you to listen to me. I don't know how much time we have before Roark comes back to get me."

Her heart thudded, pounding her chest. She wouldn't let him go. No matter what he said.

"If I don't manage to escape, I want you to call out to Raphael. I assume he showed you how to do that."

Red nodded.

"Good," Morgan said. "Call to him. I'm sure he'll hear you and come."

She shook her head. "I think he might be too far away. I've already tried."

"Try again. He'll be looking for you. I know I would be," he said with a small smile. Morgan reached out and their fingertips brushed.

"I will," she said. "But we still have time to figure a way out of here."

Morgan stared at her, his heart in his eyes. "You really are beautiful," he said softly. "Remember that I love you."

Tears blanketed her lashes, but she refused to let them fall. "I will."

"I want you to do one more thing for me," he said, watching her closely.

"What's that?" Red asked, biting her trembling lower lip. One wrong word and she'd shatter.

"I want you to give Raphael a second chance." Morgan's voice cracked.

"What?" She couldn't have heard him correctly. There was no way he'd just asked her to be with Raphael, not after everything they'd talked about.

"He's a good man. I've known him for years. He'll take care of you."

Her eyes narrowed. "I don't need anyone to take care of me. What I need is you."

Morgan's gaze was steady. "You have me. Forever. But I need you to think ahead right now. I know this conversation isn't pleasant, but these things have to be said. Raphael will come for you. And he will protect you if I'm gone. Let him."

Red shook her head in denial. He was giving up. She could hear it in his voice. "You don't know what you're asking."

"Yes." Morgan swallowed hard, as if the words were clogging his throat and he needed to clear them before he choked. "I do."

"It won't come to that." Red searched frantically for escape. She wouldn't allow it to come to that. She'd think of something. She always did.

Morgan's head shot up and his attention locked on the door. "It already has," he said as the door slid open and Roark walked in.

Red couldn't breathe. She wouldn't allow Roark to take the man she loved away from her again. She needed to keep him distracted. "Back to taunt us some more?" she asked, venom dripping from her words.

"Now, would I do that?" he asked.

She cocked a brow. "Yes, you would, because you're an asshole."

Roark laughed. "You have such a way with words. No wonder the monster likes you so much."

"You won't be laughing soon," she warned.

"Why? What are you going to do?" he asked, looking at her chains. "Oh, that's right. Nothing." Roark stepped forward, swatting at her as Red tried to get her hands on him. If she could just reach a little farther, she'd have him. But she knew that was the point. He kept himself just out of range. She tried again. As long as she continued to struggle, he wouldn't take Morgan. At least until he tired of their game.

Raphael stared at Demery. "Are you sure you can do this?"

"I can, if you shut up and let me concentrate." He shot him a dirty look through his protective suit. "I need absolute silence in order to get in the right frame of mind to remote view."

Demery went back to concentrating. It would take awhile for him to hone in on Red's location. He pictured her, then let his mind drift across the land, seeking the threads that would eventually narrow down his search.

His eyes darted side to side beneath his lids as various images flashed in his mind. Sand, lots of sand. It was too general. He focused harder, controlling his breathing within his trancelike state. Buildings popped into his mind. Too nondescript to be of help. He latched onto their cylindrical shape anyhow and pulled his mind forward for a closer look.

A building with gold lettering came into view, then stairs leading down into darkness. He saw rooms, many rooms, and then bars. Demery came out of the trance with a start and grabbed a pad of synth-paper. He started to draw everything he'd seen. After a few minutes, the shapes took form. When he was sure he had all the information down on paper, he turned and gave it to Raphael.

"Do you recognize this place?" he asked.

Raphael's lips thinned. "Yes, I do. It's Roark Montgomery's offices. Or at least the building they're housed in. I was there not long ago, visiting my brother."

Demery met his gaze. "That's where he's keeping her. She's in the dark somewhere beneath the stairs."

"Then we have no time to lose. Gather your equipment.

We leave for the Republic of Missouri within thirty minutes."

Roark had left them after an hour. He'd been called away. Had he not been, Red was convinced he would've taken Morgan and killed him. She looked around the cramped cage he kept them in. Morgan was sleeping again. He'd been doing that a lot. Enough to make her fear for his health. If he'd been able to change, he could've healed himself by now. But he wouldn't. Not as long as Roark continued to record their movements.

It was like seeing a glimpse of freedom outside your window and knowing you could never get there. Red slumped against the wall and rubbed her tired eyes. Her hands were filthy from twisting the chains and she'd have to burn her boots if she ever made it out of here, because the stench would never leave them. She wasn't sure if it would ever leave her. It would take at least three showers to even break through the first layer of grime.

She glanced at the door. Roark could return any minute. She needed to come up with a plan. She tried concentrating on Raphael. He hadn't responded thus far. Not that she'd thought he would. There seemed to be a distance limit to his abilities. She'd only spoken to him for a short while and that was at close range. Or maybe it was her. First an inability to shift and now this. Red concentrated and sent out her plea.

Raphael, if you can hear me, I need your help.

Silence met her.

Red kicked the wall hard enough to make her toe throb. Morgan started from his sleep.

"What?" he said, his voice disjointed. "Has he returned?"

"No, he's not back yet." Red reached out to touch him, only able to brush his fingertips. But it was enough. "Rest. I'm keeping watch."

Roark returned hours later. He looked haggard and a five o'clock shadow covered his jaw.

"What's the matter, meeting go bad?" Red asked.

His eyes narrowed. "The republic leaders are often short-sighted. That will change once I show them the threat the Others pose to our way of life."

Red snorted. "The Others? Please, you're the one living in a fantasy world. The republics don't want a new leader. They already have their leaders in place. Your dream is dead."

Roark's face reddened. "It's not over. It is just beginning. Once I air my proof, things will change. You'll see. Unfortunately, your friend here," he pointed to Morgan, "won't be around to witness the change. Perhaps I'll see if Raphael is available."

Fear vibrated through Red's entire body until she was trembling from head to foot. "I won't let you have him," she said quietly. Had the room not been silent, she doubted Roark would've heard. "I'll kill you first."

"Are we talking about Raphael or Morgan? Either way, you don't have a choice," he said stepping toward the cage. He produced a key and opened the door. It creaked ominously under its own weight.

Red stood perfectly still, her mind a mixture of panic and rage. She glanced at Morgan. He was awake now and watching Roark's every move. The politician reached into his jacket pocket and pulled out a laser pistol. He waved it in front of Red's face.

"Anticipation makes the wait so much better. Don't you think?" Roark asked, teasing her as he swung the weapon between the wall and Morgan. "Where will the first shot land?" he asked.

"You bastard," she cried, taking a swipe at him.

"Tsk, tsk," he said. "So close, but not quite close enough." Roark laughed. "Maybe if your arms were a little longer."

Red zeroed in on him. All her life she'd felt like an outsider. Been treated as something less. Even among the people who should've accepted her. She'd feared the beast lurking beneath her skin. Feared what it would do if it ever got out. But not anymore. Red closed her eyes and reached for the wolf with both hands, embracing the thing that scared her the most.

Warmth swept over her body, followed by excruciating pain. She opened her eyes and knew without seeing them they were glowing. The room looked different. The shadows were gone. Everything held a crimson haze.

Roark dipped toward her, a smile splitting his face. This time when she reached out, she latched onto him. Red wasn't sure who was more surprised, her or Roark. His pistol clattered to the floor and his eyes widened as he looked down. Red followed his gaze and saw that her hands had grown claws. She'd hooked the trunk of his body, sinking in to the knuckles. Her arms still looked like her arms, until they reached her hands. Gone were her fingertips and soft palms. They'd been replaced by rough pads.

Red met his eyes and smiled, running her tongue over her canines. She glanced at the camera and pulled him closer. From this angle, it would look like she was hugging Roark. Only she, Roark, and Morgan knew the truth.

"You're a—" Roark said, unable to get the words out.

"I know," Red said, giving him a genuine smile. "Surprise." She flexed her fingers.

Roark winced in pain and sweat beaded his brow.

"Now, you are going to give me the key to these shackles and we are going to walk out of here together. If you even think about calling Michael or anyone else for help, I will slice you open. Do you understand me?"

Roark nodded and he slowly reached toward his pocket. His eyes narrowed as he dug inside for the key.

"One wrong move and you'll be picking your intestines up off this godforsaken floor."

Roark plucked the key out of his pocket, using two fingers. "Good, now hand it to Morgan."

Red turned him, keeping her claws buried in his flesh. Blood seeped beneath her hands and down the front of his dark shirt. A few drops hit the floor with a thick, fat splat. Roark reached out as far as he could.

"A little farther," she said, putting pressure on his abdomen. Roark cried out.

"That's it. Easy does it," Red said.

He leaned as far as he could, then dropped the key into Morgan's palm. Morgan quickly unlocked the chain around his wrist, then moved to his legs. He held himself up against the wall, attempting to shake out his limbs. As soon as he was steady, he walked over and unlocked the chain binding Red's ankle.

She turned Roark and guided him back to the wall where Morgan had been kept. "Raise your arms," she said.

Morgan rushed forward and clamped the shackles onto Roark's wrists. Red pulled her hands out and watched in astonishment as her claws receded, morphing into her body. Morgan had made sure to block the vid recorder's view.

"You're going to pay for this," Roark said, as she clamped the chains around his ankles.

Red looked him in the eye, letting him see the wolf surface. "I already have."

The door burst open as Red rose to her feet. Morgan was already moving toward the pistol that Roark had dropped. Roark looked up in anticipation. His expression changed when he saw the men in the doorway.

Red glanced over and smiled. "Took you guys long enough to get here. Don't come any farther. The room's wired with recording vids."

Demery held the hood of his white protective suit in his hands. "Told you I could find you anywhere, mon." He grinned, flashing dimples and fangs.

Raphael smiled when his gaze landed on her. It brightened even more when he saw Morgan. "You look a little worse for wear, my friend," he said. "But it's good to see you all the same."

Morgan met Raphael's dark gaze. Something flashed between the two men, then it was gone. "Thank you for taking care of Gina while I was gone."

Raphael's lips twitched. "Anytime."

"I'll take it from here," Morgan said. There was something in his voice. A warning perhaps.

"I figured you'd say that," Raphael said.

"I hate to break up this reunion, gentlemen," Red said, watching them closely. Her body tensed, ready to separate them if necessary. "But we need to get out of here."

"Of course," Raphael said. "What about him?" He indicated Roark.

"Leave him. If we kill him, it'll be harder to prove our innocence," Morgan said.

Red stared at him, torn between the need to end this and the logic behind Morgan's words. If they killed Roark, they might never get the proof they needed to put an end to his machinations. Yet the wolf in her wanted blood. More blood than he'd spilled on the floor. It wanted blood for all the pain he'd put them through. She thought of her grandfather, her navcom Rita, Jesse Lindley, Michael Travers, Kane Hunter, and all the other people who'd been affected by his treachery.

"He deserves to die," she said.

"No one here will disagree," Morgan said, pressing a battered hand to her shoulder. "But we have to look at this as a battle, not the war."

Red nodded in agreement, even though it pained her to do so. They left the room with Roark locked in the cage. The four of them raced outside. When they reached the back of the building, Red saw Catherine Meyers waiting with Juan and Takeo.

"What is she doing here?" she asked.

Raphael looked at the woman and his eyes glittered. It was impossible to miss the predatory look he gave her. "She's our insurance policy. We needed her to get in. We might need her to get back out."

"What could she do that you weren't able to?" Red asked.

Raphael smiled. "Just watch."

They made their way to the entrance to the domed city. When they approached the guards, Catherine stepped forward. Within seconds the guards became disoriented and couldn't remember why they were there. The group walked past without having to present their I.D. chips.

"That's handy," Red said.

"Yes, she's quite remarkable," Raphael said, staring at Catherine.

Red watched their exchange and understanding dawned. She'd been replaced and she'd never been more happy about it. Red smiled as they made their way to the shuttle that Raphael had parked a few miles away.

When they reached the shuttle, Takeo tossed Morgan and Red some food along with fresh clothes and a canteen of water. "What now?" he asked, looking at the group.

Morgan ate, slowly chewing his food. "We can't go back to Nuria," he said eventually. "Other than to gather supplies."

"Why not?" Red said.

"Because it will be the first place that Roark checks when he gets loose."

Red frowned. "We can't go to IPTT because my grandfather will have to escort us to the Taos detention center."

Morgan shook his head. "We couldn't do that to him."

Raphael grew pensive. "I have a few places that no one knows about. I suppose you could stay there for a while."

"No," Morgan said. "They're going to be looking for us. The first place they'll check is where our friends reside. We have to go somewhere they won't think to look. We can wait in the ruins of Kane's house while we decide. The walls of his home have a built in chip blocker, no one will be able to track us there."

Demery, Juan, and Takeo frowned.

What about no-man's-land?" Red asked, even though her mind rebelled at the thought. It was the only place that Roark wouldn't think to look.

"You wouldn't survive there," Raphael said.

"We won't survive here, if we stay," Red countered.

Morgan looked at her. "It would be hard. I'm not sure what we'd be up against. I've only heard rumors. If there's any truth to them, the place redefines lawlessness. We'd definitely need to stop by Nuria to get some supplies and weapons, then we'd have to figure out how to cross the boundary fence. We don't have to decide this second."

Raphael piped up. "I believe Catherine could help with that. Couldn't you?"

She blushed and nodded.

"Thanks for the offer." Red looked at the woman. "I'll contact my grandfather to make sure you still have your job, if you want it."

"Thanks," Catherine said. "I appreciate it."

"She won't be going back," Raphael said, his tone leaving no room for argument.

Red arched a brow, but didn't say anything. She wished she could stick around to see this battle of wills.

Catherine scowled.

"I'll contact my brother once you've gathered your supplies and crossed the fence," Raphael said.

"You may not want to do that," Morgan said, placing a hand on Raphael's shoulder.

"Why? What's happened?" Raphael went from tough to vulnerable in seconds.

"Roark's done something to Michael," Red said. "He's changed."

"Oh no," Morgan said.

"What?" Red turned to him. Every eye was upon Morgan.

"I forgot to grab the device Roark carried in his pocket."

Raphael frowned. "What device?"

"He's chipped Michael's brain. Somehow he caught Michael feeding. He found out he was an Other," Morgan said. "I'm afraid he's not *your* Michael anymore."

Raphael looked off at the domed city in the distance. "We have to go back."

"We can't," Red said. "I'm sorry. It's too dangerous."

He met her gaze and Red cringed at the pain she saw lurking in the dark depths of his eyes.

"I'm so sorry," she said.

His mouth opened and closed a couple times. "I can't just leave him. He's my brother."

"I know." Red stared down at the sand. "You can't go in there alone. Once Roark's free, he'll arrest you. And I don't know what Michael will do."

"My brother will not harm me," Raphael said, but doubt flashed across his face. "I must go."

"I'll go with you," Catherine said.

"So will I," Takeo added. "They haven't seen me."

Raphael gave them a curt nod of thanks, then turned back to Red. He reached for her hand and pulled it to his mouth. He pressed his lips to the back of her knuckles. "Looks like this is where we part ways. Take care of yourself."

"You, too. And thanks," she said, slipping her hand free.

Morgan watched the exchange, but said nothing. Instead, he stepped forward and held out his hand. Raphael shook it. "Good luck," he said.

"I'll need it," Raphael said.

"Same here. We better get moving," Morgan said.

"Need some company, mon? I happen to know of a way into no-man's-land, if the woman is going to stay here."

They turned to look at the hooded vamp.

"You don't have to do that, Demery," Red said. "You risked enough by coming here."

"I know." He grinned. "But this is the most fun I've had

in a long time. Thought I might keep the party going for a while. We can have some laughs and do a little business while we're in no-man's-land."

Red chuckled. "Are you sure?"

"Yeah, mon," he said, tossing his helmet into the shuttle as the sun dropped below the horizon.

Juan walked up to Red. "It's not over," he said.

"I know," Red said.

His brown eyes glazed as his psychic vision struck. "He'll come back stronger than ever."

She stilled when she saw the expression on his face. He was awake, but not with them. "Can we stop him?" Red asked, terrified of the truth.

Juan shook his head. "I don't know. I see pain ahead. And blood. Lots of blood." He glanced at Demery with unseeing eyes.

Red touched his arm. "Anything else?"

Juan nodded. "In the end, you'll have to choose whether you want to continue to run or stand and fight. The world as we know it hangs in the balance." He sighed, his head slumping forward. A moment later, his chin shot up and he looked around wide-eyed. "What happened?" he asked.

"I think you had a vision," Red said.

"Was it good news?" Juan asked.

"That depends on if you think being responsible for the world is a good thing or a bad thing," Red said.

"I know what I think," Morgan said. "We'd better go."

Juan and Demery piled into the shuttle with Red and Morgan. Raphael, Takeo, and Catherine stood back as they started the engine and shifted the shuttle into gear. Red pressed her palm to the glass as they sped away. She watched Raphael, Takeo, and Catherine grow smaller and smaller until they disappeared completely.

She turned away from the window. "Do you think they'll make it?" she asked no one in particular.

"I don't know," Morgan said.

"What about us?"

"Our chances are about even with theirs. We've been through worse," Morgan said, reminding her of their time in the cage.

"Yes, but not much," Red said, as the scope of what lay ahead of them began to sink in. She contacted her grandfather to let him know they were alive and on the run. She didn't stay on the line long because she knew it was his duty to report the incident. He'd free Roark eventually, but promised to wait as long as he could before doing so. Red said her good-byes, then slumped in the chair, her bones suddenly too weak to support her.

"Don't worry," Demery said. "I know where I'm going."

"Yes, but do we?" Red looked back out the window at the endless miles of sand, as Morgan pointed the shuttle toward Nuria and on to no-man's-land.

Jordan Summers's

GRITTY AND SEXY WEREWOLF SERIES
CONTINUES WITH BOOK THREE

Crimson

Having nowhere else to turn, Morgan
Hunter and Gina "Red" Santiago must enter
the wastelands of an already barren land.

"Red Santiago is a heroine with fire
 befitting her name.... Summers has
 a winner with this one!"
> —Cathy Clamp, *USA Today*
> bestselling author

"Dark, action-filled, and hot!
 This heroine is a wolf dressed in
 Little Red Riding Hood's clothing."
> —Jeaniene Frost

NOVEMBER 2009   978-0-7563-5916-2

TOR

TOR-FORGE.COM
JORDANSUMMERS.COM

TOR
ROMANCE

Believe that love is magic

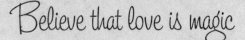

P lease join us at the Web site below
for more information about this
author and other great romance
selections, and to sign up for our
monthly newsletter!

www.tor-forge.com